Courtesy of the authors

ABOUT THE AUTHORS

NEIL GAIMAN is the *New York Times* bestselling author of numerous books, including *Neverwhere*, *Stardust*, *Coraline*, *American Gods*, *Anansi Boys*, and the Sandman series of graphic novels, among others. Originally from England, he now lives in the United States.

ROGER AVARY is the writer-director of the neo-noir crime thriller *Killing Zoe* and the filmed adaptation of the Bret Easton Ellis novel *The Rules of Attraction*. In 1994 he was awarded an Academy Award for his work as a writer with Quentin Tarantino on *Pulp Fiction*. Originally from the United States, he now lives in England.

BEOWULF

THE SCRIPT BOOK

beowulf

THE SCRIPT BOOK

with insights from the authors, their early concept art, and the first and last drafts of the script for the film

NEIL GAIMAN AND ROGER AVARY

HARPER**ENTERTAINMENT**

NEW YORK · LONDON · TORONTO · SYDNEY

HARPER**ENTERTAINMENT**

BEOWULF: THE SCRIPT BOOK. Copyright © 2007 Paramount Pictures and Shangri-La Entertainment LLC. All rights reserved. Foreword and middleword copyright © 2007 Roger Avary. Afterword copyright © 2007 Neil Gaiman. Printed in the United States of America. No part of this book may be used or reproduced in any manner whatsoever without written permission except in the case of brief quotations embodied in critical articles and reviews. For information address HarperCollins Publishers, 10 East 53rd Street, New York, NY 10022.

Grendel concept art by Stephen Norrington, copyright © Roger Avary Filmproduktion, GmbH. Storyboard art by Phillip Keller, copyright © ImageMovers.

Viking ship image used by permission. Copyright © Art Parts / Ron and Joe, Inc.

HarperCollins books may be purchased for educational, business, or sales promotional use. For information please write: Special Markets Department, HarperCollins Publishers, 10 East 53rd Street, New York, NY 10022.

Designed by Nancy Singer Olaguera

Library of Congress Cataloging-in-Publication Data

ISBN: 978-0-06-135016-0
ISBN-10: 0-06-135016-8

07 08 09 10 11 ISPN 9 8 7 6 5 4 3 2 1

Contents

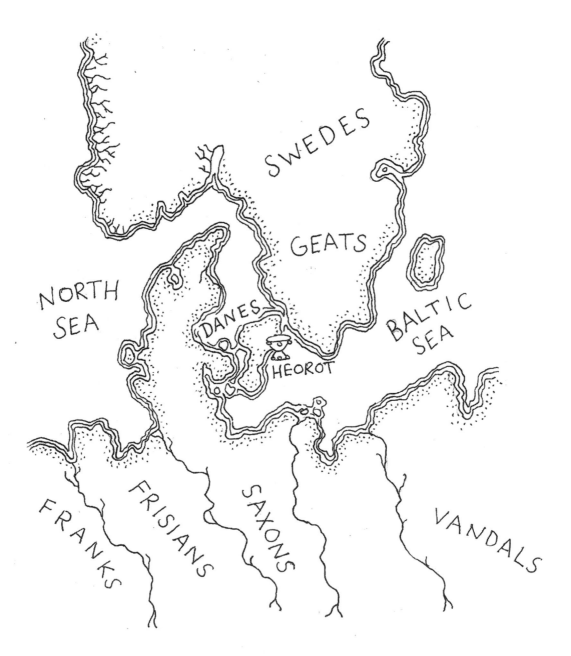

Map drawn by Roger Avary to aid in the writing of the screenplay.

PART I

THE SPRING

Foreword

BY ROGER AVARY

We've included in this book both our first draft and our final shooting script. We wanted to show the circuitous path a screenplay takes towards getting made, and to perhaps put the changes that come about over the course of development into some kind of context. So for this foreword I've chosen to tell our story of getting the film produced, rather than to analyze the work itself. I figured it would at very least be more entertaining to read.

The script for *Beowulf* was written quickly, under a palapa in a Mexican quinta I obtained for the writing process, knocking out a first draft in just under two weeks. However, the process of getting the film made took Neil Gaiman and I ten years together, and for me a total of twenty-five years from gestation to completion. During our development of this script, the Internet sprang from the mists, and our computers went from early Apple Powerbook 120's to screaming Dual Core MacBooks and 2GHz Dells, spanning Final Draft 2 to Final Draft 7. Collaboration isn't easy, but when it works, and the muse comes to you both at the same time, it's a pretty hot threesome. *Beowulf* was like that. Through it all, Neil and I have become close lifelong friends, and I love few the way I love him.

My fate was sealed for me by Lorenzo DiBonaventura, the studio honcho then running Warner Bros., who had me into his office because he loved the "manic energy" in my film *Killing Zoe*. He repeated his favorite scene to me several times—Julie Delpy being thrown naked and wet out of a hotel room and into a hallway—laughing with an odd nostalgia at how ludicrously insane and unpredictable the movie was. Then, quite to my surprise and delight, he looked me in the eye and said, "We're making a movie with you, we just need to figure out which one. I'm just gonna rattle off titles, and when you like the sound of one, stop me."

I thought to myself that this was probably the best kind of situation to be in. I sat back, and readied myself for the barrage.

"*Sergeant Rock.*" Wow. What a way to begin. "—And it's written by John Milius."

"Go on." I could barely contain my excitement. I had somehow wandered into the treasury. He went on to list several titles, some awesome sounding, some dreadful sounding. I went through the list, "yes, no, yes, no, maybe, that sounds interesting, not for me, yes, no . . . "

Then, Lorenzo casually mentioned a title that cleared the slate of competitors: "*Sandman*."

"*Sandman?*" I questioned. You mean, "*Sandman* Sandman?"

"Yes." He jumped up and walked over to a large bureau and opened it up.

"Not . . . Neil Gaiman's *Sandman?*" And in that moment he pulled out two little statues. One was of Dream, the other of Death. I literally stood up. Unable to contain myself, I gushed to Lorenzo about Neil's work, pronouncing my love of it. I was immediately attached to the film.

I had been introduced to *Sandman* in 1989, while working in the mailroom of D'Arcy Masius Benton & Bowles—the advertising agency. I had taken the job because it was next to the attorney Quentin Tarantino and I were using to put together the limited partnership paperwork for *True Romance*. I would literally shuffle mail in the mornings, load the Coke machines, and slip out for hours at a time to sit in the office building next door and prepare budgets and schedules and partnership documents. But months passed during that process, and many of my hours were spent with the ad people, sorting their mail and loading their Coke machines.

One of the executives had DC Comics delivered to him, probably for the purposes of placing ads. He never wanted them, so I ended up getting them—and so over those months, I read the serialized version of *Sandman: The Doll's House*.

It was like having a third eye open in my forehead. As I read them, I imagined the movie in my head—widescreen. Johnny Depp as Dream. Fairuza Balk as Death. I would subcontract Jan Svankmajer or the Brothers Quay to animate the transitions from the Dream realm into our own world, so as to simulate the graphic style of Dave McKean's covers. It would be a glorious and magnificent epic.

A year and a half after my meeting with Lorenzo, I politely left the production, not wanting to be the guy who ruined the *Sandman* film adaptation. I simply couldn't imagine the Lord of Dreaming throwing a punch. Just because it looked like *Batman* at first glance didn't mean that it was *Batman*. But Jon Peters, the "savant" producer Warners had attached to the project, couldn't be dissuaded. I moved on, a year and a half of my life lost to the ether. No more real to me now than the memory of a dream.

In the months that followed I tried to figure out what I would do next. I went through my files of half-finished projects and notes on things I'd always wanted to do. I stumbled upon some notes I had written in 1982, thirteen years before. They were notes on how to turn *Beowulf* into a feature film.

It was during a high school English lit class that I was first exposed to the epic poem *Beowulf*. It was the Burton Raffel translation, and its cover depicted, in stained-glass styling, a warrior driving a sword into a fiery red dragon. I was a Dungeons & Dragons geek whose favorite film at the time was *Excalibur*, and so the passing out of a fantasy book as a credit assignment was like manna from Heaven. I opened it up and read the the first verse:

> Hwæt! We Gardena in geardagum þeodcyninga þrym gefrunon hu ða
> æþelingas ellen fremedon.

This book didn't even resemble the English I knew. Even Raffel's translation taxed the cognitive capacities of my seventeen-year-old brain. I struggled with it for weeks, well after the assignment passed and I received my C−, until one night I began to read it aloud.

Beowulf was spoken and told around a fire for generations before it was put to parchment by Christian monks, and even now it demands an oral delivery. When spoken, the texture of the writing comes alive, and with breath the arcane nature of the language somehow finds life. But, as a story with an oral tradition, it was no doubt subject to alteration and embellishment. Anyone who's ever played the game Telephone Operator as a child knows how a simple sentence can transform when passed from one person to the next, and I suspect that *Beowulf* was subject to this same process. It certainly reads at times like a Paul Bunyan tall tale, with Beowulf using his near superhuman strength to slay scores of sea monsters barehanded, and fighting underwater for days on end using a single breath. Perhaps scenes had been added to spice up the tale. And perhaps, as I increasingly suspected, critical elements had been left out, edited by the passage of time.

My notes simply asked questions:

> *If Grendel is half-man, half-demon . . . then who is his father?*
>
> *Why does Grendel never attack Hrothgar, the king?*
>
> *How does Beowulf hold his breath for days on end during the fight with Grendel's Mother? Maybe he wasn't fighting her? Or maybe he isn't human?*
>
> *When Beowulf goes into the cave to kill Grendel's Mother, why does he emerge with Grendel's head instead of hers? Where's the proof that the mother was killed?*

It all seemed to add up to rather nefarious conclusions. As I reread those notes, my mind began to swim. Though it's not in the poem, clearly, Grendel was Hrothgar's bastard son. He had sired the child in exchange for worldly wealth and fame. But ill-gotten gains always come back to haunt you—at least in the epics I was weaned on as a boy. And what of Beowulf? Surely he wasn't telling his thanes the full truth. Had he given into the siren-witch and accepted her offer of gold and glory for his seed, which she needed in order to procreate? I had the time, I had the desire, I had the passion—I would write *Beowulf* into an epic. It was my intention to remain true to the letter of the epic, but I would read between the lines and find greater truths than had been explored before. It was a lofty ambition. I sat down and wrote the following treatment:

BEOWULF
a treatment for a motion picture by
Roger Avary
draft dated April 30, 1995
registered WGA/w
© copyright 1995

THE PROLOGUE . . .

A castaway ship of some ancient Nordic design is adrift in a stormy gray sea. Its large swells carry the craft with the current, as the oars are placed straight upward. It would appear that the boat has no crew . . . and no passengers.

    The boat runs ashore and is discovered by a tribe of people calling themselves the "Danes." When the tribe of people peer into the boat, they're astonished to find vast treasures of gold, myrrh, guilded weapons, and gold-encrusted armor. Surrounded by the gold is a young baby wrapped in gold-lined cloth of purest white. The baby grows to become their leader and king. The baby is the Scyld Sceafing.

    The Scyld Sceafing, having built a great kingdom, eventually dies . . . passing the throne to his son. They put the body of the dead king aboard a boat, load it with treasure, and set it adrift . . . giving him back to wherever he came from.

    Many new moons go by . . . three generations pass.

    The Scyld Sceafing's great grandson Hrothgar is now leader of the Danes. Hrothgar lives in the castle the Sceafing built (with his own hands). Hrothgar is a mediocre king . . . a bit of a lout, living off of the deeds of his forefathers. He is tormented by his mysterious and fantastic great grandfather . . . and he's tormented by the fact that he's never going to be as great a man as he was. We get the feeling that he harbors a dark secret as well.

    Hrothgar, to cover up his inadequacy complex, throws great and lavish parties where everyone gets drunk and boisterous. Because of this the land begins to suffer.

    Hrothgar's jealousy ultimately manifests itself into a large, man-like monster named Grendel, whose form we see in shadows on the flickering fire lit walls of the castle. The monster invades the drunken celebrations and devours men whole. It is a slaughter of cataclysmic horror . . . yet somehow Hrothgar is spared.

Hrothgar's thanes (and the people of his land) all look to him to save them . . . and as it turns out, he can't. He shows his true colors. Instead of standing up to the monster himself, he looks to the sea . . . looking to the same storm-covered ocean from whence his great grandfather came.

Sick with dispair, he instructs a guard to watch the coast. Many of his men secretly think he may be insane, but they watch the coast regardless . . . he is their king.

FINALLY SOMEONE COMES

From the ocean comes another craft, a Viking ship similar in design to the one that brought the Scyld Sceafing. But this boat isn't adrift . . . it's many oars strike the water and guide it through the great swells toward its destination. Its sails are filled with the wind. A man stands at its bow, looking into the storm . . . looking past the storm. The man is Beowulf.

Beowulf lands and asks the astonished coast guard to be taken to King Hrothgar. He rides a miniature horse, big enough to bring with him on his boat. It is a freakish sight, the large warrior on the little pony-sized horse. But he has many thanes with him who seem to take him quite seriously, so the guard dumbfoundedly complies.

They arrive at Heorot, the castle Hrothgar resides in, and leave their weapons outside to show that they arrive in peace. They're greeted in the great hall by King Hrothgar's aide, Wulfgar, who presents them to the King.

Beowulf tells Hrothgar that he knows about the Danes' oppression and that he has come to them because he has had experience in combat with water monsters in the past. Using his famous hand grip, he will grapple with Grendel and rid them of the monster. But one of Hrothgar's thanes, Unferth, begins to heckle Beowulf . . . suggesting that Beowulf is all words and no action. Beowulf recognizes Unferth's envy and retorts, eventually embarrassing the man. It would seem that the two are enemies.

THE COMING OF GRENDEL

After a long and drunken night of song and exchanges (like the one above with Unferth) the men all resign to sleep. It is in the darkness of night that Grendel comes from out of the dank moor . . . pained by the song and boisterousness of the thanes. As the monster picks up and rips apart one of Beowulf's men, Beowulf watches the fiend's method of attack. Then, when the monster attacks Beowulf, a terrible battle ensues that results in Beowulf ripping the monster's arm from its socket. Grendel's howls of pain echo through the hall, and with Beowulf's men together at arms against the fiend, the hideous monster runs off into the night . . . leaving its severed arm behind.

The next morning Hrothgar looks at the arm, which Beowulf has hung from the rafters as a trophy, and praises him. Even Unferth recognizes Beowulf's deed of valor. The inside of Heorot is cleaned up, new tapestries are hung, and a great feast is prepared. Gifts of helmets and mail are given to Beowulf and all the thanes continue into another of their infamous drunken parties. During this party the scop (the court singer and weaver of "history") sings about "The Fight at Finnsburg." Also at the feast, Hrothgar's wife, the Queen Wealhtheow makes a veiled pass at Beowulf.

As the party continues the men drink deeply, as they did before Grendel's raids, and all pass out . . . thinking they can sleep without fear for the first time in twelve years.

GRENDEL'S MOTHER EXACTS HER REVENGE

That night, Grendel's mother comes to revenge the death of her son. Far more horrific and terrifying than Grendel, she snatches up Aeschere, one of Hrothgar's most trusted thanes, and vanishes into the night.

Grieving for Aeschere, and perhaps even believing that he may still be alive, Hrothgar begs Beowulf to travel to where they believe Grendel's mother's lair is . . . in a dark lake underneath a fiery volcano mountain. Unferth goes as far as to offer Beowulf his family's sword to help him fight the monster . . . which is of course a veiled forfeit of heroism on his part.

THE QUEST TO DESTROY GRENDEL'S MOTHER

Beowulf and his men arrive at the cave which leads to the underground lake and find Aeschere's head on a stick. With his men terrified, Beowulf decides to go into the cave alone.

Inside of the cave Beowulf finds a vast cavern of stalagmites and stalactites leading to a mineral pool that draws Beowulf into it. He swims through the waters, *dropping his armor and avoiding strange albino water snakes until he reaches the other side . . . a sunken city, destroyed and half submerged . . . abandoned long ago by the Dwarven kind.*

Beowulf, wet and without armor, holding only his sword, wanders the dark kingdom until he finds Grendel . . . dead from Beowulf ripping his arm off. Then Grendel's mother approaches Beowulf . . . not as a hideous monster, as one might expect, but as a beautiful woman. A siren. A succubus. A demon which looks into Beowulf's very soul. He drops his sword . . . and it seems he gives in to her.

Beowulf's men have been waiting for days outside the cave. They wonder if he died at the clutches of the hideous monster that killed Aeschere. Then Beowulf emerges, pale and drained of his life force . . . half dead . . . but claiming to have destroyed the monster.

BEOWULF RETURNS "VICTORIOUS"

Beowulf is praised by Hrothgar for destroying Grendel and his mother. It isn't until Beowulf is on his ship sailing home that he confides in one of his thanes what really happened.

It seems as though Beowulf gave into the temptation of the succubus and was lost in the rapture. Grendel was half human and half demon . . . the unholy child of the bond between man and monster. Grendel's mother would send her hideous child into the world of men to steal them and bring them to her. But she was far too powerful for most men to take . . . ripping them apart as she tried to mate with them. Beowulf gave her his seed . . . and barely escaped with his life. He makes his thane vow never to tell of what had happened.

Beowulf arrives home to a hero's welcome, surely uncomfortable with his terrible secret. Hygelac, Beowulf's king, gives him his own hall and an enormous tract of land.

KING BEOWULF AND THE DRAGON

Years pass, and Hygelac and his son die in battle . . . leaving Beowulf to be king. His reign is harmonious and peaceful until one of the Geats steals an ornamented cup from a hoard in the lair of a great sleeping dragon. The dragon, furious (as dragons often become when their treasure has been stolen) lays waste to the land . . . perhaps metaphorically in the form of famine and disease.

Beowulf, now an old man, travels to the dragon's lair . . . knowing that he is too old to battle the fierce and ancient monster. The dragon (which is perhaps never seen, as I believe it is Beowulf's conscience) breathes its fiery death onto Beowulf, who is too old to kill the monster easily. Beowulf's thanes, seeing that he is being overwhelmed, all run . . . with the exception of Wiglaf. With this one trustworthy man Beowulf is able to deal a mortal blow to the monster . . . but his own wounds are so great that he dies in Wiglaf's arms, naming him the new king.

Beowulf is placed onto a splendid funeral pyre hung with helmets and shields. They ignite the greatest of funeral fires, which consumes his body into smoke and flames. There is much mourning and lamenting. The body of the dragon is thrown into the sea, and as for the treasure . . . like Beowulf's ashes, it lies buried in the earth, even now.

THE END

As you can see from my treatment, my problem was *Beowulf*'s odd two-act structure. It had always been the element that made it a difficult film adaptation. *Beowulf* is divided into major acts. The first half in Denmark, fighting Grendel and his demon mother. The second act taking place in Geatland, decades later, Beowulf now a king himself who must die killing a dragon to save the land. The two halves of the epic deal with the differences between the ambitions of youth and old age, and how it is a very different thing to rule a kingdom than it is to win one. The seemingly fractured structure of *Beowulf* is important to his arc, but in movie terms this bifurcated storyline was more of a detriment than an equity.

One day, while struggling with the second half of *Beowulf*, trying to make it work with the first half, Neil Gaiman called me. Neil had come to respect me, I believe, for leaving *Sandman* rather than bastardize it. He asked me what I was up to and I told him about my theories on *Beowulf*, not to mention my second act problem. And then, with that elegant English accent of his, he stated the obvious: "Roger, don't you see? If Grendel is Hrothgar's son, the dragon surely must be Beowulf's son—come back to haunt him."

Had it been a snake, it would have bitten me. Neil had just conceived the Beowulf Unified Field Theory, solving a problem that has plagued frustrated filmmakers for decades as if it were simple grade-school addition. I asked Neil if he wanted to collaborate with me on the screenplay, inviting him into the process. It would be a boon. His depth of knowledge of mythology and tradition would lend itself nicely to the project. His measured and sensitive dialogue would serve as a fine contrast to my more berzerk tendencies. To my delight, and my great benefit, Neil agreed.

Our deal was that Neil would receive first position, and that I, as director, would control the destiny of the material. The sale, the production, etc. I would also provide a neutral location for us to conduct the writing. Neil lived in the Midwest, and I lived in Manhattan Beach, California. For some reason, though it made no sense considering the subject matter, I chose Puerto Vallarta.

I secured a quinta with a full-time cook and bartender. It was a massive, fortress-like compound, surrounding a large pool that overlooked the Pacific Ocean. Next to the pool was a palapa, inside of which was a pool table. Neil and I would play some pool, then go in the pool, and then have a margarita—and then we would write—and then we would play some more pool, and then, of course, go back into the pool.

We wrote on two early Powerbook 120 computers, using a 3.5" floppy disk to transfer scenes back and forth. We divided the movie up between us, and then began furiously hammering out scenes. When a scene was complete, we would transfer it to the other computer, and it would be rewritten by the other writer. It went shockingly smooth, and in just under two weeks we had a first draft finished. We were also sunburned and fatter from eating burritos and drinking Mexican beer nonstop.

We returned to Manhattan Beach, looking like we were coming home from Club Med, and sent the script to our agents at the most powerful talent agency in the world, CAA.

It was around then that I discovered that in Hollywood, at that time, *Beowulf* was considered something of a joke. A sword-and-sandal hoity-toity lesson in ancient literature. People had entertained making it for years, only to be met with laughter. The truth, I imagine, is that most executives and producers would sit down to read the text and glaze over after the first paragraph. No one wants to be reminded of high school English, and this was a major strike against getting the material to be taken seriously as a Hollywood movie. My agents received the script, reminding me of this legacy, and then it sat. I assumed that they did nothing to promote the material, but I was wrong. The elves at CAA were quietly and feverishly reading it and passing it from stack to stack, and eventually it found its way into the right stack.

A few months had gone by when I received the call from ex-über-agent and former young Turk, Jack Rapke. I had always considered Jack one of the smartest agents I had ever met— and possibly one of the scariest (the smart ones are always the most terrifying). He has a slow and measured voice that articulates words so that they rise, dip, and then rise again. It's a mesmerizing pattern of speaking, and it causes you to hang on every word as if its formed from a complete story arc, with a beginning, middle, and end. I've never met a man with more experience eating at restaurants around the world. You can tell Jack that you'll be going to any city on the planet (say, Catolica, Italy), and he'll proceed to tell you the best restaurant to dine at, how to get there, and the name of the owner. For example, Catolica, Italy: "Roger, there's a little bistro off the main Rambla, on a crooked street that leads toward the basilica, just across from the butcher, but there's no sign out in front. Look for the red door. If you go there between nine P.M. and eleven P.M., on Thursday through Saturday, let yourself in and ask for Martina. Be sure to have the gnocchi—it's unparalleled." If you ever meet Jack Rapke, pick a random city and ask him where to eat. He won't disappoint you.

Jack had just left CAA and was forming a new company with director Robert Zemeckis. Jack had read the screenplay, thought it was amazing, and had passed it to Robert, who insisted that this was exactly the kind of film that their new company, ImageMovers, should be making. They wanted to option the script.

I met with Jack and Robert in their lavishly decorated Amblin offices. After a lengthy and passionate pitch trying to convince me to option them the screenplay so that they could make it as a big-budget studio epic, I explained to them that I had only written it so that I could direct it myself. They told me that no one else would be better to pull it off. I think at the time they actually believed that.

I had always seen the film as a smaller-budget epic, dirty and raw—but the promise of having the tools to make the film reach a larger audience was a dream come true. It was all happening faster than I could have hoped. Attorneys drew up contracts and money changed hands. I was now in the ImageMovers fold, and through their output deal with DreamWorks I would be making my first studio film as a director.

But Spielberg had a hair up his ass regarding the project. Maybe he didn't like the script, maybe he didn't like my work as a director, or maybe he thought it was too violent. Regardless, after a year of working on rewrites, Jack and Robert resigned themselves to the unpleasant prospect of having to set the movie up outside of their first look with DreamWorks. One thing I will say about Jack Rapke and Robert Zemeckis (or Z., as I would come to know him) is that they never stopped believing in me as the director of the film, and they stood by me through thick and thin. But soon, the option had expired.

I continued to work with Jack and Robert for another year, but it had been years since my first film, and interest in me in the marketplace had waned. Soon, through no fault of my ImageMovers partners, the project began to wither a slow death on the vine. I moved on, yet again, hoping to one day return to *Beowulf*.

Time passed and occasionally I would speak to Jack, and he would ask if I would consider allowing anyone else direct the film. "Only Terry Gilliam," I would dictate, not knowing that he had been Jack's client at one time and that Jack wasn't too keen on revisiting the manic energy of that relationship. What I didn't tell him, was that I would have let Robert Zemeckis direct the film. Besides, Zemeckis's slate was full for years to come. He was splitting the production of *Cast Away* and was squeezing in *What Lies Beneath* while Tom Hanks dropped fifty pounds. I've always loved Zemeckis's work—especially *Used Cars*. On our first story meeting, at a country club in Montecito, I brought my laser disc of *Used Cars* for him to sign. He's a great American auteur, and a man who constantly pushes the boundaries of what's visually possible to better tell his stories. The thought of him directing *Beowulf* was enough a transformation—enough of a radical departure—of what I was envisioning that it recalled my seeing Tony Scott's *True Romance* for the first time after working with Quentin Tarantino for years on his vision for the same script. But I still believed I'd one day direct the script myself—maybe I would find myself in a position to make it again.

Jack always remained polite, and supportive of me, but as we were unable to pull the financing together, our relationship waned, and we gradually drifted apart.

Eventually, I directed a low-budget adaptation of Bret Easton Ellis's novel *The Rules of Attraction*, and while doing press in Paris for the film I had dinner with producer Samuel Hadida, who had financed my first film. I love Sammy, he's always been there for me when the chips are down. His motto is "We like, we make," and when he gets it into his head that he's going to make a movie, he's relentless and passionate. His Paris-based production and distribution company had grown to the point that he was now considered one of the big players in Hollywood: the Weinstein brothers rolled into an energetic French-Moroccan with a passionate love of movies.

"I have been thinking about your *Bee-Wolf*," he told me in his highly accented English, "and I am in the zone of making epics. Why not we make this film?" It was unexpected, but welcomed. There was only one problem, and it was called . . . TURNAROUND.

In Hollywood, when you incur development expenses on a project and the project doesn't get made, the costs of development become attached to the project. DreamWorks had taken the option payments and added giant line items called simply "Development Expenses" to the turnaround on *Beowulf*, and they added up to a staggering figure. I realized that the flowers and oak and antiques in the ImageMovers/Amblin office all came at a price. Beware well-appointed production companies with comfortable chairs; they'll somehow find a way to write it all off onto dead productions. The only solution was to disregard all of the drafts that had been generated during development and go back to draft one, which Neil and I had written in two weeks while sunning in Puerto Vallarta. This was not a problem for Neil or I, for we loved that first draft. It was raw and pure. Our vision undistilled by the Hollywood process.

This is that draft . . .

BEOWULF

as told by

Neil Gaiman & Roger Avary

Draft Dated:
June 10, 1997

```
Hwæt!  We Gar-Dena      in geår-dagum,
peod-cyniga,            prym gefrunon,
hu oå æpelingas         ellen fremedon!




Listen!  We have heard  of the Spear-Danes' glory
In the old days,        the kings of tribes--
How noble princes       showed great courage!


                        "Beowulf"
                        Lines 1-3
                        Original Author Unknown
```

FADE IN:

1   EXT. HEROT - DAY   1

EXTREME CLOSE UP ON: The face of KING HROTHGAR. He is a man
past the prime of his years, but still a mighty warrior, and
a charismatic leader of men. As he bombastically talks, with
full volume, to a large audience, we SLOWLY PULL BACK.

                    HROTHGAR
          A year ago I, Hrothgar, your King, swore
          that we would celebrate our victories in
          a new hall, a mighty hall and beautiful.
          Craftsmen from all over the land of the
          Danes, and from all the civilized world
          have worked on this hall to make it the
          finest mead-hall on the face of the
          earth.

PULL BACK TO REVEAL that Hrothgar is atop his horse in front
of a huge mead hall, which is called Herot, and that around
him are a HUGE BAND OF DANES -- closest to him are WARRIORS,
and ADVISORS, including ESHER, an elderly man, and UNFERTH
(with long black hair streaming out from his winged helm and
intense black eyes).

Further away are the MERCHANTS and the WOMEN and CHILDREN and
DOGS. Everyone is Filthy. For that matter everyone in the
film is filthy.

The queen, WEALTHOW (who is less filthy than everyone else),
stands a little behind the King, with a COUPLE OF HER LADIES.
Wealthow is over thirty years younger than Hrothgar, his
second wife, and is radiantly beautiful. Her chief lady is
YRSA, a girl with intense blue eyes and contrasting black
hair to the queen's blond locks.

The King is happy, shouting loudly enough to be heard by the
furthest dog.

                    HROTHGAR (CONT'D)
                 (continuing)
          In this hall I shall have my throne. In
          this hall we shall feast and tell of
          victories. In this hall shall the scops
          sing their sagas. And in this hall we
          shall divide the spoils of victory, the
          gold and treasure. This shall be a place
          of merrymaking and joy from now until the
          end of time.

1   CONTINUED: 1

Hrothgar holds out a huge bejewelled cup to a PAGE, who pours
mead into it from a jug. Hrothgar holds up the cup.

                    HROTHGAR
          I name this hall...

He takes a huge swig of Mead. His eyes are bright. Then he
pours the rest of the mead on the doorway.

                    HROTHGAR
               (continuing)
          ...Herot!

And the crowd CHEERS.

                                                    CUT TO:

2   INT. HEROT - MEAD HALL - NIGHT   2

Everything is golden and burnished. The CROWD are NOISY AND
CHEERING and happy. We see golden mead being poured from
jugs into goblets. One warrior sticks out his helmet, mead
is poured into it and soon he is drinking from it. A brace
of golden roasted geese are brought out on wooden serving
platters. The fire is burning golden-orange in the
fireplace. It's noisy and riotous.

Hrothgar is sitting at a huge throne, and beside him is a
pile of golden treasure -- wristbands, rings, neck-rings,
helmets and the like.

                                                    CUT TO:

3   EXT. HEROT - THE MOORS - NIGHT   3

We are a short distance away from Herot. All is blue-grey
and still. Mists hang low on the moor. Smoke and MUFFLED
JUBILATION come from the Hall. A door opens and a man
stumbles out to piss.

                                                    CUT TO:

4   INT. HEROT - MEAD HALL - NIGHT   4

NOISE once more assaults our senses. Hrothgar is laughing
loudly at some dirty joke. He picks up his queen, Wealthow,
and kisses her long on the mouth, while she beats at his
chest with her fists, demanding to be put down. His WARRIOR
THANES cheer him on.

                                                    CUT TO:

5   EXT. THE MOORS - HEROT - NIGHT   5

The hall is now a tiny smudge of light in the distance. WE
ARE MOVING AWAY FROM IT, and now are slightly above the
ground. Mists writhe beneath us.

                                                CUT TO:

6   INT. HEROT - MEAD HALL - NIGHT   6

They are dividing the treasure. Hrothgar is having a great
time doing this. He's drunk, but then, everyone's drunk.
With each distribution of treasure, with every joke, THE
CROWD CHEERS.

                    HROTHGAR
               And to Wulf the Eight-Fingered, who was
               valorous in battle but puked like a seasick
               babe whenever he got into a ship--

We see WULF glowering, as his friends nudge him in the ribs.

                    HROTHGAR
                 (continuing)
               --this golden wristband, and this ring.

He tosses them into the crowd. Wulf catches them.

                    HROTHGAR
               For Unferth, my wisest advisor, violator
               of virgins and boldest of brave brawlers--
               where the hell are you, Unferth, you
               weasel-faced bastard? Here you go--

Hrothgar puts a huge golden torque or a thick gold chain
around Unferth's neck. CHEERS. A man throws down a bone for
a dog, onto the rushes of the floor.

                                                CUT TO:

7   EXT. THE MOORS - NIGHT   7

The SOUNDS OF THE REVELRY are almost lost to us now. An owl
HOOTS. We are travelling through the quiet blues and greys
of the mist on the moor. OMINOUS BASS MUSIC starts, almost
imperceptibly.

                                                CUT TO:

8   INT. HEROT - MEAD HALL - MONTAGE - NIGHT   8

IN A SERIES OF SHOTS:

The revelry in the hall is reaching a fever pitch...

9   ERICK,   9

one of Hrothgar's Thanes, is talking to the King, Esher, and
some other warriors.

>   ERICK
>   So I look up, wipe the blood from my
>   eyes, and the bastard's gone and pulled a
>   knife from his boot, he has!
>
>   ESHER
>   And what was it you did?
>
>   ERICK
>   Right. Well. I turned, like this, and I
>   stabbed out, like this, but at the same
>   time, I did this thing, right...

He's trying to show his THANE FRIENDS what he did...he lunges
forward, using a leg of goose as a sword, loses his balance,
falls back, knocking into the King, who goes down.

There is a moment of NERVOUS SILENCE in the hall -- what is
the King going to do?

Hrothgar glares, for a moment, then begins to LAUGH
UPROARIOUSLY, and the hall resumes partying.

10   WULF THE EIGHT-FINGERED   10

is in earnest conversation with a young lady, ISOLDE THE FAT.
He's holding out his golden arm-bracelet.

>   WULF
>   You want to feel it? Yeah, of course
>   it's real gold...
>
>   ISOLDE THE FAT
>   I don't think so, dearie.
>
>   WULF
>   That stuff he was saying about me puking.
>   That was just his little joke. I got a
>   stomach like a rock.

11   A BAND OF WARRIORS   11

      are together in one corner of the hall, singing an obscene
      and lusty warrior song, more or less together.

12   ROLF THE BRAVE IS CHASING GITTE THE SLUT   12

      through the hall. They are both giggling, as they play
      something close to hide and seek.

13   SEVERAL ELDERLY LADIES   13

      sit, almost unaware of the chaos around them, primly sitting
      and eating goose with their fingers. One of them BELCHES
      with relish, surprising us.

14   A KNAVE BOY   14

      is trying to pull a goose-leg away from a DOG. He succeeds,
      and begins gnawing on it himself.

      We are seeing humanity, rough-cut, having a real festival,
      feast, celebration. It's NOISY and rude, and everything is
      burnished with the glitter of gold.

                                                    CUT TO:

15   EXT. DARK FOREST - NIGHT   15

      We are at the nape of a dark primeval forest, just at the
      border of the high moors. The moon is out. It's silent --
      we are much too far away to hear the noise in the feast-hall,
      Herot. Just the WIND HOWLING, an OWL HOOTING...

      ...and the sound of SOMEONE MOANING.

      We cannot see GRENDEL properly. He is more or less a shadowy
      figure in the darkness. But he has his hands clutched over
      his ears, arms extended, and is swaying from side to side, as
      if trying to blot out a noise so loud it's filling his head.
      He is MOANING.

      Then he lowers his hands from his ears, and we hear what
      Grendel hears -- the NOISE OF THE PARTY as an obscene and all-
      engulfing babble of sound: a WALL OF NOISE.

      Grendel steps out into the light of the full moon, a dark,
      huge shape...

                                                    CUT TO:

16   INT. HEROT - MEAD HALL - NIGHT   16

The Hall. The party is in full Danish sixth century swing.

Rolf the Brave and Gitte the Slut are locked in a passionate embrace under the table, possibly fucking. Some are passed out, some are partying full bore, all are drunk. A SCOP, a Bard of the time, is CHANTING and accompanying himself on the HARP. If we can hear the words of his chant, it's about King Hrothgar killing a dragon.

The King, on his throne, one huge hand pawing his wife's waist, closes his eyes and begins to sleep.

                                          CUT TO:

17   EXT. THE MOORS - NIGHT   17

We are travelling towards the hall Herot from Grendel's POINT OF VIEW. We are about 15 feet above the ground and moving inhumanly fast. More OMINOUS MUSIC.

                                          CUT TO:

18   EXT. HEROT - NIGHT   18

A handful of THANES burst out of the great doors of Herot, and begin to adjust their clothing and to piss against the side of the wooden walls. They are chatting while they relieve themselves. They are slightly drunk, and thus taking themselves very seriously. They all have newly-awarded golden torques, armbands and rings.

                    PISSING THANE #1
          So if Christ Jesus and Odin got into a
          fight, who do you think would win?

                    PISSING THANE #2
          A knife fight?

                    PISSING THANE #1
          Any kind of fight.

And then it's the same location, but we're coming towards them from

19   GRENDEL'S POINT OF VIEW.   19

The Thanes must have heard something, because they turn towards us in horror, piss spraying each other, mouths opening soundlessly, but it's too late, because--

20   INT. HEROT - MEAD HALL - NIGHT   20

We hear SCREAMS from outside the hall. The screams of the
pissing Thanes being torn limb from limb.

Hrothgar opens his eyes, waking.

People start sitting up, worried. Warriors reach for swords,
knives, spears.

A DOG BEGINS GROWLING, its fur on end, backing away from the
great door.

There is a pause. A BEAT OF SILENCE, which goes on almost
longer than we can bear and then...

Grendel enters.

We see Grendel in fragments, glimpses. Eyes, sharp-clawed
hands, scaled golden skin, teeth. We see him in fragments
and glimpses, but we do not see him clearly or as a whole as
he seems to bring shadows in with him.

Grendel is huge.

Torches and candles snuff and go out as it enters.

We see Grendel's hand slash out, and a THANE'S HEAD goes
flying, spilling blood as it goes.

Wulf the Eight-Fingered attacks Grendel with a sword. The
sword shatters, and Grendel's fist goes into Wulf's chest,
pulling out his heart. Blood splashes.

Grendel is moving inhumanly fast.

Hrothgar, now awake, is on his throne. An arm comes hurtling
across the room, golden bracelet on its wrist, splattering
blood over him.

Grendel picks up a WARRIOR, bites off his head, sucks the
blood that pours from the neck. Drops the drained thing onto
the floor.

HROTHGAR is about to attack it himself, when Unferth pulls
him back.

                    HROTHGAR
          Let me go. Am I not the King?

20 CONTINUED: 20

> UNFERTH
> You are the King. And that is a monster
> from Hell. There is no dishonor in
> fleeing from such a beast.

Hrothgar pulls away from him, and stumbles toward Grendel,
his sword in his hand.

But Grendel avoids him, with ease.

Grendel has pulled a man apart at the legs, as if it were
splitting a wishbone. It throws the body at the fire,
putting out the last of the light.

The room goes dark.

We hear PEOPLE SCREAMING AND SOBBING, in the darkness.

Then a torch is lit, and another, and another....

In the silence, we see that the room is literally awash with
blood. And that many of the men are gone.

> WEALTHOW
> What was...that?

We spiral in, dizzyingly, into HROTHGAR's blood-spattered
face. And he says:

> HROTHGAR
> Grendel.

                                                        CUT TO:

21 INT. GRENDEL'S LAIR - NIGHT   21

Grendel shambles into his lair -- a cave mouth, beside a
pool. He is dragging two or three bodies in one hand, and
has a couple of other dead warriors slung over his shoulders.
We are watching him from behind, as he moves.

Then he steps into the water, walking down. The dead eyes of
a dead warrior stare at us sightlessly, and then vanish under
water.

                                                        CUT TO:

22 INT. THE GREAT CAVE - GRENDEL'S MOTHER'S LAIR - NIGHT   22

Somewhere under the water there is an underground cave. It
is a strange and unnerving place. There are bones, many of
them human. Greenish-golden light flickers in this place.
Old weapons, of enormous size, are strewn around, hanging on

the glimmering rock walls - particularly a huge GIANT SWORD.
There is a pool taking up some of the place.

Grendel comes, step by laborious step, out of the pool,
dragging his warrior-bodies with him.

GRENDEL'S MOTHER is sitting a little way away, on a ship-
wreck. She is in the shadows, and swathed in dark cloth.
What we can see of her skin glitters, like gold.

This is the first good look we have had at Grendel. He is
huge, and strangely misshapen. His fingernails are sharp
claws, his eyes are serpentine, his teeth are pointed. He is
hairless. But he has charisma, and we feel for him. He is
more or less naked.

Grendel's mother's VOICE is melodious and young.

                    GRENDEL'S MOTHER
          Grendel? What have you done?

                    GRENDEL
          Moth-er? Where are you?

Grendel's Mother stands up, and moves forward. We still
can't see her properly.

                    GRENDEL'S MOTHER
          Men? Grendel...we had an agreement.
          Fish, and wolves, and bear, and sometimes
          a sheep or two. But not men.

                    GRENDEL
          You like men.

                    GRENDEL'S MOTHER
          Grendel. They will hurt us if they can.
          They have killed so many of us...the
          Giant-breed, the Dragon-kind...

                    GRENDEL
          Here.

He holds out a body.

                    GRENDEL'S MOTHER
               (tired)
          Just put it down, Grendel.

                    GRENDEL
          They were making such noise. So much
          noise. It hurt my head and my mind. I
          could not think.

22   CONTINUED: (2)   22

Tears begin to run down Grendel's face. He lets go of all
the warriors he is holding, and they float on the surface of
the pool.

                    GRENDEL'S MOTHER
                (sharply)
            Was Hrothgar there?

                    GRENDEL
            I did not touch him.

Grendel squats down on the rock-floor, and, almost
absentmindedly, begins to eat the face of a warrior.

                    GRENDEL'S MOTHER
                (pacified)
            Good boy. My poor sensitive boy.

                                            CUT TO BLACK:

                    SEVERAL MONTHS LATER

23   EXT. HEROT - VILLAGE - DAY   23

It's a grey, wet, drizzling morning, wet and dull. Unferth
walks though the camp. When he gets to the hall, he sees the
great doors are open, and he goes in.

Then, a few seconds later, he runs out -- we can see that
Unferth limps as he runs -- he has sustained some kind of
injury to his legs from Grendel, since we last saw him.

                                            CUT TO:

24   INT. HEROT - HROTHGAR'S QUARTERS - DAY   24

Hrothgar and Wealthow are asleep in their bed -- a straw
pallet, covered with cloth and deer hides, and, covering
them, more deer hides and furs. They both sleep naked, but
are beneath the fur. The PITTER-PATTER OF RAIN on the roof
can be heard.

Unferth bursts in. He respectfully touches Hrothgar's
shoulder. Hrothgar opens his eyes.

Unferth talks quietly, not wanting to wake Wealthow.

                    UNFERTH
                (whispering)
            My lord?

CONTINUED:

>   HROTHGAR
>   (waking)
>   Hnh? What?

>   UNFERTH
>   My lord. It has happened again.

>   HROTHGAR
>   Grendel's work?

Unferth nods.

>   HROTHGAR
>   How many men this time?

By this time Wealthow has woken. She sits up and looks at
them. The furs have slipped off, revealing her breasts.
Unferth tries hard not to stare at her. Hrothgar, naked,
clambers up from the floor.

>   UNFERTH
>   I could not tell. They were not whole.
>   Five. Ten.

>   HROTHGAR
>   (to Wealthow -- boisterously)
>   Keep the bed warm for me, eh?

>   WEALTHOW
>   (drily)
>   Why?

We realize that all is not well for our King and Queen in the
bed department. Hrothgar ignores this insult to his
masculinity, and pulls a fur robe over his nakedness.

25   EXT. HEROT - VILLAGE - DAY   25

It's still raining, and we can see Hrothgar's bare legs and
feet beneath his fur robe, as he walks with Unferth across
the open space between his sleeping quarters and the hall.

>   HROTHGAR
>   How many does this make it?

>   UNFERTH
>   This is the second attack this moon. The
>   tenth in half a year. He's coming more
>   frequently.

Unferth, walking behind the king, goes into Herot.

26   INT. HEROT - MEAD HALL - DAY   26

The carnage left by Grendel is terrible -- body parts,
bodies, and, above all, blood everywhere -- on the floor and
the walls.

Hrothgar is standing in a puddle of blood, in his bare feet,
and he says, almost sadly:

> HROTHGAR
> When I was young I killed a dragon, in
> the Northern Moors. But I'm too old for
> dragon-slaying now. We need a hero, a
> Siegfried, to rid us of this curse upon
> our hall.

> UNFERTH
> I will not face Grendel again.

Esher, Hrothgar's counsellor, arrives, and stares at the
devastation with them.

> UNFERTH
> I say we trap the beast. Brute strength
> fails against such a brute. Let us use
> cunning.

> HROTHGAR
> These creatures know cunning, Unferth.
> They are cunning.

> ESHER
> Our people wait for deliverance, my King.
> Some of them pray to the Christ Jesus to
> lift this affliction. Others sacrifice
> goats or sheep to Odin, or Heimdall.

> HROTHGAR
> (takes a deep breath)
> This place reeks of death.
> (he turns and leaves, the
> others follow him.)
> The gods will do nothing for us that we
> will not do for ourselves. No, we need a
> hero.

Hrothgar, Esher, and Unferth walk down the

27   HALLWAY   27

Hrothgar leaves bloody, sticky, red footprints behind him,
from his bare feet.

28   EXT. HEROT - DAY   28

Hrothgar et al walk out into the village, it has begun to
rain harder.

                    HROTHGAR
          Men! Build another pyre! There's dry
          wood behind the stables. Then clean out
          the hall. Burn the dead, wash out the
          blood. Put down new straw and reeds on
          the floor.

He begins to walk through the rain, ignoring it completely.
Unferth and Esher walk with him.

                    HROTHGAR
                  (to Unferth and Esher)
          The scops are singing the shame of Herot
          as far south as the middle sea, as far
          north as the ice-lands. Our cows no
          longer calf, our fields lie fallow, the
          very fish flee from our nets, knowing
          that we are cursed. I have let it be
          known that I will give half the gold in
          my kingdom to any man who can rid us of
          Grendel. That should bring us a hero.

                    UNFERTH
          I wish you had had a son, my lord.

                    ESHER
          The country folk hereabouts have a very
          amusing saying about that. "You wish into
          one hand, and shit into the other, see
          which fills up first."

                    HROTHGAR
          There is nothing wrong with hope, Esher.
          It is all that keeps us from being
          animals. A hero will come, because a
          hero must come. We will trust to the
          sea, my friends. It will bring our
          release.

                                        CUT TO:

29   EXT. THE STORMY SEA - DAY   29

Great gray sheets of rain sweep a stormy Northern sea. The
clouds which bear the rain are so full of water they've
swollen to a blackness deep as pitch.

The sun itself has vanished beyond the dark torrent. It
seems it will never return, as sometimes it seems daylight
will never return after a nightmare. But LIGHTNING is here
instead...flashing with its sporadic brilliance, occasionally
illuminating the wave caps.

The ocean is furious. Commander of the tempest above. The
weight of it swells like an angry orchestra...CRASHING with
bombastic fervor...rising with every crescendo. Rhythm to
the melody of rain and lightning.

A man is watching natures symphony play before him. His
curious eye takes in the chaos and out of the randomness
patterns form. Nature's music is heard by him. His name is
BEOWULF.

He wears leather armor studded with hand pounded iron. At
his hip is a heavy, hand forged ancestry sword that at one
time belonged to his father's father. His cape, a tapestry
of heavy black weaves and animal skins, blows in the wind.

Beowulf is standing on the deck of a Nordic craft whose ample
span was never meant for voyages as rabid as this. The poor
vessel slams into each wave with thunderous booms that send
cascading shivers up its wooden ribs.

The red sail has been tattered by the wind -- it has been
ripped to unusable shreds. As it snaps in the gale we can
see the image of a golden dragon emblazoned on it.

At the oars sit FOURTEEN THANES. Their hands, bloodied and
pierced with slivers, tug at the wooden oars rhythmically...
pulling the craft along on its perilous journey through the
waves.

Like a toy carved from a branch the boat is momentarily lost
under the waves' event horizon.

Beowulf, his left hand holding the mast for balance, remains
undaunted by the howling winds and the walls of water
surrounding him. He continues to hold his stare at where the
horizon must be. Somewhere, beyond the dark veil of the
storm, there is a fire to guide him. Somewhere, beyond the
darkness, there will be light and placid waters.

Beowulf's Second in command, a strong Thane with wild red
hair and beard looks up to Beowulf. He is WIGLAF. He ships
his oar, and clambers up to where Beowulf is, shouting --

                    WIGLAF
               (above the wind and rain)
          Can you see the coast? Do you see the
          Dane's guide-fire?

                    BEOWULF
          I see nothing but the wind and the rain.
          And I am unimpressed!

                    WIGLAF
          No fire? No stars by which to navigate?
          We're lost! Given to the sea!

Beowulf looks at him and starts <u>laughing</u>...a laugh of
challenge.

                    BEOWULF
          Ha! The sea is my mother! She will
          never take me into her murky womb!

                    WIGLAF
          That's fine for you. But my mother's a
          fishwife in Uppland. And I was rather
          hoping to die in battle, as a warrior
          should.

He grabs Wiglaf by the shoulders.

                    BEOWULF
               (looking up to the sheets of
                falling rain)
          It's no earthly storm! That much we can
          be sure.
               (then to Wiglaf with a grin)
          It's Hrothgar's sin which shrouds his
          land in this torrent! This demon's
          tempest won't hold us out! No! For our
          journey this storm is not the worry, it's
          the return which you should fear, dear
          friend! None can leave once challenge
          met, lest challenge overcome! And who
          better than us, Wiglaf?

                    WIGLAF
               (who has noticed that Beowulf
                makes no sense what-so-ever)
          What?!

Wiglaf looks at Beowulf with wide, questioning eyes. Is
Beowulf mad? Well, even if he was, Wiglaf would follow him
into the mouth of death herself.

                    BEOWULF
          Man your oar, Wiglaf! Beyond this storm,
          as any, there is calm! As much as beyond
          the calm there will always be storms,
          ready to blow you from your path...

Wiglaf nods with a GRUNT. Good ol' Wiglaf. He turns and
grabs the oars with renewed vigor.

                                                      CUT TO:

30   EXT. THE CLIFFTOPS - DAY   30

Five spears stand together, their blades pointing to the
vertex of the Cimmerian storm above.

The spears belong to the SCYLDINGS' WATCH, a Dane whose duty
it is to watch the coast for invaders. He sits at a camp
he's set up next to some cliff side ruins. He has built a
fire in an ancient pit of unknown origin. Perhaps at one
time this place was an eternal fire to aid ships in storms
such as this. On this day it is being used to cook a kebab
of skewered field mice.

Rain surrounds on the horizons. But here, in this
encampment, there seems to be a proscenium of eerie
stillness. A bubble of barometric pressure keeping the storm
at bay.

The Scyldings' Watch stands up, his rough leather armor,
chapped and weathered, is covered by an animal skin to keep
him dry. He squints his eyes to look at the horizon. There
is nothing but the blackness of the storm clouding it.

This Dane spends his days staring at the line separating the
sea from the sky. It has become his only focus. He's sure
something is there...

And sure enough something is there. A tiny craft with bright
shields hanging from its sides.

His mouth drops open.

There is indeed a ship approaching -- a Geat ship, which
might be a raider.

He drops his mouse kebab and hastily climbs onto his horse.

30   CONTINUED: 30

After grabbing his greatest long spear from the makeshift
rack he takes one last look at the approaching craft and
rides his horse down a...

31   STEEP TRAIL   31

of bramble thicket, still misty from the afternoon showers.
Its trail to the beach below is a near vertical drop of loose
foot stones and crumbly shale.

The Scyldings' coastal guard descends the cliff side at a
fearless speed, confident to the end of his horse's footing.

Soon, he finds himself on a...

32   RECESSED BEACH   32

Nothing more than a glassy sand bar. Once this area was a
tidal plane that met the cliffs. Now it's a field of shallow
pools. A living mirage of sea birds, and the crabs they eat.
It is a scape of neither ocean nor shore, a limbo of
glistening earth, reflecting the gray light of the storm
above.

The Dane's mare, trotting sidelong in grave apprehension,
spies the Geats landing their ship on the bar's edge. It
neighs an abrupt exhalation as it clenches at its bit.

A dwarf horse is being guided off the craft, and from this
vantage point it seems to walk on water.

Scyldings' watch pushes his horse toward a

33   MOORING   33

which the foreign ship has tied on to. A number of Beowulf's
Thanes are unloading weapons from the ship.

Beowulf, standing on the bow of the ship, has been watching
the coast guard's approach.

                    WIGLAF
          He has a horse. What kind of man is he?
          Should we fight?

                    BEOWULF
          That'll be the Scyldings' coastal watch.
          We'll greet him with friendly words.

There is a stir of motion...the armed rider -- the Scyldings'
Watch -- is GALLOPING his horse toward them, over the wet
sands. He has a long spear which he lowers and points before

33   CONTINUED: 33

him, as if to impale the first man he reaches. It's a moment
of fear for Beowulf's men...but not for Beowulf.

Then he reins his horse, a few feet from our ship, in a
splash of water, and points his spear at Wiglaf's neck.

                    SCYLDINGS' WATCH
          Who are you? By your dress, you are
          warriors.

                    WIGLAF
          Yes. We--

                    SCYLDINGS' WATCH
               (not yet prepared to stop
                talking and start listening)
          For more years than you would believe I
          have been on guard here. I have guarded
          Denmark's shore from pirates and raiders,
          after our gold and our women.

                    WIGLAF
          We aren't _after_ your--

                    SCYLDINGS' WATCH
          You have no permission from Hrothgar to
          land. No safe conduct. No passport.
          Hrothgar sent no messengers to tell me
          you were coming. Why should I not run
          you through right now? _Speak_. Who are
          you? Where are you from?

                    BEOWULF
          Leave him be. We are Geats. I am
          Beowulf, son of Edgethow. We have come
          seeking your prince in friendship. We
          have no secrets from Hrothgar. They say
          you have a monster here. Some dire beast
          who comes in the night and has brought
          fear to your land.

                    SCYLDINGS' WATCH
          Is that what they say?

                    WIGLAF
          Bards sing of Hrothgar's shame from the
          frozen north to the shores of Vinland.

                    SCYLDINGS' WATCH
          It is no shame to be accursed by demons.

33   CONTINUED: (2)   33

                        BEOWULF
          It is no shame to accept aid that is
          freely given. I am Beowulf, and I have
          come to kill your monster.

The Watch lifts his glance to Beowulf, looks over him with
questioning eyes.

                                              DISSOLVE TO:

34   EXT. RECESSED BEACH - DAY   34

The Scyldings' Watch is riding upon his horse. Some rain
drops begin to fall from the colorless ether above. The
Watch is struck underneath the eye by a particularly large
drop. He flinches and then looks to the clouds, more drops
speckle his face.

                        SCYLDINGS' WATCH
          Rain.

Beowulf comes trotting ahead, past his men, upon his dwarf
horse, no larger than a Great Dane dog.

                        BEOWULF
          Just the ocean falling from the sky.
          Finding its way to its home the sea.

The Scylding's Watch looks down at Beowulf on the tiny horse.

                        SCYLDINGS' WATCH
                (slightly cynical)
          A small horse...for a Thane as "great" as
          you, Beowulf.

                        BEOWULF
          She is strong enough to bear me, or to
          bear supplies. She does not eat much,
          and takes up little space on our ship.

He nods and then looks ahead, down the

35   KING'S ROAD   35

which is not much more than a rocky road of shale stones set
into the mud. It leads into a forest.

                        SCYLDINGS' WATCH
          You know, if you turn out to be raiders,
          Hrothgar will have my head.

                        BEOWULF
          You trust us.

35   CONTINUED: 35

                         SCYLDINGS' WATCH
                I believe your words. I trust in your
                friendship. But...
                     (he looks down at Beowulf on
                      his little horse)
                ...if you or your men dishonor one
                maiden, or steal one gold ring, before
                you leave...when you come for your ship,
                I'll kill as many of you as I can, before
                you kill me.

                         BEOWULF
                     (approvingly)
                A fine sentiment.

                                                    DISSOLVE TO:

36   EXT. FOREST - THE KING'S ROAD - DAY   36

      Beowulf and his men are marching along, following the
      Scyldings' Watch. The Scylding's Watch reins his horse.

                         SCYLDINGS' WATCH
                This stone path is the kings road.
                     (with a smile)
                It was built in better times. Follow it
                to great Herot, the hall where my King
                waits. This is as far as I go. I must
                return to the cliffs.   The sea must not
                be left unguarded.

                         BEOWULF
                I thank you for your aid.

      The watch kicks his horse, and heads back the way they came.
      And then he reins in his horse and calls,

                         SCYLDINGS' WATCH
                Beowulf?

      Beowulf turns, and looks back at him.

                         SCYLDINGS' WATCH
                The creature took my brother. Kill the
                bastard for me.

                                                    CUT TO:

37   EXT. HEROT - VILLAGE - DAY   37

      There is a stir inside the village stockade, as the VILLAGERS
      see Beowulf and his 14 marching followers coming up the road
      toward them.

37   CONTINUED: 37

The villagers are terrified -- are these armed raiders, come
to carry off the young women (who are either going off to
hide, or making themselves look more desirable, depending on
their temperament) or to burn the town?

They stop marching in front of Hrothgar's mead-hall.
Hrothgar's herald, WULFGAR, a tall, dark-haired thane in his
mid thirties, is standing at the great front doors to the
hall.

                                                        CUT TO:

38   INT. HEROT - THRONE ROOM - DAY   38

We follow Wulfgar through the hall, as he makes his way to
Hrothgar's throne. Hrothgar looks even older and grayer than
he did when last we saw him. He's staring off into nowhere.

                    WULFGAR
          My lord? My lord?

                    HROTHGAR
          Hnh?

                    WULFGAR
          My lord. There are warriors outside,
          Geats. They came over the sea-road,
          bringing messages for your ears alone.
          They are no beggars -- and their leader,
          Beowulf, is a--

                    HROTHGAR
          Beowulf? Edgethow's little boy? Not a
          boy any longer...but I knew him when he
          was a boy. Strong as a grown man he was,
          back then. Yes! Beowulf is here! Send
          him in! Send him to me! Bring him in!

Wulfgar the herald hurries out.

Hrothgar begins to walk around the throne room, looking
younger and happier as he walks. He's placing all his hopes
on Beowulf.

Unferth steps backwards into the shadow at the mention of
Beowulf's name.

                    HROTHGAR
          Wealthow! Unferth! Everybody! Help is
          at hand! Beowulf is here! Treasure --
          we must give him fine gifts. And food,
          and drink, they will have been long at
                         (more)

38   CONTINUED: 38

                        HROTHGAR (CONT'D)
                sea -- bestir yourselves, you ungrateful
                louts!

                                                        CUT TO:

39   EXT. HEROT - VILLAGE - DAY   39

Beowulf and his men are standing around. Beowulf stands like
a statue.

His men, behind him, are staring at a pretty girl, YRSA, who
is eating a large, slightly over-ripe plum with gusto and
relish. Juice runs down her chin and onto her cleavage.

HONDSHEW, one of Beowulf's more ornery Thanes, stares at her
and licks his lips, but whether it's food or companionship
he's after we do not know.

                        YRSA
                Nice Spear.

Hondshew swallows with an almost audible GULP.

Wulfgar, the King's herald, comes out.

                        WULFGAR
                Hrothgar, Master of Battles, Lord of the
                North Danes, bids me say that he knows
                you, Beowulf son of Edgethow, knows your
                ancestry, and bids you welcome. You, and
                your men, shall go in to him.
                    (pause)
                Your weapons shall wait out here for your
                return.

Wiglaf, Esher, Hondshew and the others look at Beowulf for
guidance. None of the Geats is going to put down his weapon
until and unless Beowulf tells them so.

There is a CLATTERING, as Beowulf's sword and spear hit the
ground. He pulls a dagger from his belt and throws it so the
blade sticks in the ground.

His men copy him. The weapons fall to the floor. They
follow Beowulf into the Hall. Wulfgar waits for the last man
to go in. Then he glares at the plum girl, Yrsa.

                        WULFGAR
                Woman! Have you nothing better to be
                doing?

39   CONTINUED: 39

She makes no reply, but with her little finger, wipes the
drip of plum-juice from her breast, and licks it from her
finger.

                                                    CUT TO:

40   INT. HEROT - THRONE ROOM - DAY   40

The WHOLE COURT is assembled here now. Queen Wealthow and
THE QUEEN'S WOMEN, GUARDS and COURTIERS. Unferth is there,
but he is standing in the shadows to the right of the throne,
and is not visible.

Hrothgar hugs Beowulf to him, proudly.

                    HROTHGAR
          Beowulf! How is your father?

                    BEOWULF
          He died in battle with sea-raiders, two
          winters' back.

                    HROTHGAR
          He was a brave man. Need I ask why have
          you come to us?

                    BEOWULF
          They say that there is a monster who
          comes to this hall at night.

                    WEALTHOW
          And there have been many brave men who
          have come here, and have drunk too much
          of my Lord's mead, and have sworn to rid
          his hall of our nightmare. And the next
          morning, there was nothing left of any of
          them but blood to be cleaned from the
          floor and the benches and the walls.

                    BEOWULF
          I have drunk nothing. Yet. But I will
          kill your monster.

                    HROTHGAR
               (overly enthusiastic)
          He will kill the monster! Did you hear
          that? Grendel will die!

                    BEOWULF
          Grendel?

                    HROTHGAR
          The monster is called Grendel.

40   CONTINUED: 40

                    BEOWULF
          Then I shall kill your Grendel. I,
          Beowulf, killed a tribe of giants in the
          Orkneys. I have crushed the skulls of
          sea-serpents. And this...this troll of
          yours shall trouble you no longer.

The Queen is about to say something doubtful about all this,
but Hrothgar, who takes Beowulf at face value, announces to
the hall...

                    HROTHGAR
          A hero! I knew that the sea would bring
          us a hero! Will you go up to the moors,
          then, to the cave by the dark pool, and
          fight the monster in its den?

The Queen, Wealthow, looks doubtful.

Unferth glares from the shadows.

Hrothgar raises his eyebrow, wanting to hear Beowulf tell of
how he'll kill Grendel.

Beowulf steps forward and waves his hand.

                    BEOWULF
          I have fourteen brave Thanes with me. We
          have been long at sea. I think it is
          high time, mighty Hrothgar, to break open
          your golden mead, famed across the world;
          to let the scop chant, and to feast and
          boast and to make merry, in this great
          hall of yours.

Hrothgar squints.

                    HROTHGAR
          But...that will bring the beast here.

Beowulf says nothing, but a huge Cheshire smile spreads
across his face. A smile that's much too huge.

                                                      CUT TO:

41   INT. THE GREAT CAVE - GRENDEL'S LAIR - EVENING   41

Grendel is SINGING to itself, a slow, sad, tuneless sort of
noise. It is taking a soldier apart, bit by bit, and
throwing the bits of body into the water. EELS seize the
fragments of flesh and disappear back under the water with
them. Grendel LAUGHS delightedly at the eels.

>   GRENDEL
>   No more. You get fat! Fat fish! More
>   tomorrow.

Then Grendel walks over to the side of the cave, and puts the
warrior's head on a spike. He hangs the rest of the body
from a hook. He moves awkwardly. While Grendel is not
human, if he were human, he would be retarded, perhaps brain-
damaged. He is honestly a sweet and gentle person, except in
the matter of eating people, and then only when driven mad
with noise.

Grendel begins to play with the spear (and the head on it) as
if it were a puppet.

>   GRENDEL
>   (pretending he's the voice of
>   the Thane's head)
>   Da-dee-da! Da-dee-da! Who's laughing
>   now?!

There is a RUSTLE behind him. Grendel is alarmed; he drops
the head on the spear and his fingernails shoot out and
become sharp claws. His eyes narrow.

EXTREME CLOSE ON: Grendel's mother's lips. She has full
lips, tinged with gold -- almost like fish-scales. Her lips
are not the lips of an old woman. We do not know, yet,
whether or not they are the lips of a monster.

>   GRENDEL'S MOTHER
>   (a bodiless whisper)
>   Grendel.

Grendel soothes a little, his nails recess back into his
fingers.

>   GRENDEL
>   Mother? You should not be here. You do
>   not come here. We are too close to the
>   worlds of man.

>   GRENDEL'S MOTHER
>   I had an evil dream, my son. I dreamed
>   that you were hurt, and killed. I
>   dreamed that you were calling out for me,
>   and I could not come to you. And then
>   they butchered you.

>   GRENDEL
>   I am not dead. I am happy. Look, happy
>   Grendel.

He does an awkward, shuffling dance around the cave, SINGING
as he does.

                    GRENDEL
               (singing, tunelessly)
          Happy happy, happy happy, happy happy,
          happy happy...

                    GRENDEL'S MOTHER
          You must not go to the hall tonight. You
          have killed too many of them.

                    GRENDEL
          Grendel is stronger. Grendel is bigger.
          Grendel will eat their flesh and drink
          their blood and break their bones.

                    GRENDEL'S MOTHER
          Please, my son. Do not go to them.

                    GRENDEL
               (makes a whining sound)
          Oh...

                    GRENDEL'S MOTHER
          Please. Promise me this.

He sulks, defeated.

                    GRENDEL
          I swear. I shall not go to them.

                    GRENDEL'S MOTHER
          Even if they make the noises?

Grendel hesitates, then nods, reluctantly, as if it's being
jerked out of him, an awkward little boy promising his mother
something.

                    GRENDEL'S MOTHER
          Good boy.

                                                    CUT TO:

42   EXT. HEROT - VILLAGE - DAY   42

The sun hangs in the west of the sky, but is still an hour
away from setting.

We are looking at the hall from outside. Smoke is coming
from the chimneys (or from the holes in the roof that let
smoke out). We can hear, MUFFLED HARP MUSIC, the sound of
MEN TALKING, and the CLINKING OF GOBLETS.

43   INT. HEROT - MEAD HALL - DAY   43

Inside the hall, the party is just beginning. It's not the
same party as before, however. For a start there are much
fewer males, even counting Beowulf's 14 Thanes. For second,
everyone seems more subdued and miserable than they did at
the previous party -- like a party at a funeral. Still, a
HARP IS PLAYING, and people are sitting at long tables, and
maidens are pouring golden mead into cups.

Hrothgar is sitting at his throne, which has been carried
into the hall by FOUR BRAWNY THANES.

Wealthow is sitting on the side of the throne, and Hrothgar's
hands are, absentmindedly, stroking her hair.

Unferth is behind and to the right of the throne.

Beowulf is walking about the hall, deep in thought, in
another world entirely.

Hondshew is staring at Yrsa, the plum girl, who is pouring
mead somewhere across the hall.

Wiglaf is talking to the other 13 thanes.

                    WIGLAF
          Look, all I'm saying is we don't want any
          trouble with the locals. So, just for
          tonight, no fighting, and no fucking.
          Okay?

                    OLAF
          I wasn't planning on doing any fucking.

                    WIGLAF
          Well, I obviously wasn't talking to you
          then Olaf, was I?

Yrsa sticks her tongue out at Hondshew. He smiles a yellow-
toothed smile at her.

                    WIGLAF
          Hondshew. Make me feel like you're
          pretending to listen to me. It's only
          been five days since you waved your wife
          goodbye.

This maybe so, but Hondshew is still driven by his loins.

                                                  CUT TO:

44   EXT. HEROT - DAY   44

The sun continues to move West. Now the shadows are long,
and the light has taken on a late afternoon glow. We hear,
muffled, the PARTY NOISE. A little louder than before.

                                                      CUT TO:

45   INT. HEROT - MEAD HALL - DAY   45

Beowulf walks behind Wiglaf, to Hrothgar's throne.
Wealthow's face, unearthly in its beauty, stares at him.

                         WEALTHOW
                I hope that God is kind to you, Sir
                Beowulf. It would be a great shame on
                this house, if one so brave and noble
                were to die in it.

                         BEOWULF
                There is no shame to die in battle with
                evil.

Hrothgar, perhaps getting a little drunk, does not realize
that this is a private conversation, and announces, to
everyone listening, including Unferth, standing in the
shadows...

                         HROTHGAR
                Hear that? _I_ said that before I fought
                the great dragon of the Northern moors!
                Killed him, too. There's a soft spot
                beneath the dragon's chin,
                     (he points to it)
                and you go in with a knife or a dagger...

Wealthow ignores her husband. She says, directly to Beowulf,
eye to eye contact.

                         WEALTHOW
                And if you die?

                         BEOWULF
                There will be no corpse to weep over, no
                funeral to prepare, and none to mourn me.
                Grendel will dispose of my body in a
                bloody animal feast, taking my bones and
                sucking off my flesh, swallowing me down.

Wealthow is obviously sexually turned on by the thought of
sucking and swallowing on Beowulf. She swallows, moistens
her lips, slightly upset by her reaction.

45   CONTINUED: 45

She forces a smile.

                    WEALTHOW
          I would mourn you, my lord.

                    BEOWULF
          It is up to fate, and fate will go as it
          must.

Hrothgar has completely missed the moment of strange romance
between his wife and the young warrior. Or perhaps he
hasn't...either way, he begins to talk, getting up from his
chair.

                    HROTHGAR
          Your father came here fleeing the
          Wylflings. He'd killed one of them--

                    BEOWULF
          Heatholaf.

                    HROTHGAR
               (nodding vigorously and then
                continuing)
          --that was him! I paid the blood debt
          for your father, and he swore his oath to
          me. No good deed goes unrewarded,
          though. I saved his skin, now you're
          here to save ours, eh?

He SLAPS Beowulf on the back.

We hear A LOW, BITTER, LAUGH from the shadows behind the
throne. Unferth steps out of the shadows into the light,
CLAPPING his hands.

                    UNFERTH
          All hail the great Beowulf!
               (softer, to Beowulf)
          Here to save our pathetic Danish skins,
          eh?
               (bitter irony & plenty of it)
          And we are so damned grateful, mighty
          Beowulf. But can I ask a question -- as
          a huge admirer of yours?

Beowulf simply stares at him, with the sort of unblinking
stare that Clint Eastwood made famous.

                    UNFERTH (CONT'D)
          You see, there was another Beowulf I
          heard tell of, who challenged Brecca the
                         (more)

45   CONTINUED: (2)   45

> UNFERTH (CONT'D)
> mighty to a swimming race, out on the
> open sea. Was that you?

Beowulf wonders if he's being set up. But he nods.

> BEOWULF
> I swam against Brecca.

> UNFERTH
> Hmm. I thought that it had to be a
> different Beowulf. Someone else of the
> same name. You see--
>> (he has raised his voice here,
>> to try and make sure that
>> everyone in the mead hall can
>> hear him)
> --the Beowulf I heard of swam against
> Brecca, and lost. He risked his life,
> and Brecca's, in the deep ocean to serve
> his own vanity and pride. A boastful
> fool. And he lost. So I thought it had
> to be someone else...

Beowulf stands, and slowly walks toward Unferth. You could
hear a pin drop. All the Thanes, both Hrothgar's and
Beowulf's, are preparing themselves for a brawl to break out
between the two men.

> BEOWULF
> I swam against Brecca.

> UNFERTH
>> (loudly)
> But victory was his, not yours. A mighty
> warrior who cannot even win a swimming
> match. Speaking only for myself here, I
> not only doubt that you will be able to
> stand for a moment against Grendel, but I
> doubt you will even have the guts to stay
> in the hall all night.

He grins up at Beowulf. This is a drama, being enacted for
everyone else, and we should get REACTION SHOTS from some of
the people around -- Wealthow and Hrothgar, but also the
commoners. Beowulf's Thanes, however, are not interested in
any of this -- they've heard this a thousand times.

> BEOWULF
> I find it difficult to argue with a
> drunk. And it is true that I did not win
> the race...

DISSOLVE TO:

46   THE MEMORY OF THE RACE WITH BRECCA   46

Beowulf is a tiny Jan Svankmajer doll, swimming in stop-
motion animation a race with Brecca, another doll. Bony,
strange, nightmare creatures, like marine versions of the
Wonderland inhabitants of Svankmajer's "Alice", rise up from
beneath Beowulf, and drag him down beneath the sea.

                    BEOWULF (V.O.)
                  (continuing)
            We swam for five days, neck and neck.
            And I was the more powerful swimmer. I
            was conserving my strength, for the final
            stretch. Then a storm blew up, and with
            the storm, came sea monsters.

We HEAR the Thanes in the hall MURMURING with approval.

We watch the little Beowulf killing the monsters, one by one.

                    BEOWULF (V.O.)
            One of them seized me in its jaws, and
            dragged me to the bottom. I hacked at it
            with my sword, and killed the huge beast
            with my own blade. Again and again the
            monsters attacked, dark things from the
            sea's dark depths. I was to have been
            their banquet. When morning came they
            were lying on the shore, their guts
            spilling crimson into the salt-water.Luck
            was with me, perhaps, but still, I killed
            nine of them. I did not win the race,
            but I braved their hot jaws, making those
            lanes safe for seamen, and survived the
            nightmare.

                                        DISSOLVE TO:

47   INT. HEROT - MEAD HALL - DAY   47

EXTREME CLOSE ON: Beowulf's face. We see something in his
eyes that reveals that what we have just been told may not be
the truth.

He shuts his eyes, remembering something else...something
forbidden.

                                        DISSOLVE TO:

48   THE MEMORY OF BIRTH   48

Beowulf is swimming beneath the sea. And he sees something
GOLDEN and glittering, and he swims after it. It appears

48   CONTINUED: 48

from the glimpses we get of it, to be a beautiful golden
woman, underwater. She is not a mermaid, but there is
something inhuman about her. However, we only glimpse her in
tiny fragmentary moments, never getting a good look.

DISSOLVE TO:

49   INT. HEROT - MEAD HALL - DAY   49

Beowulf shakes himself out of the memory, forcing it
somewhere deep back into his subconscious. He begins to
walk, continuing.

                    BEOWULF
          They sing of my battle with the sea
          monsters to this day, my friend. And
          they sing no such songs about Brecca.

                    UNFERTH
               (magnificently unimpressed)
          Of course. The sea monsters. And you
          killed, what, twenty was it?

                    BEOWULF
          Nine. But...will you do me the honor of
          telling me your name?

                    UNFERTH
          I am Unferth, son of Ecglaf.

                    BEOWULF
          Unferth? Son of Ecglaf? Your fame has
          crossed the ocean ahead of you. I know
          who you are...

Unferth does not know if Beowulf is telling the truth. But
he starts to preen a little...

                    BEOWULF
          Let's see....they say you are clever.
          Not wise, but sharp. And they say that
          you killed both of your brothers when you
          caught them having knowledge of your
          mother, "Unferth Kinslayer".
               (laughs)
          A crime for which you will roast in agony
          forever.

After a protracted moment of hate, Unferth throws himself at
Beowulf, growling. Beowulf steps aside and Unferth, bad leg
and all, trips and falls to the floor of the hall. Beowulf
crouches beside him. And, with a captive audience, he
continues.

49   CONTINUED: 49

                              BEOWULF
                    I'll tell you another true thing, Unferth
                    Kinslayer. If your strength and heart
                    had been as strong and fierce as your
                    words, then Grendel would never have
                    crippled you. But he murders and gorges
                    on you people, with no fear of
                    retaliation. Tonight he will find Geats
                    waiting for him: not crippled sheep, like
                    you.

Hrothgar starts CLAPPING. Is he senile, or sensibly breaking
up the fight?

                              HROTHGAR
                    That's the spirit, young Beowulf! That's
                    the spirit we need! You'll kill my
                    Grendel for me.

                                                            CUT TO:

50   EXT. HEROT - MEAD HALL - SUNSET   50

A bloody sky in the west, and the sun hangs like a huge ball
of orange fire. We hear the sound, MUFFLED, OF PARTYING. It
sounds like they're starting to have fun in the hall...

                                                            CUT TO:

51   INT. THE GREAT CAVE - GRENDEL'S LAIR - SUNSET   51

Grendel is on the floor of its cave, rolling back and forth,
moaning in misery. We cannot be sure whether or not Grendel
is even awake. We can hear, distorted, THE PARTY SOUNDS.

                                                            CUT TO:

52   INT. HEROT - MEAD HALL - SUNSET   52

The party is in full swing, and, following the fracas between
Beowulf and Unferth, everything seems to have loosened up.
The Danes know that Grendel will not be attacking until dark,
and are beginning to party.

We see the glitter of gold everywhere, rings on fingers,
light flashing from mugs and goblets (each person has his or
her own mug or goblet). Beowulf's thanes are eating, with
their fingers and with knives, from a huge cut of beef on the
table.

Hondshew cuts a slice of beef, with his knife, and puts it
into the mouth of Yrsa, who is walking past with a jug of
mead.

52   CONTINUED: 52

Wealthow has brought a huge, silver and golden jug of gold
mead out.

                    HROTHGAR
          The High King's mead! The finest mead!

                    WEALTHOW
          For our brave Geats.

Wealthow moves from Thane to thane, pouring each of them a
cup of mead, while Hrothgar says things like:

                    HROTHGAR
          I know it doesn't look like much, but
          it's the most powerful stuff we have.
          Three cups of that and they'll be
          carrying you out of here.

The mead runs out just as it gets to Beowulf. Wealthow walks
off, looking back at Beowulf.

                    UNFERTH
               (to Beowulf)
          The mead is gone, before Lord Beowulf
          mighty fighter of sea monsters had his
          cup of inspiration.

                    BEOWULF
          At least I do not get my courage from the
          mead-cup.

But at this moment Wealthow returns, bearing high a huge
golden cup crusted with jewels, the treasure cup, filled with
mead. She smiles at Lord Beowulf and passes him the cup.
The hall rings with loud CHEERS.

                                                      CUT TO:

53   INT. THE GREAT CAVE - GRENDEL'S LAIR - SUNSET   53

Grendel's eyes are open. We hear the CHEERS FROM THE PARTY,
blasting at monstrous and distorted levels. Grendel clamps
his hands over his ears and thrashes on the rocky floor of
its Den.

                                                      CUT TO:

54   INT. HEROT - MEAD HALL - SUNSET   54

Wealthow gives the cup to Beowulf. The party is loud enough
that they are able to speak quietly to each other, unheard by
everyone else. Beowulf sips the mead from the goblet.

54   CONTINUED: 54

                              WELTHOW
               The goblet is a gift for you, Beowulf.

                              BEOWULF
               You do me great honour, lady.

                              WEALTHOW
               It is we who are honoured.
                    (she hesitates then)
               Grendel. Our curse. He is my husband's
               shame.

                              BEOWULF
               Not a shame, but a curse.

                              WEALTHOW
               Shame. Hrothgar has no...other sons...
               And he will have no more, for all his
               talk.

          And with these enigmatic words, she returns to the King's
          throne, Beowulf following her progress back with his eyes.

          Someone SHOUTS "Speech!" and the CRY is taken up by the whole
          room, slamming mugs and feet against the floor and the bench.

                              ALL
                         (rhythmic chant)
               Speech! Speech! Speech! Speech!

                                                              CUT TO:

55   INT. THE GREAT CAVE - GRENDEL'S LAIR - SUNSET   55

          Grendel writhes in agony as we hear this NOISE, louder and
          harsher than anything he's heard so far. He MOANS. He hits
          his head against the cave floor, as if trying to distract
          himself from the noise, causing his forehead to bleed.

                                                              CUT TO:

56   INT. HEROT - MEAD HALL - SUNSET   56

          Beowulf clambers onto a table. He raises the goblet high...

                              BEOWULF
               When we crossed the rolling sea to come
               to you, we knew, my men and I, that we
               would either triumph over evil, or we
               should perish in Grendel's grasp.
               Tonight, here in this very hall, we shall
               live forever in greatness and courage,
               or, forgotten and despised, we shall die!

56   CONTINUED: 56

                          WIGLAF
                     (sotto voce)
               Well that pretty much covers all our
               options, doesn't it?

                                                              CUT TO:

57   EXT. THE SEA - SUNSET   57

      The red ball of the sun falls in the Western sea, and goes
      out, with an almost imperceptibly green flash. It is now
      night.

                                                              CUT TO:

58   INT. HEROT - MEAD HALL - NIGHT   58

      And now, Hrothgar leans back in his throne. He yawns,
      ostentatiously.

                          HROTHGAR
               Well, this old man needs his sleep.
               Where's my bed-mate? Wealthow my dear?
               Shall we pound the pillow?

      He claps his hand, and the four thanes lift his throne and
      carry it, and him, out of the room. Wealthow follows, and
      looks back at Beowulf.

                          UNFERTH
               Good night, Beowulf. Watch out for sea
               monsters. I'm sure your imagination must
               be teeming with them.

                          BEOWULF
               I will. Watch out for brothers.

                                                              CUT TO:

59   EXT. HEROT - NIGHT   59

      The sun set half an hour ago. Hondshew and the plum girl are
      arguing outside the mead hall, in the shadows. While the
      conversation is going on, DANES are SLIPPING OUT OF THE HALL
      and going to their homes, looking about nervously...

                          HONDSHEW
               Oh, go on.

                          YRSA
               I said no

                        HONDSHEW
            Oh go on, please...

                        YRSA
            I said no and I meant no

                        HONDSHEW
            Why not?

                        YRSA
            Because it's too late. Sorry.

                        HONDSHEW
            I could transport you to paradise, Take
            you to ecstasy and back with my magic
            spear. No other man will be able to
            satisfy you again.

                        YRSA
            I don't think so.

                        HONDSHEW
            Well how about a quick blowjob?

                                                    CUT TO:

60   INT. HEROT - MEAD HALL - NIGHT   60

Beowulf and his men are sitting around a table, drinking,
SINGING and generally having a party.

PULL BACK TO REVEAL: No one else there.

It's just Beowulf and his men. Hondshew comes back in. The
thanes HOOT AND JEER him:

                        THANES
            Oy, Hondshew. Did you get any? How was
            she?

                        HONDSHEW
            Nah. Not my type.

The rest of the thanes laugh at him.

                        OLAF
            Yeah? What's your type? A sheep that
            runs slow enough for you to catch her?
            Baaa!

Hondshew throws himself at Olaf, and they roll around on the
floor, fighting -- or mock fighting, anyway. The other

60   CONTINUED: 60

thanes are laughing, cheering for Olaf or for Hondshew,
chanting.

                    THANES
              (chanting in unison, two
              teams)
          Hondshew! Hondshew! Hondshew! Olaf!
          Olaf! Olaf!

                                                   CUT TO:

61   INT. THE GREAT CAVE - GRENDEL'S LAIR - NIGHT   61

Long shot. The mouth of the cave. We can hear, Grendel-
style, the CHANTING of 'Olaf' and 'Hondshew', but we can only
see the mouth of the cave. We are waiting for something to
happen, and then...

Grendel SCREAMS. It's a scream that tears at our hearts and
guts, a noise as animal as it is human.

                                                 DISSOLVE TO:

62   INT. HEROT - MEAD HALL - NIGHT   62

The fight between Olaf and Hondshew is pretty much over. We
hear, from a distance, GRENDEL SCREAMING. The men stop what
they're doing and look around.

                    WIGLAF
          What was that?

                    BEOWULF
          A wolf. Or an owl.

                    OLAF
          Maybe it was... Grendel...
              (then he laughs to show us he
              was only joking)

Someone cuffs him in the head. Beowulf stands up and walks
across the hall, to the fire. Then, almost like a strip-
tease, with the firelight behind him, he begins to take off
his clothes, starting with his wolf-bear fur cloak.

                    WIGLAF
          My lord Beowulf...What are you doing?

                    BEOWULF
              (continuing to undress, taking
              off his armor)
          When Grendel comes, we will fight as
          equals. The creature has no sword, no
                    (more)

62   CONTINUED: 62

                          BEOWULF (CONT'D)
              armor, no boots. I shall fight him on
              equal terms. Fate shall decide.

                          WIGLAF
              Oh.

                          BEOWULF
              Wake me when the monster comes.

He lies down on the floor, his head pillowed by his rolled-up
clothes.

                          WIGLAF
                     (repeating to himself -- not
                      quite as under his breath as
                      he thinks)
              "Wake me when the monster comes" -- what
              are we here for, then?

                          BEOWULF
                     (his eyes closed, to himself)
              Bait.

                                                    CUT TO:

63   EXT. HEROT - MEAD HALL - NIGHT   63

The moon is almost full, and is high in the sky. Night
surrounds the hall of Hrothgar like a black velvet cloak. We
can hear RAUCOUS SINGING, muffled, inside.

                                                    CUT TO:

64   INT. HEROT - MEAD HALL - NIGHT   64

Beowulf is sleeping, naked, in front of the fire.

A couple of the thanes are having a knife fight with their
hands tied together, and they have a small audience.

More of the thanes are standing around in a semicircle, arms
linked, singing. The tune is rough-and-ready, rugby song
type thing:

                          THANES
                     (singing in verse)
              There were a dozen virgins,
              All Friesians and Franks!
              We took 'em for a boat-ride,
              and all we got were wanks!
                     (chorus)
              OOohh, We are Beowulf's army, we are
              mighty thanes, we'll steal your cattle,
              and take your girls, then we'll do it all
                     (more)

64   CONTINUED: 64

                          THANES (CONT'D)
          over again!
               (verse)
          The prettiest of the virgins,
          she was the fairest swede!
          I told her I'd an urgin',
          for where to spend my seed!
               (chorus)
          Singing *we are Beowulf's army, we are*
          mighty thanes, we'll steal your cattle,
          and take your girls, then we'll do it all
          over again!
               (verse)
          The oldest of the virgins,
          she was a Vandal lass!
          I showed my mighty weapon,
          and she showed me her ass!
               (chorus)
          Singing *we are Beowulf's army, we are*
          mighty thanes, we'll steal your cattle,
          and take your girls, then we'll do it all
          over again...

They SING happily and obscenely, taking it in turns to
alternate verses, all joining in on the choruses. They are
all sweating -- the fire's heat has turned the hall into a
sauna, and anyway, they are drunk.

                                                         CUT TO:

65   EXT. HEROT - NIGHT   65

      SLOW ZOOM OUT OF Herot, its heavy stones can't hold the
      JUBILANT LAUGHTER of the rowdy Thanes. A monument to
      mankind's resilience, it may hold out warring hordes but it
      can't hold the BOISTEROUS SINGING inside.

                                                         CUT TO:

66   EXT. THE MOORS - NIGHT   66

      The song inside the mead hall seems to echo through the moors
      as if it were some great parabolic transmitter amplifying the
      fete du soir.

                                                         CUT TO:

67   EXT. DARK FOREST - NIGHT   67

      WE SLOWLY MOVE through a dark forest of primordial origin.
      The THANE'S SONG still resounding through the night,
      stillness carrying it beyond the realm of man.

                                                         CUT TO:

68   EXT. THE GREAT CAVE - NIGHT   68

SLOW ZOOM INTO the mouth of a great cave into which feeds a
mighty torrent of water. The SINGING, now louder than ever,
seems to be coming from inside the murky burrow.

The CHANTS have reached a fever pitch. Swollen to an
amplitude of unprecedented intensity. Never before has a
song of happiness seemed to warp into a TORTUROUS REQUIEM.
An aria of joy and light, underscored by darkness and self
doubt...

69   INT. THE GREAT CAVE - GRENDEL'S LAIR - NIGHT   69

To hear it all there is GRENDEL, a deformed man of gargantuan
size. His skin like stretched leather over ancient muscles.
His hands clutched tightly over the sides of his oblong
skullcap. His golden eyes pinched tightly shut, tears of
blood drip from them. This is a monster born of pain. Once
a man, now twisted into a caricature of insanity and
depravity.

He writhes in pain at the song inside his head. His naked
body scarring the sodden floor of the cave around him.

The dank walls, lichen covered and scared with roots, seem to
close in on Grendel as if the monster were inside an immense
trash compactor. A claustrophobic nightmare has manifested
itself into Grendel's twisted reality.

Indeed, the cave is growing smaller. Or is it that Grendel
is growing bigger?!

The behemoth has grown so large he can barely fit into the
room. The tiny bones of many Thanes litter the sarcophagus
chamber, some bleached with age, others still ripe with their
fruity flesh. Their armor, now dwarfed by the monster's
size, seem like small cans of ripped open tomato paste.

The monster can no longer take the haunting song of happiness
inside his twisted brain. He scrambles for the exit to this
tomb of song.

There is only one thing that can stop the noise inside his
head. Murder. Murder of all things living and good. Murder
of all things beautiful and proud.

                                                    CUT TO:

70   INT. HEROT - MEAD HALL - NIGHT   70

Beowulf, naked and laying on the floor, opens his eyes from
his slumber. Almost as if he knows what's coming.

70   CONTINUED: 70

                         THANES
                    (still singing their song in
                     verse)
               The fattest of the Virgins,
               I knew her for a whore!
               I gave her all my codpiece,
               And still she wanted more!
                    (chorus)
               Singing *we are Beowulf's army, we are
               mighty thanes, we'll steal your cattle,
               and take your girls, then we'll do it all
               over again...*

                                                          CUT TO:

71   INT. THE GREAT CAVE - GRENDEL'S LAIR - CRAWLSPACE - NIGHT   71

Grendel squirms through the tight crawlspace, big enough for
the shoulders of twenty men. The Thane's song has Grendel in
a shrieking frenzy. Anything to escape from the cave, where
the warrior's hymn echoes against the hard stone walls.

                                                          CUT TO:

72   INT. HEROT - NIGHT   72

Beowulf smiles. He knows what's coming.

                         THANES
                    (continuing their song in
                     verse)
               A virgin was from Norway,
               She cost me twenty groats!
               She showed me there was more ways,
               Than one to sow my oats!
                    (chorus)
               Singing *we are Beowulf's army, we are
               mighty thanes, we'll steal your cattle,
               and take your girls, then we'll do it all
               over again...*

                                                          CUT TO:

73   EXT. DARK FOREST - NIGHT   73

Grendel, in a frenzy of anger and hate is charging through
the forest, knocking trees down in his tortured frenzy.

                                                          CUT TO:

74   INT. HEROT - MEAD HALL - NIGHT   74

CLOSE ON: Beowulf's open eyes.

                          THANES (O.S.)
                    (singing in verse)
          There was a girl from Iceland,
          And she was mighty hot!
          She'd take a whole damn iceberg,
          To cool her burning tw--

The Thanes' song is suddenly interrupted by a BANGING on the
heavy wooden door.

                        OLAF
          That'll be Grendel now! Ooh! It's
          fucking Grendel!

The Thanes LAUGH raucously at Olaf's witticism.

Hondshew jumps from the table and turns to the other Thanes
as he walks backwards toward the hallway that leads to the
door.

                       HONDSHEW
          It's Yrsa, my sweet plum! She's changed
          her mind and is ready to allow me to
          taste her ripe and juicy fruit!

The Thanes LAUGH LOUDLY. Hondshew, drunk as a particularly
drunk drunkard, stumbles down

THE HALLWAY

to the large main double doors to open them up.

                       HROTHGAR
          Patience, my lovely! Give a Thane a
          chance to open the door and invite you...

He swings the door open only to find Grendel, looking quite
large and hideous.

                       HONDSHEW
          (continuing, but a tad more
           sober)
        ...in.

Grendel SNARLS a sort of hideous laugh.

75   INT. HEROT - MEAD HALL - NIGHT   75

The other Thanes are waiting for Hondshew to come in carrying
the fair woman.

                         THANE
               Save some for us, Hondshew! We've got
               pricks that need a waxin', as well!

Suddenly Hondshew's bloodied and ripped up corpse is thrown
from the hallway and into the great hall. It flops on top of
a long table like a rag doll whose joints allow his limbs to
move in any direction.

                         THANE
               Hondshew?

But Hondshew is clearly dead as a doorknob.

And at that moment, in the flickering golden light of the
fireplace, Grendel comes from out of the hallway, his SNARL
is preceded by a horrific gaping grin that shows off his
yellow canines. His sick skin glistens a wet shade of
greenish gold, but appears to be scarred and nicked from
scratching at himself nervously. His talons are simply
broken nails as hard as marble, sharpened by scraping at the
earthen soil of his cavernous lair. Simply put, Grendel is
one scary motherfucker.

                    FREAKED-OUT THANE
               Fucking fuck! It's the monster! Get
               yourselves awake!

The freaked-out Thane kicks one of his sleeping drunken mates
to wake him, but the sad warrior has drunken himself into
oblivion. Even another, harder kick doesn't help. In fact,
most of the Thanes in the hall have drank so much mead that
they're dead to the world...passed out.

The singing Thanes (who are now the freaked-out Thanes) draw
their broadswords...but it's too late, for Grendel is upon
them.

With one mighty swing Grendel hurls the table of Thanes
aside, sending some of them into the massive firepit, and
others tumbling across the floor.

Wiglaf is awoken by the CLAMOR.

Grendel LAUGHS as he stomps on TWO SLEEPING THANES, crushing
life out of their slumbering bodies.

A few of the THANES WHO WERE THROWN INTO THE FIRE roll out
and try to beat the flames from their bodies. Some of them,
unable to continue despite being roasted alive, fall to their
knees and slump too the ground in burning heaps.

The hideous creature picks one man up, who is too drunk to
know what's happening to him, and throws him down onto his
bent leg, SNAPPING his back with a LOUD CRUNCH.

Grendel starts LAUGHING to himself with every dead Thane he
stomps on.

Then, Grendel comes to Beowulf...naked and laying on the
floor. Beowulf is like a nice, soft, shell-less morsel by
comparison to the greasy, armor-wearing thugs he's been
killing. He raises his foot to crush Beowulf.

Then, from behind Grendel...

                    WIGLAF
          Die demon!

Wiglaf strikes at Grendel's back with his sword, but the
blade BREAKS against the creatures tough skin.

Grendel spins around and strikes at Wiglaf, who manages to
hold up his small shield just before the massive arm swats
him aside like a defenseless kitten.

Wiglaf slides backwards and into a rack of spears which CRASH
down around him.

Grendel turns around and faces Beowulf again, but Beowulf
isn't there.

Grendel SNARLS.

Beowulf, naked as the day he was born, leaps onto Grendel's
back and locks his arm around Grendel's neck in a chokehold.

The monster jerks forward, causing Beowulf to topple head
over heels over Grendel's head. He lands on his back with a
HARD THUD, knocking the wind out of his lungs.

Grendel then grabs a keg of mead and raises it above his
head, with the intention of slamming it down onto the already
stunned Beowulf's head.

But before Grendel can gore Beowulf, Wiglaf is upon him,
attempting to run the monster through with a spear.

Beowulf grabs a length of golden chain -- part of Hrothgar's
treasure...

ONE OF HROTHGAR'S THANES wakes up and comes to help, or die.

Beowulf lashes the chain around Grendel's hand and pulls it
tight. The monster lets out a HORRIFIC SHRIEK and rips the
chain free from Beowulf.

Then, angry Grendel lashes the chain like a whip, causing it
to wrap multiple times around the neck ONE OF HROTHGAR'S
DRUNKEN THANES. While it can be argued that the Thane died
then and there, no one would argue that he lived after
Grendel yanked on the chain, causing the head to SNAP free
from the body and rapidly tumble across the floor toward

76   BEOWULF   76

who kicks it aside like a soccer ball.

Beowulf is PICKED UP by Grendel, like a child holding a large
doll. Grendel obviously plans to bite Beowulf's head off,
but in a maneuver made famous by Scottish soccer hooligans,
but originally invented by Swedish heroes, Beowulf HEADBUTTS
Grendel -- a head to forehead crash that leaves blood
spilling from Grendel's face.

Grendel is dazed and hurt, for the first time on one of its
nocturnal expeditions. It begins to WHIMPER.

Beowulf takes advantage of this by biting Grendel's cheek, at
the same time that his hands fasten around Grendel's throat.

Grendel shakes Beowulf as if trying to free himself from
something that's bad and hurting him, shaking himself
desperately -- and Beowulf FLIES OFF, crashing into some
dead bodies, which cushion his fall.

Beowulf then runs toward Grendel, who is trying to flee
towards the open door at the end of the hallway that leads
out of the mead hall, still dragging the chain along behind
him.

Beowulf, fearing that Grendel might escape, dives for the
chain and grabs it, causing him to be dragged along with it
into the

77   HALLWAY   77

which leads to the large main doors to Herot, and ultimately
to the outside.

In mid-slide Beowulf manages to hook the chain onto a large
nail half sticking out of a massive support beam, jolting
Grendel to a stop just in the threshold of the door, with an
unsettling POP OF DISLOCATION in his shoulder.

CONTINUED:

The chain, hooked onto the nail, has yanked at the beam so
hard that it has ripped it partially from the wall. Support
stones, wood planks, and mud-fill begin to shower down from
above as the hallway begins to partially collapse.

Grendel ROARS in agony and pain as he tugs at the chain and
claws at his wrist's shackle.

                                                        CUT TO:

78   INT. HEROT - HROTHGAR'S QUARTERS - NIGHT   78

We can hear, slightly muffled, the THUDS and CRASHES of the
battle between Grendel and Beowulf going on. Hrothgar lies
in bed, covered with furs, beside Wealthow, listening to the
noise.

Then the NOISE STOPS.

Wealthow begins, very softly, to cry.

                    WEALTHOW
            He is dead. Beowulf is dead.

                    HROTHGAR
            I had hoped it would be otherwise.

Hrothgar shakes his head. Then he moves closer to Wealthow,
and reaches out a hand to paw at her breast. Wealthow hits
at it.

                    WEALTHOW
            Monsters come out of your cock. How can
            I let you inside me, knowing you were in
            her?

                    HROTHGAR
            I should never have told you.

                    WEALTHOW
                (getting progressively more
                 turned on as she talks)
            Poor, poor Beowulf. Now he is dead, and
            he will never make love to me. He will
            never touch me with his strong hands, and
            his hot mouth.

Hrothgar looks uncomfortable at this.

                                                        CUT TO:

79   INT. HEROT - HALLWAY - NIGHT   79

Beowulf, who is by now cut, bruised, and bloodied sees that
Grendel is captured and unraveling the chain from his wrist.
Beowulf scrambles to action and runs toward Grendel.

Grendel, who sees that Beowulf is running toward him,
quickens his efforts to free himself.

But it's too late...

Beowulf slides like he was coming in to home base and kicks
the door closed with his foot, SLAMMING the heavy wooden
portal onto Grendel's arm. He has Grendel caught by the arm,
and while Grendel can flail wildly he can't seem to get
loose. The demon lets out the SCREAM OF A CAGED HOWLER
MONKEY.

                    BEOWULF
               (holding the door shut on the
                flailing arm)
          Your days of blood-letting are finished,
          demon!

                    GRENDEL
          Let...Grendel...free!

Beowulf is a little shocked. He didn't expect to be able to
hold a conversation with this nemesis.

                    BEOWULF
          It speaks!

                    GRENDEL
          I speak! I think! I am!

                    BEOWULF
          Perhaps you are...but you won't be for
          long!

He begins pressing the door shut with the wedge, causing the
sinewy tendons to begin to SNAP and Grendel's bones to POP
free from the socket. Grendel SHRIEKS.

                    BEOWULF
          Think you now of the Thanes whose lives
          you've stolen! Think you of them as you
          die your demon's death!

And with one powerful lunge with the wedge Beowulf causes the
door to SLAM shut. The arm, with a SQUISHY RIPPING SOUND,
falls free from its socket and lands on the floor with a
satisfying MEATY THUD.

79   CONTINUED: 79

Beowulf stands there, staring at the arm for a moment...when
suddenly it grabs his foot. He kicks wildly at it, finally
shaking it loose.

The arm flops around on the stone floor for a few moments
like a beached fish and then suddenly seizes into a contorted
position of agony.

Beowulf, for the first time, is freaked. He stands there,
leaning against the door, breathing heavily in great gasping
WHEEZES.

Several Thanes, swords drawn and bodies bleeding, appear at
the

80   OPPOSITE END OF THE HALLWAY   80

looking at Beowulf. Wiglaf pushes himself to the front of
them.

                    WIGLAF
          Grendel's arm! You've done it! You've
          killed him!
               (turning to the other men)
          He's done it! He's torn the limbs from
          the beast!

They all begin CHEERING.

81   BEOWULF   81

on the other hand, doesn't seem so confident. He quickly
turns and pulls the door open, revealing

82   THE OUTSIDE OF HEROT   82

As if a nightmare is over -- it's placid and quiet and there
is a marked absence of Grendel around.

                                              MATCH CUT TO:

83   THE OUTSIDE OF HEROT   83

The nightmare is over. But it is now morning, and all is
well. We hear HAMMER BLOWS, rhythmic as sex.

84   INT. HEROT - MEAD HALL - DAY   84

CLOSE ON: Grendel's arm is being NAILED into a massive
wooden beam in the mead hall.

84   CONTINUED: 84

It is Beowulf who wields the massive blacksmith's hammer.
Beowulf laughs as he nails Grendel's arm to the wall, and we
wonder, which one is the monster?

                                                        CUT TO:

85   INT. THE GREAT CAVE - DAY   85

From the inside of the great cave, the outside world is a
bright and hot place. Grendel comes stumbling in from this
world of light and heat into the safety of the cave. He is
in silhouette and we can see that he is missing his arm.

Grendel shambles awkwardly, dripping crimson blood as he
goes, toward the placid clear waters of the cavern's pool.

Grendel is making A DREADFUL SOUND as it goes, one arm
missing, into the pool, with little or no sense of balance,
stumbling and half-falling. It should take us a few moments
to realize that the noise Grendel is making is SOBBING.

Grendel falls through the dark water of the pool, blood from
his shoulder, from the missing arm, pumping out into the
water, until everything is red and we

                                                        CUT TO:

86   INT. THE GREAT CAVE - GRENDEL'S MOTHER'S LAIR - DAY   86

Grendel comes up from the pool in her cave. Tears are
running down his face. He is dying -- nearly dead.

                         GRENDEL
              Mama...mama...he hurt me...mama...

There is no answer. Grendel collapses to the floor, and then
he bellows, sobbing.

                         GRENDEL
              Mama!

There is A RUSTLING NOISE and the SOUND OF A RUSHING WIND.

Grendel's mother sits beside him. She wears a black cowl and
cloak, that covers her from head to toe, and she has her back
to us.

                         GRENDEL'S MOTHER
              Oh Grendel, my son. My poor son. I
              warned you. You must not go to them--

                         GRENDEL
              He killed me, mother.

> GRENDEL'S MOTHER
> Who killed you, Grendel my son?

> GRENDEL
> He tore my arm away, and my life's blood
> has spilled onto the ground, and it hurts
> so ... Grendel hurts so bad...

Grendel's Mother's golden hand strokes his forehead. She has
a beautiful hand, with slightly-too-long golden fingernails.

> GRENDEL'S MOTHER
> I know. Sleep now, my sweet son. Sleep
> forever. Mother is here.

> GRENDEL
> Mama? I do not know his name. So
> strong. He hurt me.

> GRENDEL'S MOTHER
> He will pay, my darling. In the fullness
> of time. I love you so much, Grendel my
> son.

The life has gone from Grendel's eyes: they have misted
over, like the dead eyes of a rotten fish. There is silence
in the hall beneath the earth.

EXTREME CLOSE ON: Grendel's mother's lips.

> GRENDEL'S MOTHER
> He will come here to me, he who did this
> thing to you. And he will pay.

87   EXT. HEROT - VILLAGE - DAY   87

Yrsa is talking to Isolde the Fat and Gitte in the muddy
grass.

> GITTE
> He's dead?

> YRSA
> The creature's arm is nailed to the wall
> of the hall. They say Beowulf ripped it
> off with his bare hands.

Isolde and Gitte look appropriately amazed.

                                                        CUT TO:

88   EXT. HEROT - STOCKADE - DAY   88

A Pyre is being assembled. Thanes are picking up the dead
bodies -- and bits of bodies -- from the night before, and
throwing them onto the pyre. Standing beside it are a
handful of WOMEN sobbing, and a few CHILDREN. And Wiglaf.

We however SWING AROUND from the pyre and ENTER THE HALL,
where Hrothgar is standing in front of GRENDEL'S ARM and is
making a speech to Beowulf and everyone else.

                    HROTHGAR
          This hall has been a place of sadness and
          misery and blood. From today the
          monster's reign has ended. And we owe
          thanks to one man and one man alone:
          Beowulf. Come here, lad.

He puts his arm around Beowulf's shoulders. Beowulf grins
out at the crowd. It's hard to believe that this grinning,
friendly guy is the same naked lunatic who ripped Grendel's
arm off the night before.

                    HROTHGAR
          Beowulf, I love you like a son. With
          Grendel dead, you are a son to me. And a
          son deserves his reward.
               (to thanes)
          Come on -- bring it out!

A couple of thanes haul out a closed chest.

                    HROTHGAR
          Well, go on, open it.

Beowulf opens the chest. It's filled with gold and silver
stuff -- goblets, rings, torques and so forth.

Beowulf turns to the crowd, grinning -- then, suddenly
serious, like a politician or a statesman.

                    BEOWULF
          I find it hard to find in my heart the
          words I should say to thank you, great
          king. And all of you, I wish you could
          have been there last night, when I killed
          the monster. And I wish his whole body
          were nailed to this wall, not just his
          arm. I was asleep when he arrived,
          growling like a wild beast...

And as Beowulf tells them the story of his genius and ability
we TRACK BACKWARDS down the hallway of Herot and

89   OUTSIDE IN THE STOCKADE   89

BEOWULF'S VOICE gets quieter and the sound of the CRACKLING
OF THE BURNING PYRE gets louder, and the WOMEN QUIETLY
SOBBING, and we end on Wiglaf...watching his friends' bodies
burning up.

                                                    CUT TO:

90   INT. THE GREAT CAVE - GRENDEL'S MOTHER'S LAIR - NIGHT   90

CLOSE ON: Grendel's very dead body.

We can hear Grendel's mother, SINGING WORDLESSLY, a song of
mourning, very gently and quietly.

Then she breaks off her song and she says to Grendel's dead
body...

                    GRENDEL'S MOTHER (O.S.)
              He must come here to me. If he has the
              courage, as well as the strength, he will
              come.

And with that she turns and walks into the pool, descending
into its black depths...

                                                    CUT TO:

91   INT. HEROT - BEOWULF'S QUARTERS - NIGHT   91

Beowulf is looking at the treasure that he has been given.
In the background we can hear a small amount of CELEBRATING
from the hall. Beowulf is in his small room, though,
examining his gold.

Queen Wealthow comes in. She stands in the open doorway, to
avoid any appearance of impropriety, and says:

                    WEALTHOW
              You are not celebrating?

                    BEOWULF
              I am celebrating in my own way.

                    WEALTHOW
              You will take our gold back to your own
              land. It does not matter. Nothing that
              is gold ever stays long.

                    BEOWULF
              Steal away from your husband in the
              night. Come to me.

91   CONTINUED: 91

                              WEALTHOW
                    You are so beautiful, Lord Beowulf. But
                    you are not meant for me. You have the
                    mark on you
                              (she reaches out and touches
                              his forehead, as if showing a
                              mark we cannot see)

                              BEOWULF
                    What mark?

          Wealthow does not answer. She touches her fingertips to her
          lips, and brushes her fingertips against Beowulf's lips, as
          she turns to leave.

                                                          CUT TO:

92   INT. HEROT - HROTHGAR'S QUARTERS - NIGHT   92

          Hrothgar is lying on the bed. The door opens, and Wealthow
          comes in. She begins to undress. Hrothgar stares at her,
          grinning.

                              WEALTHOW
                    If you touch me tonight, I will kill you.

          Her tone of voice tells us that she means it.

                                                          CUT TO:

93   INT. HEROT - BEOWULF'S QUARTERS - NIGHT   93

          Beowulf is picking up handfuls of golden rings and chains and
          letting them fall, clinking, into the chest: they glitter in
          the candle-light.

                                                          CUT TO:

94   EXT. HEROT - MEAD HALL - NIGHT   94

          The last lights go out in the hall. We hear a RUSTLING.

                                                          CUT TO BLACK:

95   INT. HEROT - BEOWULF'S QUARTERS - DAY   95

          A WOMAN'S SCREAM shatters the stillness. Day shines in.
          Beowulf was asleep on the furs, fully dressed, surrounded by
          gold. He pushes himself up off the bed.

                                                          CUT TO:

96   INT. HEROT - MEAD HALL - DAY   96

Beowulf throws open a heavy carved door. His eyes open wide
like saucers at the horror of what has become of the
remaining Danes.

Behind him, other Thanes push their way into the room. Their
eyes, like Beowulf's, betray the terror in their hearts.

The hall, once white wash over stone, has been stained with
the blood of the South Danes. Great crimson splashes paint
the ceiling. Golden tapestries have been speckled by the
milk of slaughter.

TWENTY DEAD THANES in all, their bodies ripped into pieces,
litter the soaked hall.

Thanes continue to push their way into the hall, trying to
get a good look at the carnage. But as each man enters he
becomes frozen, unable to move into the room filled with
death.

It has become a feast for the flies. Their buzz adds a
horrific edge to the already surreal bloodshed before them.

Beowulf steps slowly through the hall assessing the dead.
Not a single man lays living. Beowulf draws his sword from
his back and holds it in front of him, as if it might defend
him from the invisible air of death in the hall.

WE TRACK BACKWARDS AND OUT of a huge hole which has been
knocked through the far corner of the south hall. Great
stones lay in rubble heaps outside the massive keep.

Beowulf jumps out of the keep onto the green glade beyond the
rubble heap. He runs into an EXTREME CLOSE UP as he scans
the horizon where

97   THE MOORS   97

leads beyond Herot and into a dark forest. Close to the rim
of the tangled grove, at least a kilometer away, a SHADOWY
FIGURE runs. After an instant the figure vanishes into the
deep forest. For a moment, it seems as though it may have
never been there at all.

98   BEOWULF   98

squints his eyes in the hope of getting another glimpse at
the dark apparition.

                    BEOWULF
          What monster is this!?

CONTINUED:

Behind him, the Thanes are coming out of the huge hole in the keep. No one can seem to answer him.

> WIGLAF
> Is Grendel not dead? Has he grown his
> arm anew?

Beowulf looks at him, afraid to answer.

Then, Hrothgar is there, pushing his way through the crowd of Thanes.

> HROTHGAR
> It's not Grendel.

> WIGLAF
> Not Grendel? Then who?

CUT TO:

99 INT. HEROT - THRONE ROOM - DAY 99

CLOSE ON: Hrothgar is sitting in his mighty (and portable) throne. He is in his full compliment of battle gear.

> HROTHGAR
> Grendel's mother. I had hoped that she
> had left the land long since. True you
> killed the son. Rid us of a terror like
> we have never known. But none of us were
> reckoning with the creature's foul
> mother.

Beowulf doesn't seem to happy about this.

> BEOWULF
> Another, then another, then another. How
> many monsters am I to slay? Grendel's
> father? Grendel's uncle? Grendel's
> cousin once removed? If there are more
> please tell me now, friend Hrothgar. For
> I would like to know if I will have to
> burn down an entire family tree of these
> demons.

> HROTHGAR
> There are no more...no more of her kind
> in <u>this</u> world. And without another she
> can not procreate. With her gone
> demonkind will slip into legend.

                           WIGLAF
                 (shaking his head aghast)
           Where they belong.

                         BEOWULF
          And what of her mate? Where is Grendel's
          father?

Wealthow looks at Hrothgar with an expression that says "yes,
Hrothgar, where is Grendel's father?"

                       HROTHGAR
          Grendel's father is dead, gone with a
          bygone age. Grendel's father can do no
          harm to man.

Beowulf nods, perhaps a little suspicious.

                       BEOWULF
          Then let us destroy her.

                       HROTHGAR
          Lay into your mind what has happened
          here!

Beowulf's eyes fix into a stare as he imagines the atrocity
taking place.

                                     FLASH TO:

                       UNFERTH
          Beowulf.

Beowulf turns and looks at Unferth.

                       BEOWULF
          Unferth. What is it?

                       UNFERTH
          I was wrong to doubt you before. And I
          shall not doubt you again. The blood
          that flows in your veins is the blood of
          courage. I ask your forgiveness.

                       BEOWULF
               (perhaps a little too abruptly,
                Beowulf is uncomfortable with
                Unferth's humility)
          Forgiven.

He turns to leave.

                              UNFERTH
                    Take my father's sword.

Beowulf turns around and looks at him.

                              UNFERTH
                    It's called "Hrunting". It belonged to
                    my father's father.

                              BEOWULF
                    A sword is no match against demon magic.

Unferth looks at his father's sword which he's holding in his
hands. He looks a little sad. Unferth begins sheathing it.

                              BEOWULF
                    But--

Unferth stops short of sliding his sword into its casing.

                              BEOWULF
                    One never knows.

Unferth smiles and holds the sword out for Beowulf. Beowulf
takes it and feels it's weight.

                              UNFERTH
                    Thank you, Beowulf. I'm sorry I ever
                    doubted you.

                              BEOWULF
                    And I'm sorry I mentioned that you
                    murdered your brothers. They were...
                    hasty words.

                              UNFERTH
                    I bid you well in killing the demon's
                    mother.

Beowulf nods and turns to leave. He pauses and looks back at
Unferth.

                              BEOWULF
                    You know, Unferth...I may not return.
                    Your ancestral sword may be lost with me.

                              UNFERTH
                    As long as it is with you, it will never
                    be lost.

Beowulf nods and leaves.

                                                      CUT TO:

100   EXT. HEROT - STOCKADE - DAY   100

Beowulf comes out of the Hall to find Wiglaf, seven of his
thanes, and their little horse, loaded high with provisions,
waiting for him.

A funeral pyre is burning in the distance.

                    BEOWULF
               (puzzled)
          Where are the rest of the men?

                    WIGLAF
          Dead.
               (he points to the pyre)
          That's the last of them, over there.

                    BEOWULF
          I will kill the Monster's mother myself.
          You men will wait behind when we get
          there. We will need enough thanes to man
          the oars on the ship home. I do not want
          any more of you getting killed.

                    OLAF
               (to himself)
          How considerate.

Beowulf strides off, and his men follow him.

                                             CUT TO:

101   EXT. DARK FOREST - DAY   101

It's a wild woodland. Flies and mosquitoes BUZZ around, and
Beowulf's men, leading their little horse, are in an
appalling mood, sweating and swatting at flies the whole
time.

                    OLAF
          Damn this forest. We're not in Geatland
          anymore, that much I'll tell you for
          nothing.

                    THANE #2
          Aye. How many monsters do these bloody
          Danes have anyway? Where do they get
          them from?

                    OLAF
          Same place they get these damned
          mosquitoes from. Isn't this glorious?
          Fight in Beowulf's army -- he gets the
               (more)

101   CONTINUED: 101

                         OLAF (CONT'D)
               gold and the glory and the girls, we get
               the mosqitoes...

                         WIGLAF
               Quiet back there!

                                                          CUT TO

102   EXT. THE GREAT CAVE - DAY   102

      The great dense weald opens into the rocky mouth of a
      gigantic cave made of quartz. Into the cave mouth a river
      runs, fed by hundreds of thousands of dewy drops fallen from
      the many ferns and leaves that make up the viridian tapestry
      surrounding it. Indeed, while not raining the air is thick
      with water.

      It is a bizarre space, birds soaring about like fish in the
      sky. Their SCREECHES echo in spirals upward like whale song.

      Beowulf almost seems to be underwater already, yet he stands
      on a gray slate boulder under which glassy waters feed the
      cave.

      In them, tangled in the rocks, is the HEADLESS CORPSE OF
      ESHER which Grendel's mother must have killed. The man's
      blood stains the crystal waters red.

      Beowulf draws Unferth's sword, "Hrunting", and looks to his
      men who stand not a hundred meters away in the foliage.

                         BEOWULF
               Bring me some fire!

      Wiglaf climbs down into the gorge with a fiery torch in his
      hand. He passes it to Beowulf.

                         BEOWULF (CONT'D)
               Thank you.

                         WIGLAF
               She's a water demon. Don't meet her in
               her element.

                         BEOWULF
               I know.

                         WIGLAF
               Do you want me to go in with you?

                         BEOWULF
               No.

CONTINUED:

                         WIGLAF
           Good. I'll wait up there.

Wiglaf nods and heads back up the hill to the others.

Beowulf turns and walks along the current and into the cave,
the torch blazing in his right hand.

103   INT. THE GREAT CAVE - DAY   103

The inside of the cave is like some great cathedral of gray
slate, stalagmites, and stalactites. Pools of minerals,
millions of years in silent creation, become dazzling color
shows in the light of Beowulf's torch.

Gauging each step, he slowly enters into the great chamber
that hides an underground lake. It's waters are dark and
placid.

Across the body of water, where the cave wall should meet the
surface, a tunnel continues into darkness.

Beowulf, holding the blazing torch in his right hand and the
sword Hrunting in the left, begins to wade into the still
water.

Soon he is up to his waist in the black liquid, scaling each
step with caution, he moves closer and closer to the
narrowing end of the chamber.

The further Beowulf goes the deeper he gets, and the closer
the cave ceiling comes to the placid surface of the water.

Soon Beowulf is up to his neck in the reservoir and the cave
ceiling is no more than 25 centimeters from the surface of
the water.

He has left the main chamber behind and now finds himself
chin deep in a...

CHANNEL

of water with no more than 13 centimeters of air between it
and the cave ceiling.

He still holds the torch in his right hand, it's flame so
close to the water it could extinguish any second.

In his other hand he holds Hrunting out of the water.
Occasionally the sword dips into the water, causing it to
sing.

The light from the blaze of the torch illuminates the
causeway several meters in front of him. There seems to be
no end in sight.

Then the torch begins to go out as it touches the water.

There can't be more than 7 centimeters between the surface of
the water and the mountain of rock above it. Soon, the
entire channel will be submerged.

Beowulf begins to breathe rapidly...in gulps. His face is
now kissing the ceiling of the dank cave.

The torch, now completely immersed, extinguishes itself.

Beowulf is now...

UNDERWATER

It is dark and blue. Beowulf, still holding Hrunting, begins
to swim down the channel of stone.

Through the murky water Beowulf sees the bones of many a
Thane dragged into this liquid crypt and left to be picked by
the eels living here.

His feet kick and push at the floor and ceiling of the
channel, aiding his desperate swim.

But no end is near.

In fact, the further Beowulf swims the closer the floor seems
to be coming to the ceiling.

Beowulf scrambles through the narrow causeway, scratching at
the crevices in the stone for a finger or foot hold.

His armor has become an encumbrance in the tight crawlspace.
Beowulf claws at the straps which hold it on, desperately
trying to undo the yoke. Finally, he manages to rip his
armor from his body. He lets it fall behind him as he
advances.

Beowulf is underwater spelunking. The chamber has become a
slate coffin with no sides. A watery crypt.

He is squeezing his way through. Birthing through stone.
Scraping for air on the other side.

And he finds it.

104   INT. THE GREAT CAVE - GRENDEL'S MOTHER'S LAIR - DAY   104

The lair of Grendel's Mother once belonged to the Nibelungen,
a race of Dwarfen craftsmen. They and their treasure long
gone, all that remains here is their one time kingdom. A
great underground temple on it's side, half submerged by the
icy waters which flow into the great cave.

Beowulf emerges into this tabernacle underneath the mountain
from between two steps on an immense busted up stairway. The
steps lead to a huge statue of Odin, the gems once inlaid
into it long stolen by thieves.

Beowulf coughs as he gulps in the dank, stale air of the
great Dwarfen hall. In his hand he still holds Hrunting, the
sword Unferth gave to him.

Beowulf, standing to his waist in the water, takes in his
surroundings.

It is a bizarre chamber. A sideways world of mythic origin.
The air of magic still haunts this hall. Great fallen
pillars lay in busted up heaps. Runic writing of some
ancient long dead language are inscribed about the cracked
walls.

There are also the BODIES OF DEAD THANES scattered pell mell
about the room. Their armor ripped open like sardine cans.
Their insides spilt in hungry haste by the monster that could
be lurking in the dark shadows. On the ground lies GRENDEL'S
BODY, one arm missing. It is quite dead.

Beowulf slowly climbs out of the water and onto the collapsed
stairs. His armor was left behind in the crawlspace, and now
he only wears his soaked tunic. His teeth chatter in the
cold air, giving him away to anyone who might be listening.

From the shadows a giant lizard crawls up one of the walls of
the ruin.

Beowulf hears the scratching of it's talons against the heavy
stone walls. He spins to face the sounds, holding Hrunting
before him.

Then, it crawls into the shaft of light crossing the ceiling.
In the firelight he sees glimpses of it. Her golden
skin...shark-like, its glistening surface reflecting a deep
flaxen spectrum. Gills run the length of her shimmering
back. Her hands and feet are only parodies of human form,
they more resemble a birds.

She lifts her head to gaze more fully on Beowulf beneath her.

> GRENDEL'S MOTHER
> Are you the one they call Beowulf?

She lets loose her hold on the ceiling and drops to the floor
with a thud. This startles Beowulf a bit, he steps back and
grips his sword tighter.

> GRENDEL'S MOTHER
> The Bee-wolf? The Bear-wolf? I have
> seen the future Beowulf. When they sing
> your song they will have sung about your
> strength. But when they sing about
> me...it shall be a lie.

She steps closer into the light. Beowulf steps back, his
sword is aimed directly at the sea witch.

> GRENDEL'S MOTHER
> It has been a long time since a man has
> come to visit me.

> BEOWULF
> Stand back, witch!

> GRENDEL'S MOTHER
> As you can see, my suitors are all brave
> men like yourself...but they were brought
> to me by my son...Grendel is his name.
> And without an arm today, is he.
> But...of that I'm sure you know. If
> you've come to finish him, you're too
> late for his wound was mortal.

> BEOWULF
> I've come to finish you.

> GRENDEL'S MOTHER
> And finish me you shall. But first a
> *little death*. You shall give me your
> seed of life. You shall give me back the
> son you stole from me.

> BEOWULF
> Nothing will bring your demon child back.

Beowulf lifts his sword to strike the monster.

In an instant she has TRANSFORMED HERSELF into a beautiful
woman. Her long hair is now silken, her skin like golden
milk. She seems to radiate from within, like the moon. She
has transformed from a hideous lizard demon into beautiful
goddess of shimmering golden flesh. It is perhaps more
terrifying to Beowulf that she isn't a gruesome monster, but

a beautifully sexy siren with firm breasts, long legs, and
full lips.

                          BEOWULF
            Demon!

He raises his sword to strike her, but cannot.

                     GRENDEL'S MOTHER
            Not a demon, but a woman of many names.
            Lorelei to some. Calypso to others. My
            song brings death to men driven by their
            loins...sea-men...like yourself.

She approaches Beowulf like a cat descending on its prey.
Her long fingers, webbed like a fish, caress the sides of
Beowulf's face.

He drops the sword. It shatters like glass into a million
shards.

Fear has paralyzed the great warrior. All he can do is stare
into the eyes of his enemy. Eyes that reflect a thousand
starry nights, eyes as full as the night sky. Mesmerized,
Beowulf's eyes dilate. She has hold of him.

                          BEOWULF
            I... I should... I should kill you...

                     GRENDEL'S MOTHER
            But you don't want to, do you, my love?
            If you wish to kill me, though, you may.

She walks over to the wall, and pulls down a huge sword -- a
giant's sword, -- that is hanging on the wall.

                     GRENDEL'S MOTHER
            This blade is old, and not of this world.
            It will even end the life of such a thing
            as me.

She passes it to Beowulf.

                     GRENDEL'S MOTHER
            I'll even show you where to plunge it...

She begins to unfasten her top, displaying her chest.
Beowulf swallows, holds the huge sword, breathing heavily,
and then, suddenly, turns and crashes the blade down on
Grendel's dead neck. The blade severs Grendel's huge head
from its body, but the blood of Grendel turns much of the
sword blade to liquid mercury, which dribbles and rolls away.
We are left with only a couple of inches of blade and the
huge hilt.

                        BEOWULF
          Why?

                        GRENDEL'S MOTHER
          You took a son from me. Give me a son,
          brave thane. Stay with me. Love me.

This really seems to send horror into Beowulf's heart.
Beowulf shakes his head, but is still walking towards her.

She leans forward and after a moment's hesitation gently
kisses him with her full, golden lips. Beowulf closes his
eyes...

                                                     CUT TO:

105   EXT. THE GREAT CAVE - MORNING   105

Beowulf's remaining Thanes have set up camp and look to be
living off the land fairly well.

                        WIGLAF
          It's been eight days.
               (pause, as he's coming to a
                decision.)
          I think we should go in after him.

Consensual groans come from the group of Thanes. The men
start to stand up and strap on their weapons.

                                                     CUT TO:

106   INT. THE GREAT CAVE - UNDERWATER - DAY   106

Beowulf is swimming through the murky causeway, in his hand
he holds a sack.

                                                     CUT TO:

107   EXT. THE GREAT CAVE - DAY   107

Beowulf's men are now fully dressed and ready for battle.
They all have lit torches in their hands and are preparing to
enter the cave. One particularly NERVOUS THANE looks at
Wiglaf, who is heading them in.

                        NERVOUS THANE
          Creatures like this eat men whole. The
          hands and feet as well. I don't like it
          at all.

                        WIGLAF
          Neither did Beowulf.

                    NERVOUS THANE
          Ha! He couldn't wait to get in.

Just as they approach the cavern's lake, something starts to
emerge. The Thanes all prepare to hack whatever it is to
bits.

Beowulf emerges from the water, soggy and wet. No armor, no
weapons...just the sack.

                    BEOWULF
          I hope you're not planning on hacking off
          my head?

They all lower their swords, joyous to see Beowulf.

                    WIGLAF
          You're alive!
              (to the other men)
          Beowulf lives victorious!

They CHEER and help him out of the water.

                    WIGLAF
          Eight days, to slay one monster. What
          took you so long, Beowulf?

They all start LAUGHING. But Beowulf seems a different
person. No sense of humor at all.

                                                    CUT TO:

108   INT. HEROT - THRONE ROOM - DAY   108

Everyone is assembled in the throne room of Herot. Hrothgar
sits on the throne. Wealthow stands beside him. Everybody
seems on tenterhooks. Then Beowulf enters, carrying his
sack.

                    HROTHGAR
          Well?

In reply, Beowulf grins, and opens the sack he is carrying
over his shoulder. Grendel's huge head (and the hilt of the
giant sword) tumbles out onto the floor.

An excitable woman SCREAMS.

                    BEOWULF
              (calming the lady down, and
               talking about the head)
          He's dead, my lady. Nothing to worry
              (more)

CONTINUED:

> BEOWULF (CONT'D)
> about. I cut the brute's head off, after
> I finished off his monstrous mother.

> HROTHGAR
> Then our curse has been lifted!

Hrothgar looks the happiest we have seen him since Grendel's
first attack.

Everyone CHEERS.

> HROTHGAR
> So tell us the tale Beowulf! Tell us so
> my scop can weave a song of your battle.
> I want to be able to hear it every night
> of every day for the rest of my years.
> Tell us the tale.

Beowulf looks around the hall. Everyone is silent, waiting
for him to begin.

> BEOWULF
> Well... I dived into the pool, and
> immediately found myself surrounded by
> loathsome water-beasts. Each time one
> would get close to me, I would crush its
> skull with my hands. After 24 hours of
> swimming, I found myself deep in the
> underground cavern in which Grendel's
> mother made her monstrous home...

As Beowulf continues to lie -- or tell the version of the
truth that he thinks will go down best in history -- his lips
move but we no longer hear a word he says. Instead, the
SOUNDTRACK gives us the movements of the people we are
looking at, enormously magnified: Hrothgar SCRATCHES HIS
NOSE; Unferth PICKS AT HIS NAILS with a dagger; the SWISH as
Wealthow shakes her head and her hair swings back and forth;
the CLATTER as a small boy drops his wooden ball.

> BEOWULF
> ...and with that, the hell-spawned
> creature lay dead on the body of her
> monstrous son, and I alone remained to
> tell the tale.

                                                        CUT TO:

109   INT. HEROT - MEAD HALL - NIGHT   109

We are in the final festivities at the mead hall (our fourth
by my count) and it has the atmosphere of a real party.
People are enjoying themselves, secure in the knowledge that
no monsters will be coming.

109   CONTINUED: 109

       Beowulf holds his golden goblet (the one he was given) out
       for mead, and Yrsa pours him some mead, with a grin. He
       walks

110   OUTSIDE IN THE STOCKADE   110

       The night is clear and warm. Beowulf stands on his own, just
       listening -- as Grendel once did -- to the sound of the
       revelry. Unferth comes out of the door, looks around -- he's
       looking for Beowulf -- and heads over to him.

                         UNFERTH
                My lord Beowulf. Our people shall be
                grateful until the end of time. And, um,
                as for me, I want to make it clear that I
                believe all nine of those sea-monsters.

                         BEOWULF
                Thank you, Unferth.

                         UNFERTH
                Did Hrunting, my father's sword, did it
                help you destroy the witch?

                         BEOWULF
                It...it did. The demon would not be dead
                without your father's sword. High on the
                wall was a giant's sword, forged by magic
                and sharpened by dwarfen whet
                stones...but with the strength of your
                father's sword I had no need of such
                sorcerous weaponry. I plunged Hrunting
                into the chest of Grendel's Mother. And
                there I left it, to keep her dead until
                the sun falls into the sea.

       Unferth nods, it is a noble enough image for him to relay to
       his children's children.

                         UNFERTH
                Thank you, so much, Beowulf. Thank you.

       He goes. Beowulf downs some mead. Pull back to reveal
       Wealthow standing beside him. She holds a jug of mead.

                         WEALTHOW
                I thought you might need some more to
                drink.

                         BEOWULF
                Aye.

       She pours for him.

> WEALTHOW
> All the things you say about yourself,
> Beowulf. Are any of them true?

> BEOWULF
> (speaking quite honestly)
> I say nothing that I do not believe, my
> lady.

> WEALTHOW
> That was what I was afraid of. The hall
> will be quiet when you are gone. But you
> must go soon. Or I will make love with
> you, and then you will have to fight my
> husband, and kill him, and then we will
> have to hang you from the highest oak-
> tree, and I will be so sad. So you see,
> you must leave soon.

She goes up on tiptoes and kisses him, gently, on the cheek.
And then she goes away.

Beowulf begins to walk along, on his own, while the party
sounds happen in the background.

And he sees Hrothgar, standing beside a wall, waiting for
him.

Hrothgar takes Beowulf aside and holds him by the arm. They
walk together.

> HROTHGAR
> Have you seen my wife?

> BEOWULF
> She went back into the hall. She said
> she thinks I should leave soon, so that
> she does not have to make love to me, and
> then hang me for your murder.

> HROTHGAR
> That's a woman for you. They're so
> sensible. And talking about women --
> Tell me...You brought back the head of
> Grendel. But what about the head of the
> mother?

> BEOWULF
> With her body, sunken into the mire. Is
> it not enough to return with one
> monster's head.

                         HROTHGAR
              You <u>did</u> kill her?

                         BEOWULF
              Why do you ask?

                         HROTHGAR
              I was a young man once too, Beowulf.
              Answer my question straight -- it's
              important for me to know: You did kill
              her, did you not?

Beowulf stops walking and looks Hrothgar dead in the eye.
There is a long moment between them.

                         BEOWULF
                    (in a way that could be
                     construed as an accusation)
              Would I have been allowed to escape her
              had I not?

Hrothgar knows the answer, and it chills him to the bone. He
begins to step away.

                         HROTHGAR
                    (trying to convince himself)
              Grendel is dead. That's all that matters
              to me. Grendel will bother me no more.

                         BEOWULF
              And if the mother did still live, would
              you care then?

                         HROTHGAR
              She is <u>not</u> my curse. Not any more.

Hrothgar reaches one hand to his other arm, and pulls off a
big golden armband. It's worth a King's ransom.

                         HROTHGAR
              Catch!

                         BEOWULF
                    (catching it)
              You are too generous.

                         HROTHGAR
              Aye. Maybe I am at that. The wind
              stands fair to the west. How soon can
              you be gone?

                         BEOWULF
              Tomorrow morning.

110   CONTINUED: (3)   110

                         HROTHGAR
              Make sure you are.

He walks away. Beowulf smiles, uncaring, tosses the armband
in the air, and catches it. Then he toasts it, with his
goblet, and drinks from the goblet, and we

                                              FADE TO BLACK:

111   EXT. THE QUIET SEA - DAY   111

The ocean is as calm as the deep azure sky above it is clean.
A perfect day. Sea-spray is liquid drops of diamonds. It's
a great day to be alive -- the first real sunshine we've seen
in the film so far.

112   EXT. RECESSED BEACH - DAY   112

Four of Beowulf's thanes push the boat off the sandbar and
into the sea, clambering in at the last moment, pulled in by
the men in the boat. Strong winds, all blowing toward
Geatland, fill the red newly repaired sails of Beowulf's
ship, billowing the golden dragon.

113   EXT. THE CLIFFTOPS - DAY   113

The Scylding's Watch stands on his cliff, with his arms
folded, and stares out at Beowulf going away.

114   EXT. THE QUIET SEA - DAY   114

Beowulf and his men are LAUGHING as they scud along in their
ship, in the perfect weather and the swift breeze. The oars
are shipped and unneeded. The storage hold in the middle of
the ship is piled high with glittering golden treasure.
Beowulf glances back at the shore.

BEOWULF'S POV: Wealthow is standing on the cliffs watching
him sail away. He can not see her expression.

We realize that Beowulf only has six men plus Wiglaf in the
boat. There are lots of empty seats, for the dead men they
set out with.

                         BEOWULF
                    (to Wiglaf)
              There now, old friend. The scops will
              sing of our brave deeds from now until
              the day the sun grows cold.

                         WIGLAF
              Your deeds, perhaps. Not mine.

114   CONTINUED: 114

                          BEOWULF
                     (perfectly satisfied)
                  Isn't that enough?

Beowulf is in the prime of his life. He's grinning, and
happy, and beautiful: the entire world -- the sea and the
boat and the sun and the seagulls, everything -- simply
exists as a frame to the picture, in the middle of which,
grinning like his namesake wolf, is Beowulf.

The sun glints off the golden armband he was given by
Hrothgar, and the PICTURE FREEZES.

                                        FADE TO BLACK:

                     FIFTY YEARS AFTER

115   INT. KING BEOWULF'S CASTLE - KING BEOWULF'S QUARTERS - DAY   115

We are looking, in CLOSE UP at the Golden Bracelet we last
saw on young Beowulf's arm. It is worn, now, and slightly
tarnished. As we look at it, a man's old fingers close
around it. We pull back slowly, to reveal KING BEOWULF.

He is in very good shape, for his age, which must, simple
addition tells us, be in at least his early seventies. His
hair is streaked with grey and white, his skin is liver-
spotted, and marked with old scars, long healed. He is still
tall and proud, though scarcely recognizable as the young man
he was fifty years before. He has a golden circlet, denoting
kingship, on his head. His beard is tightly trimmed.

We are in his castle, a fortified Swedish stone building, on
the moors. It is within sight of the sea. We are in his
chamber. A rough bed, consisting of a pallet and sleeping
furs, sits in one corner.

He is staring out to sea, through a window. He will not be
going to sea again.

KING BEOWULF'S POV: The winter sea, grey, stormy and fickle,
as it crashes on the rocks below. The sea has frozen to ice
where it touches the rocks. Mid-winter in sixth century
Sweden was bitter.

URSULA, King Beowulf's young mistress, comes up behind him.
He does not register her presence. She is his personal maid,
a young woman in her early twenties. Then she speaks and
startles him.

                          URSULA
                  Your majesty?

115   CONTINUED: 115

                    KING BEOWULF
          Unh? I was thinking, Ursula. Hundreds
          of leagues away, in my mind, over the
          ocean.

                    URSULA
          My lord Beowulf. They are waiting for
          you, in the throne room.

                    KING BEOWULF
          There is a moment at sunset at sea, when
          you watch the sun drop into the cold
          waters of the endless ocean, a red ball,
          and at the very moment it sinks beneath
          the horizon, it flames green as an
          emerald.

     While he is talking, Ursula is picking up a robe, bringing it
     over to him, fastening it around his neck.

                    URSULA
          I have never been to sea, your Majesty.

                    KING BEOWULF
          Who is waiting?

                                                            CUT TO:

116   EXT. KING BEOWULF'S CASTLE - DAY   116

     We see that this is an old, stone castle, built overlooking
     the ocean. Sea-spray in the foreground. Snow on the ground.

                                                            CUT TO:

117   INT. KING BEOWULF'S CASTLE - SPIRAL STAIRCASE - DAY   117

     Ursula walks down the stairs behind King Beowulf.

                    URSULA
          You are to give judgement today, your
          majesty.

                    KING BEOWULF
          Live long enough, Ursula, and they think
          you're Solomon. Who cares who owns half-
          an acre of barren land?

                    URSULA
          Well, obviously, Guthric does.

                                                            CUT TO:

118   INT. KING BEOWULF'S CASTLE - THRONE ROOM - DAY   118

GUTHRIC is staring at us, his face red with anger. He is a
young man, hot-headed and impetuous, and he is really really
angry right now.

                    GUTHRIC
               This is an outrage! That land is mine by
               right of birth!

PULL BACK TO REVEAL: We see that there are a number of other
people in the throne room: OLD WIGLAF, again, fifty years
older than the Wiglaf we knew in the earlier part of the
film, and a few other THANES who are also elderly. There are
also a couple of KING'S GUARDS. And King Beowulf himself.

                    KING BEOWULF
               You have land enough, Guthric. That land
               was due to your sister as bride-price.

                    GUTHRIC
               This is not justice! This is a travesty!

He advances on the King. The guards raise their spears.
King Beowulf does not, however, need guards, for the anger of
King Beowulf is a terrible thing to see, and now he's angry.

                    KING BEOWULF
               How dare you talk to me like that? If
               it's treason you are talking, Guthric
               Olaf's son, then it's treason I shall
               punish you for.

                    GUTHRIC
                    (chastened)
               I was not...I did not mean to--

                    KING BEOWULF
               See that you did not. The land is your
               sister's.

Guthric sets his jaw. He seems on the verge of exploding
with anger, but he somehow keeps a lid on it. What he
actually says is --

                    GUTHRIC
               It shall be as your majesty has said.

And Guthric turns on his heels and storms out.

King Beowulf turns to Old Wiglaf, and shakes his head.

118   CONTINUED: 118

                         KING BEOWULF
              It did not used to be so hard, Wiglaf,
              did it?

                         OLD WIGLAF
              He's a young hot-head. He'll cool down,
              in time.

                                                    CUT TO:

119   EXT. KING BEOWULF'S CASTLE - COURTYARD - DAY   119

      Guthric leaps onto his horse, and GALLOPS off. He looks
      furious still.

                                                    CUT TO:

120   EXT. THE GEAT MOORS - THE BARROW - DAY   120

      We see Guthric on his horse, riding past a huge barrow -- a
      raised mound -- on the snowy moors.

                                                    CUT TO:

121   EXT. GUTHRIC'S HALL - SUNSET   121

      Guthric rides up on his horse. His slave -- CAIN -- stands
      beside the horse, with his hands cupped, to help his master
      down from his horse. Guthric puts his muddy boots in Cain's
      hands as he dismounts.

      As Guthric gets down, the horse moves, nervously to one side,
      and Guthric misses his footing. He and Cain go down in the
      slush and mud together. Guthric gets to his feet as angry as
      it is possible for any human being to be.

                         GUTHRIC
              You did that on purpose!

                         CAIN
              Sire, it was your mare, she shied--

                         GUTHRIC
              You pitched me into the mud on purpose,
              you creeping maggot!

      And with that he pulls his horsewhip and commences to WHIP
      Cain within an inch of his life, while shouting--

                         GUTHRIC
              You stupid--!
                   (whip!)
              miserable--
                        (more)

121   CONTINUED: 121

                              GUTHRIC (CONT'D)
                         (whip)
                    pathetic--!
                         (whip!)
                    cankerous--!
                         (whip)
                    louse-ridden!
                         (whip!)
                    oaf!
                         (he stops for a moment to
                         catch his breath)
                    Now get out of my sight!

Cain gets to his feet, nervously, and Guthric slashes the
whip across his face. Cain's thin shirt is in ribbons down
the back and he has a bleeding welt across his face. He runs
off, and Guthric goes into the Hall.

122   INT. GUTHRIC'S HALL - NIGHT   122

A harpist is playing, and singing a ballad. The ballad he is
singing is the "Saga of Beowulf". Guthric is talking to LADY
GUTHRIC. Lady Guthric is tending to the LITTLE GUTHRICS, a
boy and a girl, who are sat on the rush-covered floor of the
Hall, playing with dolls quietly.

                         GUTHRIC
                    The senile old fool. I could have run my
                    sword through his doddering old head.

                         LADY GUTHRIC
                    Well, it's a good thing you didn't, dear.

                         GUTHRIC
                    Why? Why is it a good thing?

                         LADY GUTHRIC
                    He is King Beowulf. He killed Grendel.
                    He killed Grendel's mother--

                         GUTHRIC
                    Fucking Grendel and fucking Grendel's
                    fucking mother. Do you know how fucking
                    sick I am of fucking hearing about
                    fucking Grendel and fucking Grendel's
                    fucking mother?

                         LADY GUTHRIC
                         (points to the kids in a 'not
                         in front of the children' sort
                         of way)
                    I really don't think--

> GUTHRIC
> It was a hundred years ago! It was in
> another country! What the hell was
> Grendel anyway? Some kind of giant dog,
> or something? And his mother? She
> doesn't even have a name!

> LADY GUTHRIC
> That's not the--

> GUTHRIC
> And who was my Lord Beowulf's mother, if
> it comes to that? I tell you, he does not
> have long to live, and--

But he is interrupted by WILFERTH, Cain's sister, who runs in
and says:

> WILFERTH
> My lord Guthric! It's Cain! He's not in
> the stables! I think he's run away!

                                                        CUT TO:

123   EXT. THE GEAT MOORS - NIGHT   123

Guthric and some of his friends are riding around on horses,
calling out to Cain. As we hear them call, we also see shots
of the bleak and deserted moor. Night has not yet quite
fallen, and rock shapes twist into shapes that remind us of
monsters and demons.

> GUTHRIC
> Cain! Cain! Can you hear me! You don't
> want to stay out on the moors! There are
> things out here that'll eat your heart
> for breakfast! And you'll starve to
> death out here, you'll freeze! You'll
> die out here! If you don't come back,
> I'll fucking kill you!

Guthric's VOICE travels across the moors to

124   CAIN   124

who is cowering behind a rock, as the SOUNDS OF THE SEARCH
begins to fade.

Cain is shivering and scared. The SOUNDS OF THE PURSUERS are
fading away into the distance. And then, close to us, we
hear the HOWL of a wolf-pack...

124   CONTINUED: 124

       Cain bolts for it, running through the moors, when suddenly
       the ground gives way beneath him and he is seemingly
       swallowed into the Earth.

125   INT. THE BARROW - NIGHT   125

       Cain is under the ground. It's dark...but Cain realizes that
       we are somewhere that glimmers....that glimmers golden.

       Cain SWEARS to himself as he bumps into something...and then
       slowly his eyes begin to get used to the darkness and he
       sees...

       GOLD!

       It's a treasure horde, unimaginable to these times: rings and
       bracelets, necklaces torques and plates, coins and statues
       and goblets, piled all around. Helmets and mail-shirts,
       swords, daggers and spears, shields and harps, statues of
       hawks and horses...the world glows in gold.

       Cain moves through the gold like a dark shadow....

       CLOSE ON: Cain's feet as he walks past...

126   A SLEEPING DRAGON   126

       THE DRAGON is the color of the hoard, a glittering gold. In
       fact at first we think it is a statue. It's half-human, half
       dragon, winged and tailed (the wings are folded, the tail is
       curled) but its face is part human, part reptilian. It is
       played by the same actor who played young Beowulf, but this
       should not be immediately obvious.

       To repeat, this seems like a statue, and might indeed, for
       the first few shots, be a statue. Eyes closed...

                            CAIN
                   Such riches...

       And, as he says that, the Dragon's eyes slowly begin to open,
       and a smile spreads across its face.

       CAIN reaches out, tentatively, for a golden goblet, similar
       to the one Wealthow gave young Beowulf earlier.

                                                          CUT TO:

127   EXT. GUTHRIC'S HALL - DAY   127

       Guthric is standing at the door to his hall. Then, almost to
       his surprise, in comes Cain, edging towards him in a servile,

scared sort of way. He is cradling the goblet, so it cannot
be seen.

>   GUTHRIC
>   Cain!

>   CAIN
>   I...I'm sorry I runned away, master. I
>   brought you something -- what I found.
>   Please don't hurt me no more.

CLOSE ON: Guthric's face -- he says nothing, and then he
viciously hits Cain.

>   GUTHRIC
>   I thought you'd come back when you got
>   hungry.

Cain goes tumbling to the ground, WHIMPERING and MOANING and
pleading.

>   CAIN
>   Sorry master, sorry, please no master,
>   please no...

Guthric kicks at the fallen Cain, and the Golden cup falls
from his grasp, and rolls onto the snow.

>   CAIN
>   Brought it for you. Good master. Nice
>   master. Sorry. Sorry.

Guthric looks at Cain, and then reaches down and picks up the
goblet.

The weal across Cain's face has started to heal and scab. He
looks scared.

>   CAIN
>   Please don't kill me.

>   GUTHRIC
>   (taking the goblet)
>   This is quite exquisite. Where did you
>   find it?

>   CAIN
>   (too scared, initially to
>   speak, he says nothing but
>   points to the moors, then,
>   nervously)
>   Up there. On the moors--

127   CONTINUED: (2)

                          GUTHRIC
              You didn't steal it?

                          CAIN
              I swear I didn't master!

Guthric holds the Goblet up to the light...

                                              CUT TO:

128   EXT. KING BEOWULF'S CASTLE - DAY   128

The sea spray lashes the rocks in front of Beowulf's castle.
We are looking in at from the sea.

129   INT. KING BEOWULF'S CASTLE - ANTEROOM - DAY   129

There are A COUPLE OF GUARDS guarding the way. Old Wiglaf is
standing beside Guthric, who is holding something wrapped in
cloth at his side.

                          OLD WIGLAF
              Well, I really do not know, Guthric.

                          GUTHRIC
              It is vitally important that I see the
              King, Lord Wiglaf. I am certain that
              Beowulf wants to see what I have brought
              to him.

                          OLD WIGLAF
              Hmm...I, um, I'll tell you what, Guthric,
              you leave it with me and I'll make sure
              his majesty gets to see it. Yes?

                          GUTHRIC
                  (keeping his temper but the
                   effort is showing)
              No! Look, I have brought something for
              King Beowulf's eyes. I'm not going to
              give it to just anyone and watch it
              vanish into thin air.

                          OLD WIGLAF
              I am not just anyone. I am the King's
              chamberlain and I am certainly not going
              to--

                          GUTHRIC
              For the last time, you doddering old
              coot! I have a gift for the King, and--

129   CONTINUED:

But he is interrupted in his turn by King Beowulf. Who
entered unnoticed.

                    KING BEOWULF
          And you may at least show it to the king,
          Guthric.

                    GUTHRIC
          Thank you, your majesty. It was found on
          the moors, a gift fit for a King.

He offers the goblet, still wrapped in oilcloth, to the King.
King Beowulf unwraps the cloth.

                    KING BEOWULF
          A fine piece, Guthric. Long it is since
          I have seen something as fine, and old.
          You found it, you say?

                    GUTHRIC
          One of my slaves found it. It is a gift
          for you, my lord.

                    KING BEOWULF
          It reminds me of something...

                    GUTHRIC
          I thought perhaps we could talk again
          about my sister's bride-price.

                                              CUT TO:

130   EXT. GUTHRIC'S HALL - SUNSET   130

Guthric draws his horse up outside his hall. He's in a good
mood, and is singing happily to himself...breaks off as he
realizes there's no-one there to meet him.

                    GUTHRIC
               (calling out)
          Cain! You good-for-nothing! Help me off
          my horse!
               (to himself)
          If he's run away again...

There's a pause. No-one comes. The place is in silence.
Smoke...or mist...hangs on the air.

                    GUTHRIC
          Hello? Anybody here? Gretchen?
          Children? Wilferth?

But there is silence.

130 CONTINUED: 130

    Guthric slides off his horse, and walks into his

131 COURTYARD   131

    There, in the courtyard, stand, in expressions of UTTER
    TERROR, as if caught trying to flee, standing and lying,
    CHARCOAL-BLACKENED, CARBONIZED CORPSES of Lady Guthric,
    children, slaves...but no Cain.

    Guthric stares at them in horror. He reaches out and touches
    his wife's carbonized arm...

    It drops off and CRUMBLES to charcoal.

    Guthric looks around in terror and then he grits his teeth,
    summons what courage he has, draws his sword, and goes into
    his Hall.

132 INT. GUTHRIC'S HALL - NIGHT   132

    The hall is in darkness. The only source of illumination is
    low firelight, and the dim dusk light coming through the open
    door. Guthric's sword glitters gold in the firelight. He
    walks in nervously, looking around, whirling around to stop
    someone attacking him from behind...and then the large door
    to the hall swings closed with a loud SLAM.

    And the room is dark.

                        GUTHRIC
                Who's there?

    Silence.

    And then, from one corner of the room, there is a glimmer of
    fire and smoke, illuminating something gold that we can
    barely see.

                        GUTHRIC
                Come out and face me like a man!

                        DRAGON
                    (a low, inhuman, laughing,
                    then)
                I was asleep when he came to my barrow.
                The thief. He took something that didn't
                belong to him.

    The dragon's voice is sly, insinuating, gentle. Guthric
    cannot see him...perhaps just two golden lights glitter in
    the darkness -- the dragon's eyes.

> GUTHRIC
> Oh god. He was a slave, I'm sorry,
> they're all thieves. If it's not nailed
> down, they're off with it.
>   (trying to fake it)
> Um...what...what kind of thing was it
> that he took? Maybe it's still
> around...I could look for it--

> DRAGON
> I think you know exactly what it was. I
> can smell it on you, man-thing. I want
> it back.

> GUTHRIC
> I don't exactly have it on me at the
> present moment right now. If you could
> give me a day...

> DRAGON
> Who has it? Who has my precious prize?

> GUTHRIC
> What are you? What did you do to my
> household?

There is a GROWL -- the dragon is not pleased at all, and a
thin stream of flame hisses out from the darkness where the
dragon is, burning half of Guthric's face and hair. Guthric
SCREAMS in pain and fright.

> DRAGON
> You are trying my patience. Who has it?

Guthric cowers on the floor, his attitude the same as that of
Cain, when Guthric was whipping him.

> GUTHRIC
> I gave it to the King. To Beowulf!
> Please, don't hurt me! Please!

There is a moment of silence.

> DRAGON
> Beowulf?

The dragon LAUGHS.

Then the door opens, letting in a little moonlight, but not
showing us the Dragon, and it closes again. There is silence
in the hall. Guthric begins to sob--

132 CONTINUED: (2)   132

                        GUTHRIC
                   (sobbing and babbling in his
                    relief at still being alive)
              Oh god. Oh god. Oh thank you, thank you
              thank you god. Thank you Odin. Thank
              you Christ Jesus. Thank you Thor of the
              thunder. Thank you. Oh god oh god...

Then from outside we hear A ROARING so loud that the walls
begin to SHAKE.

And the walls of the hall begin to glow with a bright orange,
golden light. The dragon is bathing the hall in fire, but
Guthric does not realize that, as he gets to his feet trying
to work out what's going on...and then he...and we
understand...as the entire hall becomes, in the twinkling of
an eye...an exploding fireball.

                                                      CUT TO:

133 EXT. KING BEOWULF'S CASTLE - WALKWAY - NIGHT   133

The night sky shines brightly.

King Beowulf stands on the castle roof, staring up at the
constellations. He is alone. He SIGHS, and goes inside...

134 INT. KING BEOWULF'S CASTLE - SPIRAL STAIRWAY - NIGHT   134

He walks along, down the narrow winding stairs of his castle,
descending slowly.

135 INT. KING BEOWULF'S CASTLE - MEAD HALL - DAY   135

About TWENTY THANES are standing around in the hall,
partying. There is something insipid about their partying
though -- the Thanes of 50 years ago had more fun. These
guys are -- well, some of them are watching and betting on a
gambling game being played with ivory cubes, rune-dice,
others are talking by the fire.

A couple of them -- BONSTAN and FRODA -- are looking at the
souvenirs hanging on the wall: Beowulf's Bow; The hilt of
the giant sword that "killed Grendel's Mother"; a huge
shield; the wolf-skin/bear skin that Beowulf wore when he was
younger...

The Dragon Cup is on display in the hall, taking pride of
place, beside the throne.

Old Wiglaf wanders over to Bonstan and Froda, who are staring
at the things on the wall.

                    OLD WIGLAF
          That sword hilt, that's the hilt of the
          sword that the King used to destroy
          Grendel's mother. He cut Grendel's head
          off with it, and Grendel's blood burnt
          the brave blade, leaving nothing but the
          hilt, and a thumb's span of blade. They
          say it was made by the gods themselves.

                    BONSTAN
          And the bow? Was that from the fight
          against Grendel too?

                    OLD WIGLAF
          That comes from later, in the war against
          the Franks. No other man alive there is
          but Beowulf who can bend that bow.

                    FRODA
          You are jesting with us.

                    OLD WIGLAF
          No, not at all.

                    FRODA
          Well, I am a pretty strong fellow--

And over Wiglaf's protests, he reaches the bow down from the
wall. Then he tries to bend it, and fails, hurting his
finger on the string of the bow.

LAUGHING, Bonstan takes it from him and tries to bend it, and
perhaps others of them try and fail -- through all this Old
Wiglaf is saying things like--

                    OLD WIGLAF
          Please, just put it back, men, boys,
          please--

King Beowulf likes to enter unannounced it seems, as he has
done so yet again, and he says:

                    KING BEOWULF
          My old bow, eh? Put it back, Froda. It
          belongs on the wall.

                    FRODA
          Your majesty -- can you still bend it?
          The war with the Franks was thirty years
          back.

He passes the bow to King Beowulf, who looks at it, for a
moment -- will he try to bend it? We wonder -- and then King
Beowulf puts it back on the wall.

> KING BEOWULF
> Thirty years is a long time, Froda. And
> a warrior does not bend his bow unless he
> plans to kill something -- or someone...
> but we are at peace, now...the days of
> heroes are done.

> BONSTAN
> Mead, sire?

Golden Mead pours into the dragon's golden cup...and he sees,
golden and distorted, his own reflection.

                                                    DISSOLVE TO:

136   THE DREAM OF GRENDEL'S MOTHER   136

In Beowulf's dream, the Jan Svankmajer-esque doll of young
Beowulf is facing a monster -- a huge, golden, monster woman,
being animated by stop motion. The monster picks up the
Beowulf doll when suddenly the DREAM SHIFTS TO...

Grendel's Mother and Young Beowulf, in real life, kissing
each other desperately, passionately, underwater.

They break the surface and Grendel's mother begins LAUGHING,
in slow motion, water drops glistening around her and
SUDDENLY IT'S...

King Beowulf, who has replaced Young Beowulf...his old
fingers touch her cheeks and the swell of her breast.

> GRENDEL'S MOTHER
> You took my son, Beowulf. Give me
> another.

> KING BEOWULF
> But you are a monster. Your sons are
> monsters.

> GRENDEL'S MOTHER
> And you're a monster too. Part bear,
> part wolf, all monster. Now, give me a
> son.

                                                    HARD CUT TO:

137   INT. KING BEOWULF'S CASTLE - MEAD HALL - MORNING   137

CLOSE ON: King Beowulf's face. He's just woken up, sweating and scared, his head next to the tipped-up Dragon's cup.

                    KING BEOWULF
                  (shouting)
              No!

He looks around, upset, his face and hair sticky with last-night's spilled mead. Then he realizes that it was just a dream.

THANES are waking too -- looks like everyone passed out last night. Bright shafts of sunlight pierce the gloom of the hall. The fire is almost out. Everyone has a hang-over.

King Beowulf gets up, picking up the Dragon's Cup almost absentmindedly as he does so.

                    OLD WIGLAF
              My lord?

                    KING BEOWULF
              My head, Wiglaf. And such dreams. We're
              not as young as we were, eh?

                    OLD WIGLAF
              Bad news, my lord.

King Beowulf is immediately every inch the King and warrior.

                    KING BEOWULF
              What? Friesian ships sighted?

Old Wiglaf shakes his head. He points to the courtyard outside...

BEOWULF'S POV: The courtyard contains REFUGEES. They are MEN, WOMEN and CHILDREN, who are in bad shape -- they are standing, just, although many of the children are being carried. They look at us with hollow, scared, eyes. The nightmare has happened. They are, to a greater or lesser degree, burnt -- they have fled from burning huts and villages. Some of them are carrying treasured possessions they rescued from the flames. They are standing in lines, dumbly.

Beowulf rushes out into the

138 COURTYARD   138

where the refugees await him.

                    KING BEOWULF
          Who did this? Who did this?!

A WOMAN WITH A BABY steps forward. Her name is HELGA.

                    HELGA
          It came from the sky in the night, my
          lord. It burnt our houses and farms. I
          lost my husband in the flames that took
          our hearth-acre.

                    MAN #1
          I saw our whole village burn. I heard my
          friends screaming as they died.

                    MAN #2
          I saw it, your majesty, flaming like a
          comet in the night sky, vomiting fire and
          smoke.

                    KING BEOWULF
          What is this thing you talk of?

                    HELGA
          A dragon.

The OTHER BURNT AND DISENFRANCHISED TOWNSFOLK are nodding,
now, and repeating, dully, "a dragon".

                    KING BEOWULF
                (holding the dragon's cup up)
          Why? Why?!

No-one answers. We see Cain among the people, but he stares
at the ground, too scared and brutalized to say anything at
all.

                    KING BEOWULF (CONT'D)
          I cannot give you back your homes or your
          loved ones. But I can kill your monster
          for you.

And then a small child steps forward...

                    CHILD
          The dragon spoke to me. After it burned
          our house. It said that someone had
          taken its precious prize. Someone had
          stolen a goblet from its hoard. That was
          why it was burning the land. It said I
          had to tell people that.
                (a beat, then)
          It was creepy.

138   CONTINUED: (2)   138

We look at King Beowulf as the penny drops, and he turns and
walks away. The people stare at him, unspeaking, with dead
eyes, as their King walks away, holding the dragon's golden
goblet.

                                                        CUT TO:

139   INT. KING BEOWULF'S CASTLE - MEAD HALL - DAY   139

The Dragon's golden cup smashes into the far wall, where
there are a number of objects, including some primitive
glass. It hits them with a LOUD CRASH.

We look up from the mess to King Beowulf, his face is set
hard.

King Beowulf is standing in front of his wall of souvenirs.
The thanes are standing around dumbly, staring at him,
nervously, not saying anything.

Then Beowulf begins to pull his souvenirs down from the wall.
His bow, his shield, his sword, even the hilt-and-two-inches-
of-blade of the Grendel-blade, and the bear-wolf fur cloak.
They CLATTER down from the wall onto the floor.

Then he turns to the thanes.

                    KING BEOWULF
          I am going to kill a dragon. Who is with
          me?

None of the thanes says anything.

                    KING BEOWULF
          What? None of you want glory? None of
          you want gold?

After a hesitation, Froda steps forward--

                    FRODA
          I'm with you, majesty.

                    BONSTAN
          And I!

And with that the rest of them, shamed, step forward.

                                                        CUT TO:

140   INT. KING BEOWULF'S CASTLE - KING BEOWULF'S QUARTERS - DAY 140

Ursula is putting King Beowulf's old battle-robe on him, the
bear-wolf-skin. It is old, but still magnificent.

> URSULA
> I thought you were done with war and
> battles, my lord.

> KING BEOWULF
> There is never an end to battle, Ursula.
> I was sick of war by the time I was seven
> years old.

> URSULA
> But not sick of glory, my lord?

> KING BEOWULF
> How many men do you know who have killed
> dragons?

> URSULA
> Could not someone else do this?

King Beowulf shakes his head, and seems as if he is going to
say something, then changes his mind.

                                                        CUT TO:

141   EXT. KING BEOWULF'S CASTLE - COURTYARD - DAY   141

King Beowulf comes out, with guards and thanes behind him.
He looks out at the refugees in the courtyard. He speaks
loudly, saying:

> KING BEOWULF
> Does any man or woman among you know
> anything of this dragon? Where it comes
> from? What kind of beast it is?

No-one answers. King Beowulf gets angry.

> KING BEOWULF
> (shouting at them)
> Someone must know. Where do we start
> looking? In the uplands? In the fells?
> On the moor? If you know anything --
> ANYTHING -- tell me. The beast will be
> sleeping now. These creatures come at
> night.

He grabs a PEASANT by the neck, pulls him to his feet.

> KING BEOWULF
> Do _you_ know anything? Do you?

He flings the man to the ground.

141   CONTINUED: 141

His gaze sweeps across the refugees, sitting apathetically in
the courtyard. There is a slight scuffling at the far end,
and then, awkwardly, Cain gets to his feet, and raises his
hand.

He is terrified.

                                              CUT TO:

142   EXT. THE GEAT MOORS - DAY   142

King Beowulf, Old Wiglaf and eleven thanes on horseback are
riding along. On the last horse, tied to the horse to stop
him falling off, is Cain looking miserable.

It is snowing. Everyone is cold and miserable. Wiglaf spurs
his horse, until he is beside Beowulf. Then he says.

                    OLD WIGLAF
          We're too old for this. We need a hero.

                    KING BEOWULF
          There are no more young heroes. The age
          of heroes is over. There's just us.

                    OLD WIGLAF
          It doesn't seem fair. I wish that
          Unferth'd had a son, who could sail
          across the ocean and kill our monster.
          Or Hrothgar -- I wish he'd had a son.

                    KING BEOWULF
          Hrothgar had a son. We sailed across the
          ocean, and we killed him.

                    OLD WIGLAF
             (the penny sort of drops)
          Grendel?

                    KING BEOWULF
          His mother...she was very beautiful,
          Wiglaf.

                    OLD WIGLAF
             (uncomfortable with what he is
             being told, changing the
             subject)
          My lord -- your majesty -- Beowulf -- we
          are old men. Our eyes are dimmed, we are
          slow, our strength is gone...look at us.
          We cannot kill dragons.

142   CONTINUED: 142

In answer, King Beowulf draws his bow -- the mighty bow we
saw earlier that no one could bend -- and with one flowing,
easy movement, from horseback, he raises it, fits an arrow to
the string, bends it, and -- barely -- sights it and he
looses his arrow.

                                                        CUT TO:

143   EXT. THE SKY ABOVE THEM - DAY   143

Far above them, a bird flies, until, hit by an arrow, it
tumbles from the sky.

                                                        CUT TO:

144   EXT. THE GEAT MOORS - DAY   144

The bird falls to the ground with an arrow through it. Old
Wiglaf gapes at it. King Beowulf does not even turn around
to look at it. He knows that he is still stronger and faster
than any man alive. And he repeats to himself...

                    KING BEOWULF
              We shall be our own heroes.

                                                        CUT TO:

145   EXT. THE GEAT MOORS - THE BARROW - DAY   145

We stand on the clifftop. Cain is pointing.

                    CAIN
              I fell in through here. But the main
              entrance is down there.

                    KING BEOWULF
              It will not wake until sunset.

                                                        CUT TO:

146   INT. THE GEAT MOORS - THE BARROW - DAY   146

We see the Dragon's face, now, in the darkness. This is the
Dragon in Reptile form -- the nightmare face of an elegant,
golden dragon, half-way between a T. Rex and a Komodo Dragon.
It flexes its claws. Its eyes are open. It is listening.
These things have very sensitive hearing.

                    KING BEOWULF (O.S.)
              When it wakes it will come out of its
              cave. And then we shall kill it.

                                                        CUT TO:

147   EXT. THE GEAT MOORS - THE BARROW - DAY   147

    King Beowulf is standing, with his bear-wolf cloak on, over
    his armor. He is holding his shield -- a rectangular metal
    full-body shield -- and a sword, and he is practising lunging
    and parrying and moving, practising his swordcraft against
    the air. He is getting winded and he is sweating and
    breathing heavily.

    Old Wiglaf is sitting nearby, watching him work out. Wiglaf
    is toying with the giant hilt of the broken sword. He
    watches Beowulf and then, when Beowulf is winded, he says:

                    OLD WIGLAF
            You are not a hero, Beowulf. Not any
            more. You're an old man.

    King Beowulf grunts but says nothing.

                    OLD WIGLAF
            It's a dragon. It breathes fire. It
            destroys whole towns. You're an old man.

    King Beowulf says nothing in reply.

                    OLD WIGLAF
            But you've never run away from anything,
            have you?

                    KING BEOWULF
                (pauses)
            Only one thing. And she must be dead by
            now.

                                                    CUT TO:

148   EXT. THE SEA - SUNSET   148

    We see the sea, CRASHING onto the rocks. It is almost night.

                                                    CUT TO:

149   EXT. THE GEAT MOORS - THE BARROW - NIGHT   149

    There is a golden glow coming from below them. Suddenly we
    see, for the first time, THE DRAGON. It rises into the air,
    a huge, golden creature, wings flapping, long tail curling,
    and it hovers in the air fifty or a hundred feet above
    Beowulf & co.

    We are utterly convinced by it: this is where our budget is
    going. This is the dragon. Smoke drifts from its open
    mouth, smoke and flame.

THE DRAGON'S POV: Beowulf and his men are below us, being
buffeted by the wind from our wings...

                    DRAGON
        Beowulf Grendel-slayer. Greetings.

                    KING BEOWULF
            (shouting to be heard)
        Prepare to die, foul beast!

                    DRAGON
        Ooh. Scary. Now, you just hold that
        thought, and I shall be right back.
        Something I have to do. Don't go
        anywhere.

And with a beat of its enormous wings it rises into the sky.

King Beowulf stares at the beast, as it flies away.

                    BEOWULF
        No!

Froda and the rest of his men (not Old Wiglaf) begin to laugh
and cheer.

                    FRODA
        You've scared it away! It's scared of
        you!

                    BONSTAN
        Hurrah! The dragon is gone!

                    KING BEOWULF
        Did you not hear what it said?

                    FRODA
            (a little baffled)
        It said n-nothing, Lord. You shouted
        'prepare to die', and it flew away.

                    KING BEOWULF
        It spoke to me. It said there was
        something that it had to do, before we
        fought. Something it had to do...but
        what?

Beowulf watches the Dragon vanish into the distance.

                              CUT TO:

150   EXT. KING BEOWULF'S CASTLE - NIGHT   150

        CLOSE ON: Ursula is standing at the top walkway that
        circumnavigates the castle. Her eyes are trained on
        something in the horizon...something that is approaching.
        Something golden that glistens in the light of the full moon.

        The various COURTIERS and THANES at the castle suddenly call
        to arms. There is a flurry of activity as people flee and
        prepare themselves to fight.

        But not Ursula. She knows that the Dragon is undefeatable by
        them. She has been perhaps awaiting it, or some other
        monster, her whole life. She inhales, with no fear, almost
        accepting the inevitable.

        And the inevitable happens.

        The Dragon exhales and the castle is enveloped in fire.

                                                        CUT TO:

151   EXT. THE GEAT MOORS - THE BARROW - NIGHT   151

        King Beowulf and his Thanes are where last left them.
        Bonstan suddenly points to the horizon.

                        BONSTAN
                Look!

        There is a golden glow coming from ten miles down the shore-
        line...the castle is ablaze.

                        KING BEOWULF
                My hall.

        And the dragon is coming towards us now through the sky,
        ROARING and breathing fire. It is the scariest thing we have
        ever seen. Scarier than anything in "Jurassic Park".

        Beowulf's men scatter for whatever cover they can find. Only
        King Beowulf holds his position.

        The Dragon descends and curls its body, preparing to breathe
        flame.

        The flame hits his shield and is deflected by it. King
        Beowulf is not burnt, but he is thrown to his knees by the
        force of the flame.

        Bushes and scrub trees in a rough circle around King Beowulf
        ignite. Burning, they will illuminate all of the following
        scenes.

The Dragon lands in the empty space and faces King Beowulf.

>   KING BEOWULF
>   You burned my home.

>   DRAGON
>   Yes.

>   KING BEOWULF
>   Ursula.

>   DRAGON
>   The pretty girl? Friend of yours? I am
>   so pleased...

Goaded, King Beowulf springs at the dragon, and begins to
hack at it with his sword. It swats him away with one huge
blow of its clawed paw.

>   DRAGON
>   Oh. This is not even going to be any
>   sport. And I've been waiting for this
>   day for so long...let's even up the odds,
>   shall we?

And with one mighty beat of the Dragon's wings it TRANSFORMS
ITSELF INTO A GOLDEN MAN, in golden armor, but still with its
great, golden Dragon wings and long, spiked Dragon's tail.

Beowulf's mouth drops open, agape at what he sees, for the
face on the golden Dragon is familiar to him...it's his face
when he was a young man.

>   KING BEOWULF
>   No! It's not possible! Demon!

Beowulf strikes at the Dragon with his sword, but it's to no
avail as the golden man easily dodges him.

>   DRAGON
>   Not wholly a demon. But perhaps a half-
>   demon. Born of hate. Born of lust.

>   KING BEOWULF
>   And I'll kill you by the same!

Beowulf, swinging wildly, is perhaps too old to kill this
monster. His rage has unbalanced him.

The Dragon-man lands like a devil touching down onto Earth,
wings extended and his fingers touching the ground for
balance.

151   CONTINUED: (2)   151

> DRAGON
> Such a brittle and old man you are. Not
> what I had expected. Not at all.

Beowulf is breathing heavily, unbalanced. He approaches the
dragon.

> KING BEOWULF
> I'm sorry I have disappointed you. What
> did you expect?

> DRAGON
> I expected a man worth my hatred. I
> expected the worthy slayer of my half-
> brother, Grendel.

> KING BEOWULF
> Grendel -- was your brother?

> DRAGON
> We monsters are all born of the same
> mother, born of the same sin.

Beowulf hacks at the monster, who ducks and LAUGHS.

> DRAGON
> Do you know how long I have hated you? I
> have hated you so long...

> KING BEOWULF
> And I hate all monsters.

Beowulf swings again. The dragon catches the sword-blade
with the palms of its hands, brings it close, and looks up
mischievously.

> DRAGON
> Do you? Do you hate them all? Did you
> hate my mother?

The Dragon kisses the blade of the sword.

Beowulf pulls his sword out of the Dragon's grasp and swings
it again, this time striking the monster in the nape of his
neck. But instead of the blade digging deep into the
Dragon's shoulder, it shatters into a thousand shards.

There is a brief moment where the words "oh shit" could be
extrapolated out of Beowulf's eyes.

The Dragon grabs Beowulf by the neck with both hands and
suddenly lifts him high into the air. With each strong beat
of the Dragon's wings they lift higher into the sky. Beowulf

grasps at the Dragon's strong grasp, choking and turning
blue.

> DRAGON
> When I was young, in the early years of
> my life, I would dream of this moment. I
> could hear in the minds of men as they
> sung the song of the "great" Beowulf.
> But I know the truth. Mother made sure
> of it. I know you are a coward and a
> lout. I know that you are a liar. I
> know you are not of the humankind, that
> your father, Edgethow, lay with demons.
> And that history is a lie. I know <u>what</u>
> you are--

He releases Beowulf's neck and says the word that King
Beowulf has, deep down, known would be coming:

> DRAGON
> (continuing)
> --father.

Beowulf falls.

He tumbles backwards and STRIKES the ground with great force.

Beowulf rolls over, the wind knocked out of him, his ribs
broken.

> KING BEOWULF
> I am -- wounded. Where are my Thanes?
> Who will help me!

152   OLD WIGLAF   152

and the other thanes are lying on the ground beyond the fire-
circle.

> OLD WIGLAF
> We have to go to him.

> THANE
> Against that? You're mad, old man.

The Dragon-man, directly above Beowulf, TRANSFORMS back into
full Dragon form.

Beowulf tries to crawl away, but cannot. He does, however,
reach back and find the bow he used against the Franks and
his quiver of arrows.

The Dragon begins to dive, going in for the kill. It soars
downwards, picking up speed.

152   CONTINUED: 152

Beowulf pulls the bowstring and aims the arrow.

                    KING BEOWULF
               (to himself)
          Forgive me.

He fires the arrow and sends it quick and straight upwards
into the soft spot Hrothgar spoke of under the chin of the
Dragon.

With a great SCREECH the Dragon recoils and pauses its
descent...then, after a moments recognition of the wound,
free-falls on top of Beowulf.

153   WIGLAF   153

watches as the Dragon lands on top of his King, not too
unlike watching a bus fall on top of your best friend.

He runs toward the massive creature, and his lord.

154   THE DRAGON   154

lifts its head and looks at Beowulf.

                    DRAGON
          You have wounded me, father. But did you
          really think that a mortal weapon could
          send me to the hereafter? No weapon made
          by man can destroy me.

                    KING BEOWULF
          No...what about a weapon forged by the
          Gods?

And Wiglaf lunges the broken blade giant's sword into the
base of the Dragon's neck.

The Dragon SCREAMS AND ROARS a Devil's scream, a screech that
can be heard in all of Geatland, a screech that could be
heard throughout the world. The scream of a Dragon dying.

The Dragon slumps to the side, dead. Its eyes glass over,
and in the milky emptiness of them, Beowulf can see himself
reflected back.

Wiglaf gets to his feet in the light of the burning bushes.

                    OLD WIGLAF
               (to himself)
          I told you we were too old to be heroes.

Wiglaf looks back at the death scene. The Dragon has once
more become a winged human, golden and glittering, and dead:
a symphony in crimson and gold.

Then, Beowulf does something Wiglaf would not have expected.
He cradles the Dragon's head, and strokes it, and cries.

                    KING BEOWULF
          My...son...

Wiglaf hears this and it sends a chill down his spine.
Wiglaf then sees that Beowulf has been mortally wounded by
the Dragon. He is a bloodied mess.

                    OLD WIGLAF
          My lord, you're wounded.

                    KING BEOWULF
          Yes...

                    OLD WIGLAF
          We must get you to a healer.

He struggles over to Beowulf and tries to help him, but
Beowulf resists.

                    KING BEOWULF
          No.

                    OLD WIGLAF
          My lord, I must insist--

                    KING BEOWULF
          No!
               (he winces in horrific pain)
          It is a mortal wound. The same wound is
          killing us both. Leave me to my death,
          dear friend. It will relieve my pain.
               (then, he seems to be
                hallucinating)
          Do you hear it?

                    OLD WIGLAF
          What, lord?

                    KING BEOWULF
          The song. It's Grendel's Mother--

                    OLD WIGLAF
               (crying as he watches his lord
                slip into death)
          No, lord. Don't say such things. You
          killed Grendel's mother. She exists no
               (more)

154   CONTINUED: (2)   154

                         OLD WIGLAF
           more. You are a great hero...a killer of
           monsters--

                         KING BEOWULF
           I am a monster myself, dear Wiglaf, I am
           a monster myself--

And Beowulf is dead.

Wiglaf begins to SOB.

                                             FADE TO BLACK:

155   INT. THE BARROW - DAWN   155

We see, from the inside, the thanes pulling open the barrow
from outside, to allow them in. The grey-purple pre-dawn
light shines in on them. Some of them hold torches. Wiglaf
enters, holding a burning torch.

                         OLD WIGLAF
           All of it.

Warriors begin to seize shields, statues and gold, and to
haul it out of the barrow.

                                             CUT TO:

156   EXT. THE GEAT MOORS - THE BARROW - DAWN   156

it's getting light, although the sun will not rise for an
hour or so yet. We see a creaking wagon, being pulled by
huge Shire horses, moving through the moors, away from the
barrow. The warriors, thanes, Old Wiglaf, all walk along
beside it, for it moves at a walking pace. It is piled high
with gold. We move in closer, and see that on the top of the
wagon lie King Beowulf's body, and beside it, the Dragon's
body.

                                             CUT TO:

157   EXT. THE GEAT CLIFFTOP - DAWN   157

They reach the clifftop. It's a fall straight into the sea
from the clifftop. The CREAKING wagon stops.

Two Warriors -- Froda and another, on top of the wagon, toss
the Dragon's body down, roughly, to the ground from the
wagon, shouting first

                         FRODA
           Watch out below!

The dragon's body falls to the ground like so much meat.
Froda leaps athletically down from the wagon, beside the
dragon, and meets Old Wiglaf, who has walked over to it. The
dragon's body is face down. Froda reaches down with his foot
and tips the body over, so it stares out, face up.

                    FRODA
          So that was the dragon, eh? I thought
          he'd be bigger.

                    OLD WIGLAF
          They are always bigger, in life. Grendel
          was...
                    (then -- realizing that the
                     days of telling that tale has
                     finished, for him)
          Never mind...

                    FRODA
          Does he remind you of someone?

Froda is genuinely puzzled. He never knew Beowulf as a young
man, but Old Wiglaf did -- just as we did -- and he knows,
just like we do...and he says:

                    OLD WIGLAF
          Nobody at all. Let's get rid of it
          before the crowd get here.

And he and Froda roll the Dragon along to the cliff-edge.

PULL BACK TO REVEAL: The Dragon falls from the cliff into
the waves, it's body pounded by, and then lost into, the
surf.

From somewhere we hear what sounds like a WOMAN WAIL,
briefly, then no more.

                                                  CUT TO:

158   EXT. THE GEAT CLIFFTOP - DAWN   158

A long line of Geats -- MEN, WOMEN AND CHILDREN, are lined up
on the path up to the clifftop, watching a DOZEN MEN and a
couple of shire horses dragging a longship up the path
towards the clifftop.

We see a number of women and men from the front, but we stop
behind A WOMAN IN A WHITE COWL, without seeing her face.

                                                  CUT TO:

159   EXT. THE GEAT CLIFFTOP - DAWN   159

It is the grey time before dawn.

The thanes have hauled a ship up to the cliff-top, just like
the ship Beowulf went to Denmark in, at the start of the
story.

And then, slowly, in a long procession, the Geats walk past
the ship. Each of them throws a piece of wood into the body
of the boat.

                          SLOW DISSOLVE TO:

160   EXT. THE GEAT CLIFFTOP - LATER - DAWN   160

The boat is filled with pieces of driftwood.

But the Geats are still walking past -- throwing golden
things into the boat -- pulling off arm-rings, finger-rings,
necklaces -- it seems like everyone has some piece of Gold.

The ship is hung with shields and armor, and all the treasure
that was brought from the dragon's horde.

When the woman in the white cowl throws gold and wood, we
only see her from the back.

Last of all we see Old Wiglaf. He holds the Dragon's Cup,
and tosses it through the air.

It spins through the air until it lands on the firewood.

Only then do SEVEN THANES approach carrying a stretcher, on
which Beowulf's dead body has been placed, arms folded across
his chest. THE PEOPLE part to let it by, reaching out and
calling and sobbing as they see King Beowulf's body. Eva
Peron eat your heart out.

The Thanes tie Beowulf's dead body to the mast of the ship,
facing out to sea. Then

A BURNING BRAND

being carried by Old Wiglaf.

                OLD WIGLAF
        I...he was the bravest of us. The prince
        of all warriors. His name will live
        forever. He--

Wiglaf breaks down.

160   CONTINUED: 160

Wiglaf takes the burning brand and touches it to the side of
the boat. Which begins to burn.

Soon, the boat begins to pour smoke out from its hull, and
then it BURSTS INTO FLAME.

And we look at the faces of the Geats, Some of them are
weeping, some staring, stone-faced.

The flames reach King Beowulf's body, and the woman in the
white cowl begins to SING.

It's a SONG OF MOURNING AND MAGIC, a sad, wordless wail,
tuneful and dark. The song of a woman mourning her
sons...mourning her lover.

Her song is sad, beautiful and transcendent.

As the sky brightens, the woman in white walks down the path
to the sea shore, still singing. The Geats do not follow
her, but stand all around the burning ship.

Bits of burning wood and golden things begin to fall down the
cliff as the burning boat begins to crumble.

We see Beowulf's body burning...

                                              CUT TO:

161   EXT. THE GEAT SEA SHORE - DAWN   161

We are looking down from above as Grendel's Mother -- the
woman in the white cowl -- begins to drop clothes on the
beach, first her cloak and hood, then her skirt. She leaves
the clothes on the beach behind her.

She walks into the sea. Her hair streams out behind her,
like seaweed. She walks out until the sea covers her
completely...and her song is done.

We watch the sun rise slowly.

She does not reappear.

She has gone beneath the waves.

<u>THE END</u>

Concept Art

An early drawing by Roger Avary showing the size of Grendel. Note that Grendel's pose is in the style of Egon Schiele.

The first Stephen Norrington Grendel designs commissioned by Avary, who especially loved the penis taped to the leg.

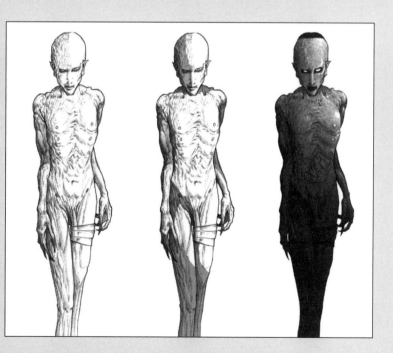

More Norrington designs.

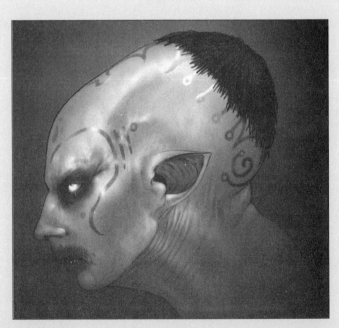

An early design of Grendel wearing a mask made of whale bones.

Another early Norrington design.

These seventeen pieces are an early storyboard that
envisions the climatic battle.

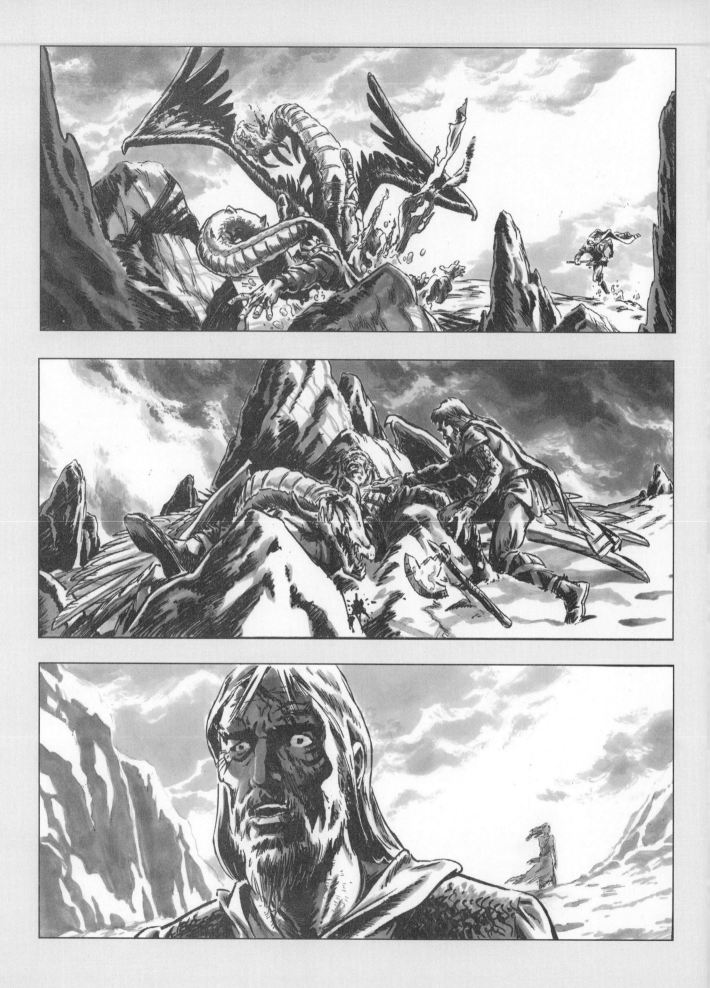

PART II

the winter

Middleword

BY ROGER AVARY

I t was December 2004 when I checked in. The hotel had once been a police station—a fascist-looking tower of a building bordering the bad neighborhoods of Toronto. My room was down the hall from the kitchen. It smelled of barbecue, which when I first checked in was delightful. But after weeks of smelling bacon fat burning on the griddle I began to feel nauseous. The stink permeated my clothes, my hair, and my dreams. But I couldn't leave the room. This was my office while I polished the screenplay of *Silent Hill* for director Christophe Gans. It was a living hell. The only escape was to take a walk in the bitter cold. Cold so intense and dry that it freezes the saline on your eyes, giving you a constant popsicle headache. I just wanted to go home to California, where it was warm and my family awaited me for Christmas. But I wasn't going to be able to leave unless I finished—and with Gans lurking over my shoulder and directing me like a French-speaking demon, finishing was difficult enough. The last thing I needed were the phone calls.

Various agents from my agency began calling me, one after the other, all on behalf of Robert Zemeckis. It seems that he had gotten it into his head after all these years that he should be the one directing *Beowulf*. He loved the script—always had. Now he loved it so much he wanted to take the reigns and "cap it," referring to the Performance Capture process of digitally enhanced live action he had pioneered with *The Polar Express*. And it made sense to cap it, because we had always had the issue of how to age Beowulf. Aging has always been difficult in movies, and I can only count three instances where I thought it was done elegantly (David Bowie in *The Hunger*, Marlon Brando in *The Godfather*, and Dustin Hoffman in *Little Big Man*). This was coming at me out of nowhere, and I was in a fragile mental state—what with the burning carcasses in the adjacent kitchen. It was a respectable offer, above my already ludicrously inflated quote. There was only one problem: I was dead set on directing the film myself.

Samuel Hadida, the producer of *Silent Hill* as well as my first film, *Killing Zoe*, was expressing interest in producing and financing *Beowulf* under the title *The Age of Heroes*. Low budget.

Raw. Dirty. Violent. It was going to be my epic. My *Excalibur*, with a bit of Polanski's *Macbeth* and Terry Gilliam's *Jabberwocky* thrown in for good measure. My hair was down below my shoulders and I had grown a Viking beard for the project. While skiing in Mammoth Mountain I had won the "Woolly Contest." It made me look sixty, and had a lightning streak of gray through it that looked rather savage. Growing the beard was an important commitment to my soul that I would make this film. My plan was to not cut it until the film was complete. I was going to direct *Beowulf*—and the beard proved it.

But the calls kept coming in. One after another, each from a more and more powerful agent. Each urging me to make the deal. Soon, they were calling Neil, but as he dutifully and politely pointed out to them, "It's Roger's film. I wrote it with him, for him. He gets to decide what happens to it." The numbers rose daily, and each time I told them "no" they would first try to talk me out of it, then bemoan my obstinacy, and then beg me to reconsider. At a certain point, when the numbers inflated beyond my expectations, I began to question my own compass. After all, it *was* the holidays—it should have been appealing. But I had NEVER made a choice in this business based on money alone. I had only followed my internal passions, and at this moment they were telling me that *Beowulf* was my calling. With hundreds and hundreds of thousands of dollars at stake, I again declined, and I was starting to become annoyed.

At this juncture, it has to be said that Neil Gaiman is by and far the most honorable and noble collaborator I will likely ever have the honor of working with. Because despite the temptation being foisted upon him, he never wavered and always stood by my decisions and our initial agreement that I would control the destiny of the material. This is especially admirable since not only would we not be able to use the many drafts written during our development with ImageMovers, but Samuel Hadida was insisting that the DreamWorks turnaround costs be totally absorbed by the writer's fee. And DreamWorks was clipping us for a percentage of every vase, Aeron chair, sushi lunch, sheet of paper, and anything else within the elegantly appointed Amblin offices of ImageMovers. This meant that if the movie got made, Neil and I would only pull in a tiny fraction of the salary, as according to Sammy's reasoning we had already been paid for the script once before, so why should he pay us again? I resigned myself to the fact that I would have to forgo my percentage of the writer's line item, which would work out to minimum wage compared to the astronomical numbers we were now being presented with.

I tried to get back to writing. Already, phone calls with Los Angeles had taken twenty hours away from my work, and ultimately, if they continued, they would rob me of Christmas with my family. I sat down to focus and began typing, the stench of pot roast in the air. Just as I was getting a head of steam, another call came in on my cell phone—the familiar 288 prefix. I gritted my teeth, and this time I told them that if they called and disturbed me one more time I would fire the agency. They then asked (and I must say very politely) if after Christmas I would talk with Steve Bing, the producer and financier, who was now Robert Zemeckis's partner. I told them that after Christmas I was skiing with my family, that I didn't want to be called during that entire period, but that he could call me on January 10, when I had returned and was back to business. I simply wanted to explain to Bing why I couldn't accept his offer.

In retrospect, as I write this, I can't help but think that I must have come across as a total asshole for my poor agents to deal with. Here they were, wrangling us the generous deal of a lifetime on a film that wasn't financed, and I'm turning my nose up at it—and turning Neil's nose for him. Perhaps my behavior can only be understood by someone who has smelled beef fat day-and-night for weeks on end. I was sickened by the stench, and with every moment that passed the stench became more and more symbolic of the life of a screenwriter. That, and the writing process on *Silent Hill,* had me yearning to get behind a camera again—out in the open air. Out in the world of the living.

I finished *Silent Hill* and traveled home for the holiday. I went skiing with my family, and I continued work on the concept art for Grendel. On my own dime I had hired Stephen Norrington, the now retired director of *Blade,* to do storyboards and concept art for me. Every day Stephen would send me a refined illustration of Grendel: one with golden tattoos running like veins through his body, one with long hair, one with short, one with moss growing on his skin. My Grendel was taking shape, and with each e-mail attachment Stephen sent me I became more and more excited to mount the production.

At 9:00 A.M. on Monday, January 10, 2005, my cell phone rang, and when I answered, Steve Bing said, "Hello." He requested that we meet, which we did the very next day at the Peninsula Hotel.

Steve Bing, for those who haven't met him in person, is an imposing figure at six foot four, and his boyish blond mop, cut bowl style, at first throws you. But it's his eyes that pull you in. One instantly knows that he's a good man in a killer business.

We sat down over tea, my beard now nearly reaching my nipples. Steve sat across from me, folding his impossibly large hands, and simply asked me what he could do to convince me to sell him the *Beowulf* screenplay. He explained that Z. had fixated on *Beowulf,* and that if he couldn't deliver this script to him, he would likely miss his window to make another Zemeckis movie. This was critical to him. Steve leaned in, very serious, and said, "Name your price."

"Steve," I said, "I only met with you so that you could see my beard and understand that I'm making this movie already. In my soul—I'm making it. I'm following my muse. If I don't direct this film, I'll die."

He didn't seem fazed by this at all, though later he told me that he had never expected my particular level and flavor of tenacity. He barely adjusted his poker gaze and said, "I respect your artistic integrity, but . . . humor me. Throw out a number."

Now, I've read about situations like this, but I'd never been in one myself. It's very unusual, and humbling. What does one do? Decline? I leaned back into my chair and the words came out: "You seem like a nice guy, and I have a great amount of respect for you, but I'm only going to tell you a number to discourage you."

I proceeded to throw out numbers that seemed impossible for him to meet. I tried to recall the largest spec screenplay sales I had ever heard of. I told him he would have to cover the DreamWorks turnaround costs. I told him he would have to cover my incurred expenses, dating back fifteen years. I told him I would need my director's compensation. I told him that since I would be walking away from one film, that I would need another—and that he would have to buy me the screen rights to a book I had my eye on. I continued on that I would need to be scanned, and that my image would have to be placed somewhere into the film. Neil Gaiman and I would have to be producers—and no other writers would be allowed to mess with the material. I asked for the moon. I did everything I could to discourage him.

He stared back at me blankly, looking rather stunned, and said, "Wow. That *is* discouraging. But . . . I think we can make a deal."

Be careful what you wish for—you might get it. And I got it. And I cried for days when I realized that I had agreed to let go of this thing that I loved—this movie that I had already filmed in my head, but wanted to give to the world. I had never made a deal against my passion and for the money. Now, I had no film. I had done what I never thought I would do—I went against my artistic desires. I was depressed. I cried for nearly a week . . . until the check came in.

Let me tell you, nothing dries tears like money. But more important than money, and twice as unexpected, was the level of collaboration and the warmth of acceptance that Neil and I received from Robert Zemeckis and his producing team. I had thought, perhaps naively, that by giving up the director's chair I was simply being bought out. But Z. wanted our creative collaboration and input—he had paid well for it, that's for sure. I knew I had passion for the material, but I had underestimated the level of Z.'s passion. And because of the unique process of digitally enhancing the live action, we would, as writer-producers, have a vast amount of input throughout the production and well into post—unusual for a writer. And since the Performance Capture process essentially builds the film in reverse, we would be able to fine tune our material up to the bitter end.

Neil flew to Ojai and checked into an artsy little hotel near my home so that we could continue the writing process for Z., whose ImageMovers offices were now in neighboring

Carpinteria—just a short drive away. Neil was no longer exclusively Apple Macintosh–based, and had a tiny little Dell as his laptop. But somehow, in the ten years since we first began writing in Mexico, the chasm between the Mac and PC worlds had narrowed, and the system itself no longer mattered. We were both writing in Final Draft, on two different operating systems, but our connectivity was as elegant as had we been writing on the same OS. Now, instead of passing a disk back and forth, we Bluetoothed our scenes from one system to the next.

Z. had numerous changes he wanted to make, which surprised me. But he has a writer's mind, and none of his ideas were the "bad ideas" that usually get thrown at you for the sheer sake of making a change. Most of his notes involved taking advantage of what digitally enhanced live action could do to further unite the two halves of the epic. Instead of having Beowulf return to Geatland, he would have him inherit Hrothgar's kingdom, riches, and women. We would be able to see Herot transform under Beowulf's rule. The passage of time would not only age Beowulf, but we would keep Wealthow for the second half of the epic—as well as Unferth. Beowulf would visit the dragon in the very same cave in which he succumbed to the mother. Also, as Z. excitedly told us: "With Performance Capture everything costs the same. Whether you're showing someone sitting in a chair or a dragon burning up a village—it all costs the same. So don't hold back, boys—don't let your imaginations be restrained by the limits of traditional 2-D filmmaking. Write whatever you ever wanted to write but didn't think you could. Go hog wild!"

So we did. We were no longer making a Roger Avary film—it was now a Robert Zemeckis film, and it needed to feel like one. A major change was the conflict between the dragon son and Beowulf. Less talk, more action. Make it big. Make it a thrill ride. It was an exciting process, rather liberating, letting go of my darlings and giving Z. what he wanted. Robert is like a wide-eyed kid, playing with his toys—smiling the entire time like he's getting away with murder.

I never wanted to get in the way of the production, thinking that I might not be welcome as the "other director." But Robert never stopped quizzing me about what had been in my head. What were the color schemes I had been thinking (grey to green to white, to illustrate the seasons passing, but with a vein of gold running through the entire film)? What were the casting choices we had in mind? And this is where I believe we scored our greatest victory. I had always envisioned the heroes of the film to be in the design of Gustav Klimt, while the monsters would be fashioned after the work of Klimt's twisted contemporary, Egon Schiele. And there was no actor who represented the sinewy, angular lines of Shiele better than Crispin Glover. I mentioned the idea of Crispin as a choice to play Grendel, and at first Z. glazed over. I expressed my belief that it would be a geek victory—the return of McFly to the Zemeckis fold. The two had locked horns during *Back to the Future 2*, when Zemeckis used his cinematic trickery to place the image of Glover into the sequel, which Glover had declined. Glover sued, and to this day the verdict protects actors from having their likeness used without their blessing. Z. began to regale us with stories of how eccentric Glover had been. How he couldn't hit his mark, but in Z.'s eyes you could see that while he may be a control freak, he had fond memories of the results of Glover's eccentricities. Besides, in the realm of digitally enhanced live action he wouldn't have to worry about hitting his mark since there was no actual camera to focus. Most of all, you could see that Z. knew. He knew that Glover was the best choice for Grendel, so he did what was best for the movie and put aside the past. Glover elevated the role, and brought a depth of torture and sensitivity to the character. I am more proud of his involvement in this film than of any other element. He is the anchor to what Roger Avary's *Beowulf* might have been, had I directed the movie—but under Zemeckis's direction, and cloaked in a virtual monster suit, he is well beyond what I could have hoped for.

Being on the Performance Capture stage was an odd experience. No sets to speak of, only house lights. It looked a little bit like the holodeck in *Star Trek: The Next Generation*, and the actors all looked like they were in costume for *Tron*. Anthony Hopkins, the man who handed me my Oscar for *Pulp Fiction*, wandered in wearing a skin-tight Lycra bodysuit, with tiny positioning dots covering the contours of his face. The word HROTHGAR was written on his chest, as if anyone could forget which part he was playing. But the entire cast *was* wearing the exact same Lycra bodysuits. He picked up a prop of a goblet, but even that was wireframe so that the watching computers could see through it and capture the spacial positions of the dots in 3-D space. It was a strange way to be making a film that should be dirty and muddy—and yet, much of our script played like a chamber piece. And I could see that these veteran actors, well used to performing Shakespeare on stage, were liberated by the process. They didn't need to worry about hitting their marks or finding their light, and no interruptions occurred during a scene for cameras to be repositioned and lights adjusted. Performance Capture is closer to theater in the round—and it allows the actors, unencumbered by the mundane annoyances of production, to fall deeper into the performance.

I had once heard a story about how Z. had digitally grafted an eyebrow from one take of Jodie Foster in *Contact* onto her face in another take—because he liked qualities of both takes. I thought it was silly at the time, the indulgences of a supreme control freak—so much a control freak that he's literally reinvented the production process to allow himself to tweak every element to his exacting specifications. But as I've come to learn, Robert's imagination won't be restrained by the chaos of the universe. He's a reality bender, and a man with a highly specific vision. But most of all, he likes to play. Every day I came into the Carpinteria offices to see the progress on the film, I would discover new technologies he had invented to advance his medium. One day, when Neil and I visited, we were presented with Z-Cam: a video camera with sensors on it so that it could be tracked in 3-D space. Using the Z-Cam we were able to playback the recorded Performance Capture data and line up shots in virtual environments. In this fashion, we were invited to throw in the occasional shot. The process wasn't invented so much so that Z. could exercise his authoritarian control, but so that group collaboration could make the movie the best it could possibly be.

Gradually, we watched the film go from wireframe to something that looks like an early PlayStation One videogame to what Z. calls "Michelin Man" to finely rendered frames that border on eerie realism. I am proud of my involvement in this film, and of the friendships I've made—most of all with Neil. For the two of us, it has been a long and circuitous route, an epic journey.

This second script, the shooting script, represents a different director's vision—a different film than I would have made. In the end I've come to realize that Neil Gaiman has been the cohesive glue that's held both works together. His voice is the constant by which we've managed to hold our course through the choppy waters of Hollywood. And the shore we've anchored on, though it's a different land than we first set sail for, is as lush and green as the one we first held in our imagination.

BEOWULF

as told by

Neil Gaiman & Roger Avary

Hwæt! We Gar-Dena   in geår-dagum,
peod-cyniga,   prym gefrunon,
hu oå æpelingas   ellen fremedon!

Listen! We have heard   of the Spear-Danes' glory
In the old days,   the kings of tribes--
How noble princes   showed great courage!

"Beowulf"
Lines 1-3
Original Author Unknown

FADE IN:

OVER BLACK: **NORTHERN DENMARK**

                              518 A.D.

                        THE AGE OF HEROES

1   INT. HEROT - MEAD HALL - NIGHT   1

We hear a VOICE. A young soprano voice SINGING a solemn
descant. Chanting and trolling in a haunting, ancient
dialect.

                        SINGER (O.S.)
                *Hwaet! We Gar-Deena in gear-dagum
                peod-cyninga prym gefrunon,
                hu oa aepelingas ellen fremedon...*

Now we see a beautiful FEMININE FORM of glittering gold,
shimmering with light reflected. It's all unclear,
however, as if we're seeing it through an underwater
dream, or perhaps a memory from which all detail has
faded. The slinky form rotates in a slow dance, briefly
revealing what looks like a long tail.

PULL BACK TO REVEAL that the entire image is inside the
pupil of an EYE, and the feminine form is actually a
reflection of fire.

The eye belongs to KING BEOWULF (50).

Bearded and grey, yet mighty and strong despite his age.
His eyes burn with dark, guarded secrets. His expression
is removed and somber. Wearing a fur cape and a gold
crown (its engraving depicts a dragon with a sword
through its heart). Beowulf sits on an elaborately carved
wooden throne. Firelight dances on his face.

AN OFF CAMERA ORATOR speaks over the SINGING. The orator
is WULFGAR, the king's herald. He is old and grey, in his
eighty's, but his voice is strong and commanding.

                        OLD WULFGAR (O.S.)
                Hwaet. We Gardena in geardagum,
                peodcyning, prym gefrunon,
                hu oa aepelingas ellen fremedon,
                Beowulf...

The King's throne sits in a raised stone alcove. A
smaller throne: the Queen's throne, sits next to Beowulf.
It's empty.

URSULA, seventeen and lovely, stands on the other side of
King Beowulf. She fills his goblet (silver and adorned)
and smiles when she catches his eye.

CONTINUED:

Behind King Beowulf stand MEMBERS OF THE COURT including
WIGLAF (late 50's), Beowulf's adviser and closest friend.

Beowulf, along with the court, are watching something...

PULL BACK TO REVEAL...

A TROOP OF DWARF ACTORS putting on a play. They're
accompanied by MUSICIANS playing instruments of the
period. A young boy SCOP SINGS. (the source of the
soprano voice). The young scop is blind, his eyes are
clouded by an eerie grey film.

The HERO ACTOR, wearing only a loincloth, swings a wood,
prop sword at a tall, grotesque MONSTER. The "monster",
made of shredded rags and animal skins, is articulated by
two little people on stilts.

This is a performance of "Beowulf".

> OLD WULFGAR (CONT'D)
> *Da com of more   under mist-hleopum*
> ***Grendel** gongan,*
> *Nu ic, **Beowulf**...*

CONTINUE PULLING BACK...

Beowulf's mead hall is massive in size. Immense timber
columns and beams are carved with totems, depicting
glorious battle scenes. Giant wrought iron chandeliers
hang from huge chains and the walls are covered with
weapons and shields.

All of Beowulf's subjects are present. SERFS and SLAVES,
OLD WOMEN and MAIDENS, KIDS and DOGS.

And in the center of the room...THANES (knights) sit at
long tables surrounding a large fire-pit. Its blazing
flames we saw earlier reflected in Beowulf's eye.

THE CAMERA CONTINUES PULLING BACK...RISING above the
hall's great door...REVEALING...

A WITHERED AND MUMMIFIED GIANT'S ARM with horrible web-
fingers and long, spike fingernails. This rotted trophy
looks more like a demon's talon than a human hand. This
is, of course, the arm of Grendel, who Beowulf killed
decades ago.

THE AUDIENCE GASPS as the hero actor throws down his
sword and leaps onto the monster's back...

WIGLAF, who knows this story by heart, doesn't
react...but sees A DARK HOODED FIGURE standing in the
anteroom...

2   INT. ANTEROOM   2

         A small room off the throne platform, furnished with just
         a single chair and table. A fireplace on one wall and a
         small balcony overlooking the sea.

         The hooded figure, with snow still on his boots, holds
         something wrapped in cloth.

         Wiglaf's BREATH STEAMS as he enters the cold room.

                         OLD WIGLAF
                   Unferth, you're not celebrating your
                   King's glory tonight?

         UNFERTH (80) has intense black eyes and long grey braids
         streaming out from under his hood. In his eighties, he's
         frail but very wily. In deference to the Christianity
         that's taking over the North, he's wearing a cross.

         Unferth lifts the wrapped object in his hands.

                         OLD UNFERTH
                   I have something for the King.

3   BACK IN THE MEAD HALL   3

         THE HERO DWARF rips a fake arm off the "monster". The
         monster hobbles off stage HOWLING in pain.

         THE AUDIENCE in Beowulf's court CHEERS and lift their
         cups. BEOWULF applauds politely.

         THE HERO DWARF victoriously raises the arm over his head
         and bows repeatedly.

4   IN THE ANTEROOM   4

         Wiglaf and Unferth are having a hushed but vocal
         argument.

                         OLD WIGLAF
                   You'll show it to me first.

                         OLD UNFERTH
                   Bollocks, Wiglaf. I'll show it first to
                   Beowulf. *The king needs to see it!*

CONTINUED:

                         KING BEOWULF (O.S.)
                    The king needs to see *what?*

KING BEOWULF stands in the doorway of the anteroom. His 7
1/2 foot frame casts a large shadow on the two old men.

                         OLD UNFERTH
                    Lost and now found, a gift fit for a
                    King.

Unferth unwraps the oilcloth...REVEALING...

A GOLDEN HORN...a cone shaped drinking goblet of ancient
origin, adorned with a gilded cast DRAGON. The dragon is
contorted in a way that reveals its underside. A
SPARKLING RUBY is inlaid in the center of the dragon's
neck.

The King looks at it. His eyes widen...stunned.

                         OLD UNFERTH (CONT'D)
                    Do you recognize it?

Beowulf stares at the horn. It has a hypnotic, magical
quality about it, not only does it glisten and glimmer,
but seems to EMIT ITS OWN GOLDEN LIGHT.

                         KING BEOWULF
                    Where did you find...this?

                         UNFERTH
                    On the moors. My slave Cain...he found it
                    on the barren hill...where nothing grows.
                    I beat him for treading near such an
                    unholy place...however...

Unferth smiles, snake-like but proud, and lifts the
drinking horn closer to Beowulf...

                         OLD UNFERTH
                    My lord, isn't this...

WHACK!!! With an angry sweep of his arm, Beowulf knocks
the horn out of Old Unferth's hands and sends it SKIDDING
across the stone floor.

THE GOLDEN HORN lands next to a pair of embroidered
slippers. After a beat, the horn is lifted by...

QUEEN WEALTHOW: Striking with unique purple eyes, she's
heart-stoppingly beautiful despite being in the autumn of
her life.

CONTINUED: (2)

Her hair, streaked with grey is wound into a long braid.
She wears no gold or jewelry, only a simple pewter
circlet to identify her position as Queen.

She looks at the horn...not impressed.

                    QUEEN WEALTHOW
          So, lord Beowulf, it's come back to
          you...after all these years.

CLOSE: WEALTHOW

She lifts the horn and suddenly...everything in frame,
except the horn...FADES TO BLACK...

FLASHBACK: Now, the image around the horn FADES
IN...REVEALING...

THE HEROT OF HROTHGAR -- MEAD HALL - NIGHT

WEALTHOW is now THIRTY YEARS YOUNGER, still with haunting
purple eyes. As a girl-queen she's happily adorned in
gold and jewels. She carries the HORN across...

Everything has FLASHED BACK to the Herot of **thirty years
past.** The MEAD HALL is still grand and magnificent, but
less adorned and refined...we have gone back to a time
when Herot was under the rule of a different King...

Following Wealthow and the horn (now brimming with mead),
we pass...

A ROARING fire blazing away in a massive fire pit.
Suspended over the flames by a long sword, a pig roasts
happily away.

The hall is full of the KING'S SUBJECTS and his THANES
all drinking mead. They are NOISY AND CHEERING and happy.

A brace of roast goose is brought out on a wood platter
along with platters heaped with boar and rabbit. SLAVES
carry baskets full of apples and pears to a table of
ROWDY THANES as MAIDENS pour them mead from giant
pitchers. The inebrious thanes fondle the maidens and
give them sloppy drunken kisses. ONE WARRIOR lifts his
helmet, mead is poured into it and soon he is drinking
from it.

We are seeing humanity, rough-cut and rude and awash with
mead.

CRACK!! The door flies open revealing...FOUR THANES
carrying a large portable throne.

5   CONTINUED: 5

On the throne sits HROTHGAR, as fat a king as you're ever
likely to see. His rotund body is haphazardly wrapped in
a bed linen. He wears the same gold crown old Beowulf
wore, its engraving depicting a sword piercing a dragon's
heart.

He spots Wealthow and the golden horn...

                    HROTHGAR
          Ah, MEAD!!
               (he grabs the horn from
               Wealthow)
          Thank you my lovely Queen!!

He pours the mead into his mouth, slobbering half of it
down his chin and on to his big pink belly.

Wealthow HEARS GIGGLING and looks into the anteroom...

TWO MAIDENS scamper out from behind a screen and up a
staircase, covering their nakedness with bedsheets.

Angry, Wealthow turns to confront Hrothgar but...

THUD!! The throne is dropped onto the dais, nearly
crushing Wealthow, and coming to rest on her dress. She
pulls at it, RIPPING the cloth.

Hrothgar LAUGHS and grabs Wealthow, pulling her toward
him and forcing a long, wet kiss on her lips as she beats
at his chest with her fists, demanding to be put down.

His WARRIOR THANES CHEER him on.

Finally she breaks free and spits on him...he opens his
mouth and asks for more with a LAUGH.

His thanes ROAR their approval. Hrothgar turns to them,
his face red with drunken excitement, standing on his
throne.

                    HROTHGAR (CONT'D)
          A year ago...I, Hrothgar, your King,
          swore that we would celebrate our
          victories in a new hall, mighty and
          beautiful. Have I not kept my oath?!

DRUNKEN CHEERS resonate from the mob of thanes.

                    HROTHGAR (CONT'D)
          In this hall we shall feast and tell of
          victories. In this hall shall the scops
          sing their sagas.
               (MORE)

5   5

CONTINUED: (2)

> HROTHGAR (CONT'D)
> And in this hall we shall divide the
> spoils of our conquests, the gold and
> treasure. This shall be a place of
> merrymaking and joy and
> fornication...from now until the end of
> time. I name this hall...Herot!

A ROAR OF CHEERS all around.

> HROTHGAR (CONT'D)
> (turning to Wealthow)
> Let's hand out some treasure, shall we my
> beauty?!

Wealthow couldn't care less.

Hrothgar lifts the lid of a chest and dunks his hand into
it. He pulls some treasure out and tosses it into the
crowd. Hrothgar is having a great time throwing gold,
but then, he's drunk, everyone's drunk.

Now he lifts up a huge golden torque, THE CROWD CHEERS.

> HROTHGAR (CONT'D)
> For Unferth, my wisest advisor, violator
> of virgins and boldest of brave brawlers--
> where the hell are you, Unferth, you
> weasel-faced bastard? Unferth--

UNFERTH, now thirty years younger, his lengthy braids are
now jet-black. He stands with his back to us, urinating
into...

THE PISS PIT

A large hole in the ground at one corner of the hall
(filled with piss and other floating debris). Standing
next to Unferth is AESHER (40), also one of Hrothgar's
advisers. Both men are urinating, and holding a
conversation...

> UNFERTH
> ...I'm telling you Aesher, we have to
> start taking this seriously. I'm told the
> believers now extend from Rome all the
> way north to the land of the Franks.

> AESHER
> Well answer me this...who do you think
> would win a knife fight, Odin or this
> Christ Jesus?

Aesher LAUGHS at his own joke. Unferth shakes his head.

                         HROTHGAR (O.S.)
          Unferth!

Unferth cuts his pee short and turns.

                         UNFERTH
               (to himself under his breath)
          What now?

BACK AT THE THRONE DAIS

Hrothgar shifts to one side in his throne and lets loose
a RIP ROARING FART. Relieved, he brightens his
expression and holds up the torque...

                         HROTHGAR
               (in a genuine loving way)
          Where are you?! You ungrateful lout!!

UNFERTH wanders through the crowd of thanes, tieing up
his cod and mumbling under his voice. He then shifts his
expression to a well practiced smile and holds his hand
in the air.

                         UNFERTH
               (in a not-so-genuine loving
                way)
          I'm here, my king!

                         HROTHGAR
          Here you go--

Hrothgar puts a huge golden torque around Unferth's neck.
He turns and faces the thanes. CHEERS.

WULFGAR, (the king's herald) now thirty years younger,
begins SHOUTING a rousing chant...

                         WULFGAR
          Hrothgar Hrothgar
          Hrothgar Hrothgar...

A band of warriors join in...pounding their fists and
cups on the table...

                         WARRIORS
          Hrothgar Hrothgar...

Now a SHIT-FACED THANE, leaps onto a table and begins
STOMPING his feet and SINGING...

                         SHIT-FACED THANE
          He faced the demon dragon
          When other men would freeze
          And then my lords
               (MORE)

5   CONTINUED: (4)   5
                          SHIT-FACED THANE (CONT'D)
                     He took his sword
                     And brought it to its knees...

Hrothgar's MUSICIANS join in...and soon EVERYONE IS
SINGING ALONG...

                          SONG
                     Hrothgar Hrothgar
                     The greatest of our kings
                     Hrothgar Hrothgar
                     He broke the dragon's wings...

6   THE CAMERA PULLS BACK IN ONE LONG IMPOSSIBLE SHOT...   6

       OVER THE FIRE PIT and up through the mead hall chimney (a
       gaping hole in the roof) and into the winter, MOONLIT
       NIGHT...

7   EXT. MEAD HALL - NIGHT   7

       CONTINUE PULLING BACK OVER the roof of mead hall and into
       the castle keep...Herot is built of log and stone, with a
       single tall turret overlooking the sea cliffs.
       Magnificent for its time, rudimentary by folklore/fairy
       tale standards.

       PULL BACK PAST the sharp, pikes of the fortress wall. A
       lone SENTRY on the wall warms himself by a fire burning
       in an iron caldron...

       BACK PAST decaying skulls of boar, wolves and other
       beasts, mounted on spikes that border the approach to the
       castle gates (an ominous warning to any would be
       invader).

                                                  DISSOLVE TO:

8   EXT. RAVINE -- SAME   8

       A MASSIVE BRIDGE made of logs and stone, spans a wide
       ravine. In the distance is Herot. The fire at the gate
       GLOWING brightly. **Note: throughout the following
       transitions the gate FIRELIGHT will remain in a constant
       position (ala Citizen Kane).** WE PULL BACK ACROSS THE
       RAVINE AND...

                                                  DISSOLVE TO:

9   EXT. DARK FOREST -- SAME   9

       Move past barren gnarled trees...

                                                  DISSOLVE TO:

10   EXT.   THE MOORS -- SAME   10

        CONTINUING BACK along the frozen bog, over the dreary,
        snow covered shrubs. The firelight at Herot's gate is
        still visible in the distance.

                                                    DISSOLVE TO:

11   INT. THE GREAT CAVE - ENTRANCE -- SAME   11

        We enter the cave, past it's craggy, dank walls. Now
        something strange happens. The SINGING from the mead hall
        becomes louder, tremendously amplified. It ECHOES and
        reverberates off the stone walls.

                          SINGING (O.S.)
                    He offered us protection
                    When monsters roamed the land
                    And one by one
                    He took them on
                    They perished at this hand

                    Hrothgar Hrothgar
                    We honor with this feast
                    Hrothgar Hrothgar
                    He killed the fiery beast...

        WE CONTINUE PULLING BACK into the cave and come upon...

        A HIDEOUS, BLEEDING, PUSTULAR OPEN SORE...the sore is on
        the back of a massive deformed cranium...mutilated and
        covered with scars and scabs. This mangled scalp is
        attached to some creature of indeterminate size and
        shape.

        The SOUND of the REVELRY in the mead hall is DEAFENING.

        Silhouetted by the moonlight...the creature raises its
        massive hands to clutch and grasp at the sides of its
        head, vainly attempting to hold out the sounds of the
        party.

        WE MOVE IN ON the creature's misshaped ear...the exposed
        membrane of the creature's eardrum QUIVERS in rhythm with
        the THUNDEROUS SINGING from the mead hall.

        The creature MOANS a GHASTLY WAIL...painful, sad,
        fearful...

                                                    CUT TO:

12   INT. HEROT - MEAD HALL - NIGHT   12

In a series of shots:

The WASSAIL in the hall is reaching a fever pitch. The
party is in full Danish sixth century swing...

THE WARRIORS continue to SING THEIR SONG. Some are
passed out, some are partying full bore, all are drunk.

We are in a WASH OF NOISE...

                    SONG
          Tonight we sing his praises
          The bravest of the Thanes
          So raise your spears
          We'll have no fears
          As long as this King reigns...

YRMENLAF (30) a tall, dark-haired thane, is chasing GITTE
(16) through the hall. GIGGLING, they play something
close to hide and seek.

YRSA, a curvaceous maiden with auburn hair, sits on
WULFGAR'S (50) lap. His ornamented helm and adorned
breastplate tell us he's an Officer (Hrothgar's Herald).

Wulfgar lifts his goblet to Yrsa's lips, dribbling mead
down her ample bosom...he hungrily licks the spilled
nectar off her chest.

UNFERTH stands behind Hrothgar's throne...pissed-off,
looking for someone...

                    UNFERTH
          Boy! Where's my mead?!

CAIN a young slave boy (10) with flaming red hair hurries
though the crowd carrying a large goblet. Running with a
limp, he slips on the dais stairs and spills some mead.

                    UNFERTH (CONT'D)
          You're spilling it! You're spilling it!!!

UNFERTH grabs a walking stick from Aesher and hits Cain
in the head. Cain spills more mead....Unferth clobbers
Cain again...he spills more mead...

                    UNFERTH (CONT'D)
          You clumsy idiot!! How dare you waste the
          King's mead!!

CONTINUED:

Unferth beats Cain until he gives up, drops the goblet,
and runs away.

EVERYONE LAUGHS at such good sport...the drunken SINGING
continues...

                         SONG
                    Hrothgar Hrothgar
                    As every demon fell
                    Hrothgar Hrothgar
                    He dragged them back to hell

                    He rose up like a savior
                    When hope was almost gone
                    The beast was gored
                    And peace restored
                    His legend will live on...

SEVERAL ELDERLY LADIES, unaware of the chaos around them,
primly sit eating goose with their fingers. One of them
belches with relish.

A KNAVE BOY is trying to pull a goose-leg away from a
dog. He succeeds, and begins gnawing on it himself.

YRMENLAF catches GITTE and they tumble behind an
overturned bench...the last thing we see is Gitte's dress
fly up over her head.

HROTHGAR, flanked by Aesher and Unferth, with Wealthow
and her ladies off to the side, surveys his raucous mead
hall.

                         HROTHGAR
                    (half drunk, to Aesher)
                    Are we not the most powerful men in the
                    world? Are we not the richest? Do we
                    not merrymake with the best of them? Can
                    we not do as we please?

                         AESHER
                    We can.

                         HROTHGAR
                    Unferth?

Unferth doesn't answer.

                         HROTHGAR (CONT'D)
                    Unferth?

                         UNFERTH
                    (grudgingly)
                    We do. We do.

12   CONTINUED: (2)   12

          Hrothgar, as content as any man could be, slips into a
          drunken catnap.

                                                    SMASH CUT TO:

          CRACK!!! A TREE LIMB EXPLODES IN FRONT OF THE CAMERA...

13   EXT. - THE MOORS - MOVING - NIGHT   13

          We are travelling towards the hall Herot from the
          creature's POINT OF VIEW. We are about 15 feet above the
          ground and moving inhumanly fast.

          THE FOLLOWING POV IS ONE CONTINUOS SHOT:

          WE'RE RUNNING straight toward a thick, black tree
          trunk...the creature lifts his hand and stiff-arms the
          tree...SMASH!! It splinters into a million pieces...

          WE'RE BOUNDING across the moors covering 30 or 40 yards
          with each stride...the creature flushes a covey of red
          grouse...the birds take-off like F-18s. WE easily
          overtake the lead bird, leaving it flailing in the slip-
          stream...

          WE VAULT over the ravine with a single bound...side
          swiping one of the timber guard-rails, ripping it
          apart...

          WE BLAST through a hedge...startling a herd of
          deer...before they can react, we clip one of them in the
          rump...sending it tumbling ass over tea kettle...

          We SPEED toward the castle...mowing down the spikes
          holding the skulls...

          OUR SHADOW looms up over the GATE SENTRY and...

          WE ABRUPTLY STOP!! Standing fifteen feet above the
          fortress wall and the lone guard. The CAMERA PULSES in
          rhythm with the creature's labored BREATHING...each RASPY
          BREATH fanning the cauldron flames.

          The terrified sentry slowly turns to look over his
          shoulder...his eyes widen in horror...and...

                                                    SMASH CUT TO:

          CLOSE ON A DOG...GROWLING...

14   INT. MEAD HALL   14

The dog is at the base of the throne dais, its fur on
end, backing away from the great door.

UNFERTH notices this, his eyes narrow with suspicion.

Everyone else in the hall is oblivious...the REVELERS
revel on...

                    SONG
          Hrothgar Hrothgar
          Let every cup be raised
          Hrothgar Hrothgar
          NOW AND FOREVER PRAIS...

BLAMM!!!!

Something of tremendous force RAMS into the great door
splintering the wooden frame and buckling the great iron
hinges...but the door holds.

HROTHGAR'S eyes go from sleepily closed to wide as
saucers.

THE SINGING stops. WARRIORS reach for their swords.

There's a long PAUSE...then...

SMAAASH!!!

The massive door BLOWS off its hinges!!

The mighty concussion SNUFFS OUT THE FIRE PIT and every
candle...plunging the mead hall into DARKNESS!!!

HROTHGAR rises in his seat, terrified. UNFERTH AND
AESHER, draw their weapons. WEALTHOW stands bravely.

Past the shattered door, SILHOUETTED against the
MOONLIGHT...we see the disfigured black shape of the
giant monster...heaving and pitching as it WHEEZES and
HISSES. Then suddenly...

THE MONSTER lets out an EAR-PIERCING SCREAM as it leaps
into the mead hall!! At that same moment...

THE GREAT FIRE PIT ROARS larger and wilder than before,
becoming a dangerous and ominous pillar of flame!! A HOT-
WHITE PHOSPHORUS-TORNADO...rising to the ceiling and
whipping around furiously...BLINDING our clear view of
the monster!! But we can SEE...

FOUR THANES, swords drawn, charge the beast...

THE MONSTER grabs the first thane by a leg and flails him
around like a rag doll!! Then it uses the SHRIEKING man's
torso to club and pummel the other three
thanes...walloping two thanes into the crowd...CRASHING
into chairs and tables...

THE FORTH THANE is flung over Hrothgar's head and SMASHES
into the wall behind the throne...

                    HROTHGAR
                   (terrified)
            My sword!   My sword!

THE MONSTER, still holding the FIRST THANE by the leg,
bashes the mangled warrior on the floor a few times, then
tosses him into the blazing fire pit...

The fire FLASHES...the burning THANE SCREAMS!!

The MONSTER SCREAMS!!!

The panicked CROWD SCREAMS!!!

MAYHEM ENSUES...WOMEN and CHILDREN flee to take
cover...THANES rush the weapons racks, grabbing spears
and axes.

Aesher takes Wealthow and shoves her down, behind an
overturned table...

                    AESHER
            Stay down, my Lady!!

She immediately PEEKS up over the table...

WEALTHOW'S POINT OF VIEW:

THE FIRE, flaring violently, screens most of what
Wealthow can see, however the INTENSE LIGHT projects a
large, strobing SHADOW OF THE MONSTER on the walls...

THE MONSTER/SHADOW swipes at a thane...sending him
crashing into a rack of battle axes...impaling him!

ANOTHER THANE is thrown up onto a chandelier...landing on
the iron candle spikes!

THE MONSTER/SHADOW SCREAMS as it comes up with the red-
hot roasting spit (the crispy pig still attached) and
skewers three thanes...their cauterized blood sending
acrid smoke billowing into the air.

A PEASANT is hurled through the blazing pillar of flame, his hair and clothes burning...the flaming body flies inches over Wealthow's head, landing on top of a huddled GROUP OF WOMEN. Their clothes catch fire...

WEALTHOW grabs a pitcher of mead and splashes it on the women to douse the flames, then scurries back behind her table...

SMASH!!! A DAGGER BLADE pierces the table...an inch from Wealthow's face. Wealthow peeks over the table top and sees...a dismembered arm...its hand still gripping the DAGGER HILT...

YRMENLAF, the young warrior, comes up from behind Unferth and Aesher with a battle ax and throws it at the monster. The ax hits the monster in the leg but bounces off...

THE MONSTER'S SHADOW turns toward the throne platform. Unferth, Yrmenlaf and the King, GULP...in an instant the monster lunges...BUT GRABS AESHER!!!!

THE SHADOW/MONSTER lifts Aesher up above its head...there's a HORRIFIC RIPPING SOUND and Aesher's shadow is suddenly TWO SHADOWS, a pair of legs and an upper torso.

THE SHADOW/MONSTER throws Aesher's lower torso at the King...but HITS UNFERTH, knocking him to the floor...

AESHER'S UPPER TORSO is tossed onto a feast table, clearing it...Aesher's torso lands in front of Wealthow, literally sitting on a silver platter! She covers her mouth to hold back a scream, but sees...

HROTHGAR stumbling from his throne...fat and covered with a sheet, holding a sword...

YRMENLAF screaming like a berserker rushes the monster, his sword held high above his head...

UNFERTH, still on the floor and white with fear, scampers backward, on his hands and knees...right into the piss-pit!!

THE SHADOW/MONSTER holds Yrmenlaf by the leg, swinging him around until his leg snaps into multiple fractures. Then it throws him on the floor and begins jumping on him. Madly, insanely, jumping up and down like a kid on a trampoline...Yrmenlaf's blood runs across the floor! (Mercifully, the white phosphorous fire-light de-saturates the color so the blood looks more black than red).

THE SHADOW/MONSTER punts Yrmenlaf's head (or maybe just his helmet) across the room, right at Wealthow!! She ducks...BAM!! Yrmenlaf hits the table!! A second later...

CRUNCH!! The monster's scaly, talon-like HAND sinks into the table, just above Wealthow's head! It lifts the table like it was a balsawood toy, then clubs and pummels the last of the charging thanes...

HROTHGAR, trembling violently, stumbles towards the monster, waving his sword...

                    HROTHGAR
              (screaming at the beast)
          Fight me!! Fight ME!!!

There's a pause...none of the surviving thanes move...

THE MONSTER slowly turns to face Hrothgar. With every move the monster makes, it MOANS and WAILS! Its crippled joints CRACKING and POPPING. The creature stands right over Wealthow, its deformed legs straddling her head. Putrid yellow drool pools onto the floor in front of her...

                    HROTHGAR (CONT'D)
                   (in tears)
          Fight me! Damn you! Fight me!

THE MONSTER suddenly ROARS a painful, angry, and tormented BELLOW...right in Hrothgar's face...

                    GRENDEL
          NNNNAAAAaaaaaaaaay!!!!!

THE MONSTER'S foul breath ruffles Hrothgar's sheet, nearly blowing it off...knocking Hrothgar backward, onto his ass!

WEALTHOW, watching from the floor, realizing that something odd is being played out, more than just a garden variety monster attack.

With one hand, the monster grabs two dead thanes by the legs...and rockets up through the chimney!!!

WHOOOOSH!!! A GIANT RUSH OF WIND as the fire pit FLARES and WHIPS...and the room goes dark.

We HEAR PEOPLE SCREAMING AND SOBBING, in the darkness.

Then a torch is LIT, and another, and another....

14   CONTINUED: (4)   14

In the silence, we see that THE MEAD HALL has been
destroyed.

UNFERTH emerges from the piss pit, covered in excrement --
but alive.

WEALTHOW approaches Hrothgar, her face pale with shock.

                    WEALTHOW
          What was...that?

WE SPIRAL IN into HROTHGAR's blood-spattered face. And
he says:

                    HROTHGAR
          Grendel.

                                                  CUT TO:

15   INT. THE GREAT CAVE - NIGHT   15

The monster (who we now know is named GRENDEL),
silhouetted by the cool light of the full moon, shambles
into his lair -- a cave mouth, inside of which is a
placid pool of clear water.

Grendel drops the bodies of the dead warriors onto a
corner of the cave where the bones of men, both bleached
and fleshy litter the floor. It is a strange and
unnerving place.

We only see Grendel in fleeting glimpses and in shadows.
But from what we see he is huge, and strangely misshapen.
His eyes are empty and sanguine, but his corneas are
flecked with glittering gold. His teeth are horrible
atrocities of nightmarish proportion. He is more or less
naked, and hairless.

WE HEAR A WOMAN'S VOICE...melodious and young. This is
GRENDEL'S MOTHER.

                    GRENDEL'S MOTHER (O.C.)
          Grendel? Hwaet oa him weas?

Grendel turns suddenly, surprised by her voice. Like a
boy who has been caught masturbating.

                    GRENDEL'S MOTHER (O.C.)
          What have you done? Grendel?

16   HIGH ANGLE -- GRENDEL'S MOTHER'S P.O.V.   16

The CAMERA is on the ceiling, looking down at Grendel and
the pool.

                         GRENDEL
                Moth-er? Where are you?

                         GRENDEL'S MOTHER (O.C.)
                Men? Grendel...we had an agreement.

The CAMERA DROPS off the ceiling and SPLASHES into the
pool...a moment later WE SURFACE and "SWIM" toward
Grendel. Floating inches above the waterline.

                         GRENDEL'S MOTHER (O.C.)
                Fish, and wolves, and bear, and sometimes
                a sheep or two. But not men.

                         GRENDEL
                You like men. Here...

It offers the CAMERA a body. We "swim" closer...

                         GRENDEL'S MOTHER (O.C.)
                Not these fragile creatures, my darling.
                Remember, they will hurt us. They have
                killed so many of us...of our kind...

                         GRENDEL
                They were making so much noise. They were
                making so much merry...it hurt. Hurt my
                head.

Tears begin to run down Grendel's face. He drops the
warriors, they float on the surface of the pool.

                         GRENDEL'S MOTHER (O.C.)
                    (sharply)
                Was Hrothgar there?

                         GRENDEL
                I did not touch him.

Something SLITHERS past the CAMERA...something GOLD and
SCALY, perhaps a tentacle, or a long lizard's tail...

                         GRENDEL'S MOTHER (O.C.)
                Good boy. My poor sensitive boy.

16   CONTINUED: 16

The tentacle reaches out for Grendel and gently caresses
his tortured, pitiful head.

                                                    CUT TO:

17   EXT. HEROT -- DAWN   17

THE DULL SUN peeks out from under the dark, cold clouds.
Hard frozen snow covers the ground. TIME HAS PAST, it's
the dead of winter

The castle and it's keep are covered in a blanket of new
snow. A WOMAN'S SCREAM pierces the frigid air...

                                                    CUT TO:

18   INT. HEROT - HROTHGAR'S QUARTERS - MORNING   18

Hrothgar and Wealthow are asleep in their bed -- a straw
pallet, covered with cloth and deer hides.

UNFERTH appears and respectfully touches Hrothgar's
shoulder.

                         UNFERTH
                     (whispering)
                My lord?

                         HROTHGAR
                     (waking)
                Hnh? What?

                         UNFERTH
                My lord. It has happened again.

                                                    CUT TO:

19   EXT. MEAD HALL DAY   19

HROTHGAR, UNFERTH AND WULFGAR (the King's Herald) along
with a CONTINGENT OF THANES stand before the mead hall's
great new doors. The doors are much thicker and fortified
with great iron straps.

                         HROTHGAR
                How many this time?

                              UNFERTH
              I could not tell. They were not whole.
              Five. Ten...it was Nykvest's daughter's
              wedding feast.

                              WULFGAR
              He's coming more frequently.

The three men stare at the pink spreading on the snow
from under the door's threshold.

                              HROTHGAR
              The new door hasn't been touched.

                              UNFERTH
              Nay. The Grendel devil obviously came and
              went through the skorsten.

Unferth points to the smoke vent in the hall's roof...a
blood stained trail cuts through the snow...down off the
roof, and across the compound grounds.

                              HROTHGAR
                    (almost sad)
              When I was young I killed a dragon, in
              the Northern Moors. But I'm too old for
              demon-slaying now. We need a hero, a
              cunning young hero, to rid us of this
              curse upon our hall.

                              WULFGAR
              I wish you had a son, my lord.

                              UNFERTH
              You can wish into one hand, Wulfgar, and
              shit into the other, see which fills up
              first.

Hrothgar turns to the small crowd of subjects who have
gathered...

                              HROTHGAR
              Men, Build another pyre! There's dry wood
              behind the stables. Then burn the dead.
                    (now louder, with royal   authority)
              And close this hall! Seal the doors and
              windows! And by the King's order: There
              shall be no further music, singing or
              merrymaking of any kind!!
                    (takes a deep breath and
                     turns away)
              This place reeks of death.

CONTINUED: (2)

Hrothgar shuffles off through the snow. Unferth and
Wulfgar fall-in alongside...

                    HROTHGAR (CONT'D)
                 (quietly to Unferth and
                  Wulfgar)
The scops are singing the shame of Herot
as far south as the middle sea, as far
north as the ice-lands. Our cows no
longer calf, our fields lie fallow, the
very fish flee from our nets, knowing
that we are cursed. I have let it be
known that I will give half the gold in
my kingdom to any man who can rid us of
Grendel.

                    UNFERTH
My King, for deliverance our people
sacrifice goats and sheep to Odin or
Heimdall...with your permission, shall we
also pray to the new Roman God, Christ
Jesus...maybe He can lift this
affliction?

                    HROTHGAR
The gods will do nothing for us that we
will not do for ourselves. No, we need a
hero.

THUNDER RUMBLES!!

CRACK!!! LIGHTNING FLASHES...

Illuminating WAVES...200 feet tall...

20   EXT. THE STORMY SEA - DAY   20

Great gray sheets of rain sweep a stormy Northern sea.
The clouds, black as pitch. The ocean is furious.
CRASHING like an angry orchestra!!

A Nordic sailing vessel (under full sail) crests a giant
wave and thrusts...

BEOWULF straight toward the LENS...into an EXTREME CLOSE
UP...this is the same man we saw earlier, in the autumn
of his life, but now he's in his twenties.

Standing on the deck...he wears leather armor studded
with hand pounded iron. At his hip is a heavy, hand
forged ancestry sword.

CONTINUED:

His cape, a tapestry of heavy black weaves and animal
skins, blows in the wind. Freezing rain pelts his
chiseled face.

At the oars sit FOURTEEN THANES. Their hands, bloodied
and pierced with slivers, tug at the wooden oars.

Beowulf, holding the mast for balance, remains undaunted
by the HOWLING WINDS and the walls of water surrounding
him. He stares at where the horizon <u>must</u> be.

WIGLAF, now in his late thirties, clambers up to where
Beowulf is standing...

>   WIGLAF
>   (shouting above the wind and
>   rain)
>   Can you see the coast? Do you see the
>   Dane's guide-fire?

>   BEOWULF
>   I see nothing but the wind and the rain.

>   WIGLAF
>   No fire? No stars by which to navigate?
>   We're lost! Given to the sea!

Beowulf looks at him and starts <u>LAUGHING</u>...a laugh of
challenge.

>   BEOWULF
>   Ha! The sea is my mother! She will
>   never take me back into her murky womb!

>   WIGLAF
>   That's fine for you. But my mother's a
>   fishwife in Uppland. And I was rather
>   hoping to die in battle, as a warrior
>   should.
>   (he becomes more serious)
>   The men are worried the storm has no end,
>   Beowulf...

Beowulf rests his hand on Wiglaf's shoulder.

>   BEOWULF
>   (looking up to the sheets of
>   falling rain)
>   This is no earthly storm! That much we
>   can be sure. But this demon's tempest
>   won't hold us out!
>   (then to Wiglaf with a grin)
>   Not if we <u>really</u> want in.

CONTINUED: (2)

Wiglaf looks at Beowulf with wide, questioning eyes. Is
Beowulf mad? Even if he was, Wiglaf would follow him
into the mouth of death herself. Wiglaf turns to the
other thanes, whose morale needs charging as well.

                         WIGLAF
                Who wants to live!?

All of the thanes HEAVE A MUTUAL RESPONSE...they do.

                         WIGLAF (cont'd) (CONT'D)
                Then pull your oars! Let's see you do it!
                For Beowulf! For gold! For glory!!
                HEAVE!!!

Good ol' Wiglaf. He's managed to get the men GRUNTING
ENTHUSIASTICALLY with every stroke. He looks at Beowulf,
illuminated by a FLASH OF LIGHTNING. Who wouldn't follow
him?

                                              CUT TO:

21   EXT. THE DANISH CLIFF TOPS - STORM   21

Five spears stand together, their blades pointing to the
vortex of the Cimmerian storm above.

The spears belong to the SCYLDINGS' WATCH, a Dane whose
duty it is to watch the coast for invaders. He sits at a
camp set up next to some ancient cliff-side ruins of
unknown origin. He cooks a field mouse over a small fire.

At sea...LIGHTNING FLASHES.

The Scyldings' Watch jumps up, squinting his eyes to scan
the horizon...something's there.

ANOTHER FLASH...and sure enough something is there. A
tiny craft with bright shields hanging from its sides.
And a golden dragon is emblazoned on its sail.

His mouth falls open. He drops his mouse kebab and jumps
onto his HORSE, grabs his greatest long spear, then spurs
his horse down a near vertical drop of the cliff-side.

                                              CUT TO:

22   EXT. SEA SHORE -- LATER   22

In the rain, Beowulf and his men are hauling their boat
up onto the beach.

WIGLAF sees something...he points down the beach.

THE SCYLDING'S WATCH is galloping full-out down the
beach...coming straight towards us, he lowers his long
spear...ready to impale the first man he reaches.

Beowulf takes a few steps toward the armed rider,
unafraid.

Faster and faster the rider and his spear come at
us...closer and closer...until the spear point fills the
screen...then...

The rider STOPS...the spike an inch from Beowulf's nose!!
Beowulf didn't flinch.

> SCYLDINGS' WATCH
> Who are you? By your dress, you are
> warriors.

> WIGLAF
> Yes. We--

> SCYLDINGS' WATCH
> Speak! Why should I not run you through
> right now? Who are you? Where are you
> from?

> BEOWULF
> We are Geats. I am Beowulf, son of
> Edgethow. We have come seeking your
> prince, Hrothgar, in friendship. They say
> you have a monster here. They say your
> land is cursed.

Scyldings' Watch doesn't move.

> SCYLDINGS' WATCH
> Is that what they say?

> WIGLAF
> Bards sing of Hrothgar's shame from the
> frozen north to the shores of Vinland.

> SCYLDINGS' WATCH
> It is no shame to be accursed by demons.

> WIGLAF
> It is no shame to accept aid that is
> freely giv...

> BEOWULF
> (cutting off Wiglaf)
> I am Beowulf, and I have come to kill
> your monster.

22   CONTINUED: (2)   22

The Watch lifts his spear, he looks over Beowulf's men
with questioning eyes.

                    SCYLDINGS' WATCH
          You'll need horses.

                                                    CUT TO:

23   EXT. KING'S ROAD/BRIDGE/RAVINE DAY   23

The storm has subsided, but the sky is still very dark
and ominous.

Leading from the massive wooden bridge is a rocky road of
shale stones, perhaps recycled tombstones, set into the
mud and lined by large stone monoliths. The lone turret
of Castle Herot can be seen in the distance.

BEOWULF'S MEN are riding along on shaggy ponies,
following the Scyldings' Watch.

SCYLDING'S WATCH reins his horse at the threshold of the
bridge...

                    SCYLDINGS' WATCH
          This is as far as I go. I must return to
          the cliffs. The sea must not be left
          unguarded. The stone path is the king's
          road.
                    (with a smile)
          It was built in better times. Follow it
          to great Herot, where my King waits.

                    BEOWULF
          I thank you for your aid.

                    SCYLDINGS' WATCH
          Our monster is fast and strong.

                    BEOWULF
          I too am fast and strong.

                    SCYLDINGS' WATCH
          So were the others who came here to fight
          it. They're all dead. I thought no more
          heroes were foolish enough to come here
          and die for our gold.

                    BEOWULF
          If we die, it shall be for glory, not for
          gold.

23   CONTINUED: 23

The watch kicks his horse, and heads back the way they
came. And then he reins in his horse and calls--

                    SCYLDINGS' WATCH
          Beowulf?

Beowulf turns, and looks back at him.

                    SCYLDINGS' WATCH (CONT'D)
          The creature took my brother. Kill the
          bastard for me.

                                              CUT TO:

24   INT. HROTHGAR'S ANTEROOM/OFFICE DAY   24

HROTHGAR stares out the window at the angry sea. He looks
even older and grayer than he did when last we saw him.
Unferth sits at the desk organizing treasure.

WULFGAR enters...

                    WULFGAR
          My lord? My lord?

                    HROTHGAR
          Huh?

                    WULFGAR
          My lord. There are warriors outside,
          Geats. They are no beggars -- and their
          leader, Beowulf, is a--

                    HROTHGAR
               (interrupting)
          Beowulf? Edgethow's little boy?

UNFERTH'S eyes narrow at the mention of Beowulf's name.

                    HROTHGAR (CONT'D)
          Not a boy any longer...but I knew him
          when he was a boy. Strong as a grown man
          he was, back then. Yes! Beowulf is
          here! Send him to me! Bring him in!

                                              CUT TO:

25   EXT. HEROT - STOCKADE - DAY   25

There is a stir inside the village stockade, as the
VILLAGERS gather around Beowulf and his 14 thanes.

BEOWULF AND HIS MEN sit astride their mounts...perfectly still...hands hovering near their sword hilts...their eyes scanning the crowd.

YRSA is eating a large plum, letting its juice run down her chin and cleavage. She has her eye on...

HONDSHEW, an ornery Thane, and almost as big as Beowulf himself. He wears a large winged helm and has an oversized broadsword slung over his back.

He stares at Yrsa and her plum, and licks his lips..

WULFGAR appears, also on a horse...

                    WULFGAR
          Hrothgar, Master of Battles, Lord of the
          North Danes, bids me say that he knows
          you, Beowulf son of Edgethow. Knows your
          ancestry, and bids you welcome. You, and
          your men, will follow me...your helmets
          and armor are approved...but your shields
          and weapons will remain here until
          further notice.

WIGLAF gives Beowulf a look...he doesn't like this.

                    WULFGAR (CONT'D)
          I assure you...they won't be disturbed.

Hondshew and the others look at Beowulf for guidance.

CLANK! Beowulf's sword and spear hit the ground. He pulls a dagger from his belt and throws it so the blade sticks in the ground.

His men copy him. Their weapons fall to the ground.

HONDSHEW'S giant broadsword CLATTERS to the ground...

                    YRSA
          My...that's a big one you've got there,
          outlander.

Hondshew swallows with an almost audible GULP.

Wiglaf pulls his horse up and glares at Yrsa...

                    WIGLAF
          Woman! Have you nothing better to be
          doing?

25   CONTINUED: (2)   25

She makes no reply, but with her little finger, wipes the
drip of plum-juice from her breast, and licks it from her
finger.

                    HROTHGAR (O.S.)
          Beowulf!!

                                                    CUT TO:

26   EXT. MEAD HALL   CLOSE HROTHGAR DAY   26

The WHOLE COURT assembled on the stone steps in front of
the shuttered and barred mead hall. Queen Wealthow and
THE QUEEN'S WOMEN, GUARDS and COURTIERS. Unferth is
there, but he is standing in the shadows. RAYS OF
SUNLIGHT briefly appear streaming though the clouds

Hrothgar hugs Beowulf to him, proudly.

                    HROTHGAR
          Beowulf! How is your father?

                    BEOWULF
          He died in battle with sea-raiders, two
          winters back.

                    HROTHGAR
          He was a brave man. Need I ask why have
          you come to us?

                    BEOWULF
          I've come to kill your monster.

The sheer arrogance of this statement sends a LOUD MURMUR
through the crowd. Even Hrothgar is taken aback.

Beowulf smiles, having stirred things up.

                    BEOWULF (CONT'D)
          ...and taste that famous mead of yours.

Hrothgar LAUGHS with a hearty ROAR. The tension in the
crowd is eased.

Now Wealthow steps forward...

                    WEALTHOW
          And there have been many brave men who
          have come here, and have drunk too much
          of my Lord's mead, and have sworn to rid
          his hall of our nightmare.
                    (MORE)

> WEALTHOW (CONT'D)
> And the next morning, there was nothing
> left of any of them but blood to be
> cleaned from the floor...and the
> benches...and walls.

Beowulf and Wealthow lock eyes...a long, penetrating
look.

> BEOWULF
> I have drunk nothing. Yet. But I will
> kill your monster.

> HROTHGAR
>   (overly enthusiastic)
> He will kill the monster! Did you hear
> that? Grendel will die!

> BEOWULF
> Grendel?

> HROTHGAR
> The monster is called Grendel.

> BEOWULF
> Then I shall kill your Grendel. I,
> Beowulf, killed a tribe of giants in the
> Orkneys. I have crushed the skulls of
> sea-serpents. And this...this troll of
> yours shall trouble you no longer.

The Queen is about to say something, but Hrothgar
announces to the assemblage...

> HROTHGAR
> A hero! I knew that the sea would bring
> us a hero!

A weary, half-hearted CHEER comes from the crowd. They
heard all this before. Wealthow looks doubtful. Unferth
glares.

Then, Hrothgar raises an eyebrow...

> HROTHGAR (CONT'D)
> Will you go up to the moors, then, to the
> cave by the dark pool, and fight the
> monster in its den?

Beowulf steps forward and waves his hand.

> BEOWULF
> I have fourteen brave Thanes with me. We
> have been long at sea.
>   (MORE)

26   CONTINUED: (2)   26

                          BEOWULF (CONT'D)
              I think it is high time, mighty Hrothgar,
              to break open your golden mead, famed
              across the world; and to feast in your
              legendary mead hall.

Unferth steps forward...

                          UNFERTH
              The mead hall has been sealed...by his
              lord's order. Merry-making in the hall
              brings the devil Grendel.

Beowulf gives Unferth a long, cold look. Then like a
politician on a soapbox...

                          BEOWULF
                    (loudly, to the multitude)
              Has closing this hall <u>stopped</u> the
              slaughter?

                          HROTHGAR
              Nay, the demon-murderer killed three
              horses and a slave in the stable a fort-
              night ago.

Beowulf says nothing, but a huge Cheshire smile spreads
across his face. A smile that's much too huge.

                          BEOWULF
              Well then...

Hrothgar nods and smiles back. He raises his arms in a
dramatic gesture...

                          HROTHGAR
              OPEN THE MEAD HALL!!!

                                            CUT TO:

27   INT. HEROT - MEAD HALL - DAY   27

CLACK! CLACK!! TWO THANES turn a large crank, pulling a
chain to lift the huge timber that bars the mead hall
door.

SPLASH!! Water is poured over one of the long feasting
tables.

SLAVE BOYS lay fresh straw on the floor.

AN OLD WOMAN blows on some embers to start a fire in the
great fire-pit.

27   CONTINUED: 27

BEOWULF'S 14 THANES are gathered around a table in the
corner, strapping on their weapons and adjusting their
gear.

BEOWULF wanders though the hall, checking it out. He
sizes up the huge entrance door with its complicated
security bar and heavy iron strapping

HONDSHEW is staring at Yrsa, the plum girl. She bends
over a table, scrubbing it. Her breasts straining her
halter.

WIGLAF kicks Hondshew in the ass...

                    WIGLAF
                (lecturing his thanes)
          We don't want any trouble with the
          locals. So, just for tonight, no
          fighting, and no swifan. Okay?

OLAF, a hulking, muscle-bound thane with a speech
impediment, draws his dagger and strikes a combat
stance...

                    OLAF
          I wa...wa...wasn't p...p..planning on
          doing any swi...swi...swi...swifan.

Hondshew flashes a lascivious, yellow-toothed smile at
Yrsa...

                    HONDSHEW
                (mimicking Olaf)
          I wa...wa...was!

                    WIGLAF
          Hondshew. Make me feel like you're
          pretending to listen to me. It's only
          been five days since you waved your wife
          goodbye.

                    HONDSHEW
          Five days!! In the name of Odin...no
          wonder my loins are burning!!

Yrsa sticks her tongue out at Hondshew. The thanes ROAR
with laughter.

                                              CUT TO:

28   INT. THE GREAT CAVE - GRENDEL'S LAIR -- SAME   28

CLOSE ON A LAMPREY SUCKING MOUTH

CONTINUED:

As it grabs a chunk of flesh...

GRENDEL is feeding bits of a dead thane to a school of
blind white MORAY EELS. The horrible sea snakes teem in
the cave's black pool.

Grendel SINGS to itself, a slow, sad, tuneless sort of
noise. It holds a spike topped with a decapitated
warrior's head, playing with it as if it were a puppet.

                    GRENDEL
              (pretending he's the voice of
               the Thane's head)
          Da-dee-da! Da-dee-da!
          Who's laughing now?!

If Grendel were human, it would be considered retarded,
perhaps brain-damaged...it's actually sweet and
gentle...except in the matter of eating people, and then
only when driven mad with noise.

AN EEL leaps out of the water striking the warrior's
head, tearing off an earlobe...

GRENDEL LAUGHS delightedly at the eels.

                    GRENDEL (CONT'D)
          No more. You get fat! Fat fish! More
          tomorrow.

A LOUD HISS burbles from somewhere in the pool...

GRENDEL is alarmed; It jumps up. Its fingernails shoot
out and become sharp claws. Its deformed torso begins to
expand and enlarge. Its eyes narrow.

EXTREME CLOSE ON: GRENDEL'S MOTHER'S LIPS...wet, full,
with golden scales...cold-blooded.

                    GRENDEL'S MOTHER
              (a bodiless whisper)
          Grrrrendellllll.

GRENDEL soothes a little, its nails recess back into its
fingers. Its torso begins to shrink back to "normal"
size.

                    GRENDEL
          Modor?

GRENDEL'S MOTHER'S POV: The CAMERA emerges from the water
and slowly floats toward Grendel. Grendel's mother
WHISPERS.

                        GRENDEL'S MOTHER
             I had an evil dream, my son. You were
             hurt. I dreamed that you were calling
             out for me, and I could not come to you.
             And then they butchered you.

                        GRENDEL
             I am not dead. I am happy. Look, happy
             Grendel.

Grendel does an awkward, shuffling dance around the cave,
SINGING as he does.

                        GRENDEL (CONT'D)
                  (singing, tunelessly)
             Happy happy, happy happy, happy happy,
             happy happy...

                        GRENDEL'S MOTHER
             You must not go to them tonight. You
             have killed too many of them.

                        GRENDEL
             Grendel strong. Grendel big. Grendel
             will eat their flesh and drink their
             blood and break their bones.

                        GRENDEL'S MOTHER
             Please, my son. Do not go to them.

                        GRENDEL
                  (makes a whining sound)
             Ohhhh ...

                        GRENDEL'S MOTHER
             Please. Promise me this.

Grendel sulks, defeated.

                        GRENDEL
             I swear. I shall not go to them.

                        GRENDEL'S MOTHER
             Even if they make the noises?

Grendel hesitates, then nods, reluctantly, as if it's
being jerked out of him, an awkward little boy promising
his mother something.

                        GRENDEL'S MOTHER (CONT'D)
             Gut. Man medo.

                                                    CUT TO

29   INT. HEROT - MEAD HALL - SUNSET   29

A giant copper vat, brimming with golden mead is carried
into the hall. BEOWULF'S THANES CHEER!!

But everyone else seems subdued -- like a reception at a
funeral. Still, MUSIC IS PLAYING, and maidens are
pouring mead.

BEOWULF stands on the dais steps, looking quizzically at
a primitive sundial carved into the wall. A prism mounted
on the anteroom balcony focuses a point of sunlight on
the dial face.

                    WEALTHOW (O.S.)
          It can measure the length of a day.

Beowulf turns to find WEALTHOW. She points to the dial...

                    WEALTHOW (CONT'D)
          ...when the sun touches the lowest
          line...soon the day will be finished.

                    BEOWULF
          And Grendel will arrive?

She stares at him, her face, unearthly in its beauty.

                    WEALTHOW
          I hope that God is kind to you, Sir
          Beowulf. It would be a great shame on
          this house, if one so brave and noble
          were to die in it.

                    BEOWULF
          There is no shame to die in battle with
          evil.

                    WEALTHOW
          And if you die?

                    BEOWULF
          There will be no corpse to weep over, no
          funeral to prepare, and none to mourn me.
          Grendel will dispose of my body in a
          bloody animal feast, taking my bones and
          sucking off my flesh...swallowing me
          down.

Wealthow is a little turned on by the thought of
swallowing Beowulf. She collects herself, upset by her
reaction.

                              WEALTHOW
                   I would mourn you, my lord.

She looks up at him. It's a moment of romance, or naked
lust...

                            HROTHGAR (O.S.)
                   Ah, Beowulf...there you are.

FOUR BRAWNY THANES lower HROTHGAR and his portable throne
to the floor. He gets up and approaches Beowulf. His
court assembles behind him.

                          HROTHGAR (CONT'D)
                   ...I was thinking about your father.
                   There was a feud, I believe. He came here
                   fleeing the Wylflings. He'd killed one
                   of them with his bare hands.

                              BEOWULF
                   Heatholaf.

                             HROTHGAR
                       (nodding vigorously and then
                        continuing)
                   --that was him! I paid the blood debt
                   for your father, and he swore his oath to
                   me. No good deed goes unrewarded,
                   though. I saved his skin, now you're
                   here to save ours, eh?

He SLAPS Beowulf on the back.

We hear A LOW, BITTER, LAUGH from the shadows behind the
throne.

UNFERTH steps out of the shadows into the light, CLAPPING
his hands.

                             UNFERTH
                   All hail the great Beowulf! Here to save
                   our pathetic Danish skins, eh?
                       (bitter irony & plenty of it)
                   And we are so damned grateful, mighty
                   Beowulf. But can I ask a question -- as
                   a huge admirer of yours?

Beowulf simply stares at him, with the sort of unblinking
stare that Clint Eastwood made famous.

29   CONTINUED: (2)   29

                          UNFERTH (CONT'D)
              You see, there was another Beowulf I
              heard tell of, who challenged Brecca the
              mighty to a swimming race, out on the
              open sea. Was that you?

Beowulf wonders if he's being set up. But he nods.

                          BEOWULF
              I swam against Brecca.

                          UNFERTH
              Hmm. I thought that it had to be a
              different Beowulf. Someone else of the
              same name. You see--
                   (he raises his voice)
              --the Beowulf I heard of swam against
              Brecca, and lost. He risked his life,
              and Brecca's, in the deep ocean to serve
              his own vanity and pride. A boastful
              fool. And he lost. So I thought it had
              to be someone else...

Beowulf slowly walks toward Unferth. You could hear a
pin drop.

                          BEOWULF
              I swam against Brecca.

                          UNFERTH
                   (loudly)
              But victory was his, not yours. A mighty
              warrior who cannot even win a swimming
              match. Speaking only for myself here, I
              not only doubt that you will be able to
              stand for a moment against Grendel, but I
              doubt you will even have the belly to
              stay in the hall all night.

Unferth downs his cup of mead and grins.

                          BEOWULF
              I find it difficult to argue with a
              drunk. And it is true that I did not win
              the race...

                                              DISSOLVE TO:

30   EXT. OPEN SEA -- DAY -- FLASHBACK   30

Beowulf is swimming in a race with BRECCA, a young
warrior the same age as Beowulf.

CONTINUED:

Great swells of the sea lift and toss the two swimmers
like driftwood, but the two men power alongside each
other. Brecca swims with a dagger in his mouth, Beowulf
with a sword in one hand. The rugged coast of Finland can
be seen in the distance.

                    BEOWULF (V.O.)
          We swam for five days, neck and neck.
          And I was the more powerful swimmer. I
          was conserving my strength, for the final
          stretch.

Beowulf pulls ahead...

                    BEOWULF (V.O.)(CONT'D)
          ...Then a storm blew up, and with the
          storm, came sea monsters.

We HEAR the Thanes in the hall MURMURING with approval.

A SERPENTINE SEA MONSTER -- comes up from the depths. Its
tentacles grabbing Brecca, crushing his rib cage and
causing Brecca to loose his dagger.

For a moment, Beowulf looks satisfied. He can win the
race. But he knows what he must do...

He sighs then plunges down, and with his sword, stabs the
serpent...in the eye. Purplish blood stains the ocean.

The serpent relaxes it's grip on Brecca...but Brecca
swims on...Beowulf on the other hand isn't going
anywhere...

ANOTHER SERPENT emerges and wraps its tentacles around
Beowulf's legs. Beowulf slashes at its throat.

                    BEOWULF (V.O.)(CONT'D)
          I hacked and lashed at these foul beasts
          with my sword...spilling their guts into
          the sea.

THEN ANOTHER SERPENT APPEARS and Beowulf slices off its
tentacle...

THEN FIVE MORE SERPENTS APPEAR AND Beowulf quickly
dispatches each of these terrifying, deep-sea
monstrosities...

                    BEOWULF (V.O.)(CONT'D)
          Again and again the monsters
          attacked...dark things from the sea's
          dark depths.

30   CONTINUED: (2)   30

Exhausted and bleeding, Beowulf breaks the surface and
swims mightily. With his sword still in hand, he pulls
even with Brecca.

The shoreline and finish are a mere 50 yards ahead. A
DOZEN GEATS CHEER them on from the beach.

Beowulf passes Brecca and is ahead by a length when...

                    BEOWULF (V.O.)(CONT'D)
          Then...

Beowulf is suddenly pulled violently underwater...

31   BACK TO THE MEAD HALL   31

EXTREME CLOSE ON: Beowulf's face, remembering something
else...something forbidden.

                    BEOWULF
          ...one of them seized me in its jaws, and
          dragged me to the bottom...

Something in his face tells us we may not be hearing the
truth. He shuts his eyes...

32   EXT. SEA -- DAY -- FLASHBACK   32

Underwater...Beowulf raises his sword at the creature
that has him by the legs...but stops!!

What Beowulf sees is not a sea-serpent, but A BEAUTIFUL
GOLDEN WOMAN...not human, but some sort of Mermaid-form,
with sea kelp hair and glistening, golden skin (She has a
striking resemblance to Grendel's Mother).

BEOWULF is awestruck, mesmerized by her beauty.

THE WOMAN seductively beckons Beowulf to swim closer...

                    BEOWULF (V.O.)
          ...I killed the monster with my own
          blade...plunging it into it's heart...

THE WOMAN wraps her golden arms around Beowulf and kisses
him...Beowulf kisses back.

                    BEOWULF (V.O.)(CONT'D)
          ...I did not win the race.

BACK TO THE MEAD HALL

Beowulf shakes himself out of the memory, forcing it
somewhere deep into his subconscious. He continues...

                    BEOWULF
          They sing of my battle with the sea
          monsters to this day, my friend. And
          they sing no such songs about Brecca. But
          I braved their hot jaws, making those
          lanes safe for seamen...and survived the
          nightmare.

                    UNFERTH
               (magnificently unimpressed)
          Of course. The sea monsters. And you
          killed, what, twenty was it?

                    BEOWULF
          Nine. But...will you do me the honor of
          telling me your name?

                    UNFERTH
          I am Unferth, son of Ecglaf.

Beowulf addresses the thanes like a seasoned politician.

                    BEOWULF
          Unferth? Son of Ecglaf? Your fame has
          crossed the ocean ahead of you. I know
          who you are...

Unferth does not know if Beowulf is telling the truth.
But he starts to preen a little...

                    BEOWULF (CONT'D)
          Let's see....they say you are clever.
          Not wise, but sharp. And they say that
          you killed both of your brothers when you
          caught them having knowledge of your
          mother, "Unferth Kinslayer".
               (laughs)
          A crime for which you will roast in agony
          forever.

After a protracted moment of hate, Unferth throws himself
at Beowulf, growling. Beowulf steps aside and Unferth
trips and falls to the floor. Beowulf crouches beside
him.

33   CONTINUED: 33

                         BEOWULF (CONT'D)
              I'll tell you another true thing, Unferth
              Kinslayer. If your strength and heart
              had been as strong and fierce as your
              words, then Grendel would never feel free
              to murder and gorge on your people, with
              no fear of retaliation. But tonight will
              be different. Tonight he will find Geats
              waiting for him: not frightened
              sheep...like you.

     SUDDENLY, DANES on the side of Unferth, pull their
     weapons and take an angry step toward Beowulf...

     BEOWULF'S THANES draw their swords and daggers...the two
     lines of warriors stand eyeball to eyeball...then...

     HROTHGAR starts CLAPPING. Is he senile, or sensibly
     breaking up the fight? He steps out between them.

                         HROTHGAR
              Well done! That's the spirit, young
              Beowulf! That's the spirit we need!
              You'll kill my Grendel for me. Let's we
              all drink, and make celebration for the
              kill to come! Eh?!

     Beowulf smiles and places his hand on Hrothgar's
     shoulder. Everyone relaxes.

                                                  CUT TO:

34   INT. MEAD HALL -- LATER   34

     A FINGER PLUCKS a harp string. PULL BACK TO REVEAL
     WEALTHOW SINGING a balled, beautiful and melancholy.

     Beowulf's thanes are eating, with their fingers and with
     knives, from a huge cut of beef on the table.

     Hondshew cuts a slice of beef, with his knife, and feeds
     it to Yrsa, who passes with a jug of mead.

     Beowulf sits in a place of honor at the bottom of the
     throne dais. Gitte arrives and re-fills Beowulf's cup.

     Hrothgar calls down to Beowulf...

                         HROTHGAR
              The High King's mead! The finest mead!
              Careful. Three cups of that and they'll
              be carrying you out of here.

CONTINUED:

Beowulf raises his cup and toasts...Wealthow.

Still strumming the harp, Wealthow nods and smiles what
looks like an inviting smile.

Hrothgar has completely missed the moment of strange
romance between his wife and the young warrior. Or
perhaps he hasn't...

                    HROTHGAR (CONT'D)
          Beowulf, son of Edgethow...come close, I
          want to show you something...

Hrothgar claps his hands then motions to Unferth to get
out of his seat. Hrothgar pulls Unferth's chair next to
his throne and Beowulf sits. Wulfgar arrives with a
carved wooden box.

CLOSE ON BOX:

Inside is the ROYAL DRAGON HORN that we saw in the
opening scene.

BEOWULF'S EYES WIDEN at the sight of the horn, gleaming
in the firelight.

                    HROTHGAR (CONT'D)
          The Royal Dragon Horn.

Hrothgar hands the horn to Beowulf. He holds it up...

                    BEOWULF
          It is beautiful.

                    HROTHGAR
          Isn't she magnificent? The prize of my
          treasury.

Beowulf runs his fingertips over it.

                    HROTHGAR (CONT'D)
          I claimed it after my battle with Fafnir,
          the dragon of the Northern moors. It
          nearly cost me my life.
                    (confiding with a loud
                     whisper)
          There's a soft spot just under the neck.

Hrothgar points to the ruby set in the dragons throat.

                    HROTHGAR (CONT'D)
          *You go in with a knife or a dagger...it's
          the only way you can kill a dragon.*
                    (MORE)

34   CONTINUED: (2)   34

                          HROTHGAR (CONT'D)
                        (admiring the horn)
                I wonder how many men have died for love
                of this beauty?

The light glints off the cup alluringly.

                          BEOWULF
                Can you blame them?

Hrothgar takes the horn, holds it up in front of Beowulf.

                          HROTHGAR
                If you can take care of Grendel, she's
                yours forever.

                          BEOWULF
                You do me great honour.

Wealthow finishes her song.

                          WEALTHOW
                It is we who are honoured.

Another furtive look between Wealthow and Beowulf.
Unferth watches this exchange from the shadows.

Beowulf clambers onto a table. He takes an ordinary
goblet from a thane and raises it high...

                          BEOWULF
                My lord, my lady, people of Herot. When
                we crossed the rolling sea to come to
                you, we knew, my men and I, that we will
                either triumph over evil, or we will
                perish in Grendel's grasp. Tonight, we
                shall live forever in greatness and
                courage, or, forgotten and despised, we
                shall die!

CHEERS from the hall. Wealthow smiles sadly.

                                                        CUT TO:

35   INT. MEAD HALL - SUNSET   35

CLOSE ON THE SUNDIAL: The pinpoint of sunlight focused on
the carved wall...extinguishes.

Hrothgar points to the dial...

                          HROTHGAR
                Ah, I see the hour is upon us.

CONTINUED:

He yawns, ostentatiously.

                    HROTHGAR (CONT'D)
          Well, this old man needs his sleep.
          Where's my bed-mate? Wealthow my dear?

Hrothgar holds out his hand to Wealthow.

                    WEALTHOW
          In a moment.

                    HROTHGAR
          Come my beauty. Shall we pound the
          pillow?

Hrothgar grabs Wealthow by the arm...she violently pulls
it away. There's a sudden vehemence in her voice.

                    WEALTHOW
          Don't touch me!

Everyone is stunned. Hrothgar freezes, anger rising in
his face.

Wanting no part of a marital squabble, Beowulf steps
forward in an attempt to mediate the situation...

                    BEOWULF
          Perhaps her majesty could grace our ears
          with one more melody... before we all
          retire.

Wealthow walks past Hrothgar and picks up her harp.

                    WEALTHOW
          It's the least I can do.

Hrothgar ignores her and instead, speaks to Beowulf.

                    HROTHGAR
          I hope to see you in the morning,
          Beowulf...Odin willing. Be sure your
          thanes secure the door.

His four thanes lift his throne and carry him, out of the
room. Unferth follows, but turns back to Beowulf...

                    UNFERTH
          Good night, Beowulf. Watch out for sea
          monsters. I'm sure your imagination must
          be teeming with them.

35   CONTINUED: (2)   35

Beowulf brushes past him and sits beside Wealthow. She
begins to PLAY. Again the song is sad. She SINGS directly
to Beowulf, her eyes full of romance and longing.

                                                    CUT TO:

36   INT. THE GREAT CAVE - GRENDEL'S LAIR   36

We can SCARCELY HEAR Wealthow SINGING in the distance.

GRENDEL bolts upright!! And SCREAMS!!

                                                    CUT TO:

37   EXT. HEROT - OUTSIDE MEAD HALL   NIGHT   37

HONDSHEW and YRSA are outside the mead hall, dallying in
the shadows.

GRENDEL'S SCREAM breaks the night...

                    HONDSHEW
                (thinks he's being cute)
            Is that your demon?

                    YRSA
            That was a wolf. You don't hear Grendel
            when he comes.

                    HONDSHEW
            No? Well, you'll hear me, I promise.

Yrsa shoves him away. He pulls her back...

                    HONDSHEW (CONT'D)
            Come on, my mighty lustleomb can
            transport you to paradise...to ecstasy
            and back...no other man will ever be able
            to satisfy you again.

                    YRSA
            Sorry...

While the conversation is going on, DANES are SLIPPING
OUT OF THE HALL, looking around nervously. Hondshew
presses Yrsa closer.

                    HONDSHEW
            Aw, come on...

37   CONTINUED: 37

                          YRSA
              I said no and I meant no.

                          HONDSHEW
              Why not?

                          YRSA
              Because it's late...and it's dark...and
              the monster could arrive at any moment.

                          HONDSHEW
              Well, then...how about a quick gobble?

Yrsa SLAPS him hard across the face.

                                              CUT TO:

38   INT. MEAD HALL -- NIGHT   38

Wealthow finishes her song. Beowulf smiles, there is a
moment between them.

                          BEOWULF
              That was beautiful. But you need to go
              now, your majesty.

                          WEALTHOW
              Of course, Grendel.

Beowulf begins removing his breastplate and weapons belt.

Wealthow sets down her harp, then turns back to Beowulf.

                          WEALTHOW (CONT'D)
                    (she hesitates, and then...)
              The demon is my husband's shame.

                          BEOWULF
              Not a shame. A curse.

                          WEALTHOW
              No, shame. My husband has no other...no
              sons. And he will have no more, for all
              his talk.

Beowulf frowns, not exactly understanding her enigmatic
words. Then...

                          THANES (O.S.)
              Oy, Hondshew. Did you get any? How was
              she?

HONDSHEW enters the hall. Yrsa's handprint burned in on
the side of his face. The thanes HOOT AND JEER him:

> HONDSHEW
> Nah. Not my type.

OLAF playfully tosses a half-eaten goose leg at him.

> OLAF
> Yeah? I n...n...know your type. *Baaa!*
> *Baaa! Baaaaa...*

Hondshew throws himself at Olaf, and they roll around on
the floor, fighting -- or mock fighting, anyway.

The other thanes CHEER and LAUGH. We see that Beowulf's
thanes are all that's left in the hall. Not a Dane in
sight.

The two wrestling thanes knock over a table.

> WEALTHOW
> Why don't you stop them?

> BEOWULF
> It's just high spirits.

Without taking his eyes off Wealthow, Beowulf lifts his
tunic over his head.

> BEOWULF (CONT'D)
> You really need to go now, your majesty.

Then, very slow, like a strip-tease, he begins unhooking
his chain mail.

> WEALTHOW
> My lord Beowulf... What are you doing?

> BEOWULF
> (continuing to undress)
> When Grendel comes, we will fight as
> equals. The creature has no sword, no
> armor. And I have no weapon capable of
> slaying a monster. But I have teeth, and
> sinews of my own. Armor forged of man
> will only slow me. We will fight as
> equals. Fate shall decide.

CA-CHINK!! Beowulf's chain-mail drops to the floor...now
naked, except for his loincloth, Beowulf's perfectly
chiseled pecs glisten in the fire-light.

CONTINUED: (2)

WEALTHOW blushes. Then, flees through the anteroom door.
WE HEAR it being triple-bolted from the other side.

BEOWULF, lost in his thoughts, stares at the door.

CLOSE ON THE MAIN DOOR:

FOUR THANES are securing the main door. A thick chain
lowers the massive wooden bar into the door's iron
brackets.

PULL BACK TO FIND WIGLAF supervising this procedure.

                    WIGLAF
          That's good...tie it off with more chain.

Now Wiglaf grabs a bucket of water and throws it on
Hondshew and Olaf who are still rolling around on the
floor.

                    WIGLAF (CONT'D)
          All right girls...enough frican' about!!

BEOWULF strips off his loincloth and lies down on the
floor, his head pillowed by his rolled-up cape.

WIGLAF approaches and LAUGHS...

                    WIGLAF (CONT'D)
          You're mad, you know that?

                    BEOWULF
               (his eyes closed, to himself)
          Yes.

Wiglaf continues to stand there...wanting to say more.

                    BEOWULF (CONT'D)
               (his eyes still closed)
          Something vexes you, my Wiglaf?

                    WIGLAF
          Aye, I don't like the smell of this one,
          my lord. The men are not prepared.
          They're distracted. There's too many
          untended women here. Abstinence prior to
          battle is essential. A warrior's mind
          must be unblurred...focused.

                    BEOWULF
          You worry too much, Wiglaf.

>   WIGLAF
>   Of course. That's my job!

Beowulf opens his eyes and gives Wiglaf a "you worry way
too much" look.

>   BEOWULF
>   Good night, Wiglaf.

>   WIGLAF
>   And while you're sleeping, what are we
>   meant to do?

>   BEOWULF
>   Sing. Loudly.

Wiglaf turns to the gaping thanes.

>   WIGLAF
>   You heard him. He wants us to sing...

Nobody does anything.

>   WIGLAF (CONT'D)
>   So...SING!
>   (kicks Olaf)
>   Olaf...SING!!

Olaf takes his cue, the tune is upbeat, rowdy, rough-and-
ready:

>   OLAF
>   (singing in verse)
>   There were a dozen virgins,
>   Friesians, Danes and Franks!
>   We took 'em for some swifan'
>   And all we got were wanks!
>   OOoohh...

>   THANES
>   (chorus)
>   *OOohh, We are Beowulf's army,*
>   *Each a mighty thane,*
>   *We'll pummel your asses, and ravage your*
>   *lasses,*
>   *Then do it all over again!*

>   HONDSHEW
>   The prettiest of the virgins,
>   She was the fairest Swede!
>   I told her I'd an urgin',
>   For where to spend my seed!

38   CONTINUED: (4)   38

                          OLAF
              Y..you g...g...go, Wiglaf.

                          WIGLAF
              The oldest of the virgins,
              She was a Vandal lass!
              I showed my mighty weapon,
              And she showed me her ass!

                                              CUT TO:

39   INT. THE GREAT CAVE - NIGHT   39

SLOW PUSH INTO the great cave. The SINGING, now LOUDER
than ever, REVERBERATING inside the murky
burrow...reaching a fever pitch.

                          THANES (O.S.)
                       (chorus)
              OOooohh, *We are Beowulf's army,*
              Each a mighty thane,
              We'll pummel your asses and ravage your
              lasses,
              Then do it all over again!

GRENDEL writhes in pain...the SONG SMASHING inside his
head. His hands are clutched tightly over his skull. His
golden eyes pinched tightly shut, tears drip from them.
The dank walls, seem to close in on Grendel. Is the cave
growing smaller, or is Grendel GROWING BIGGER?!?

                                              CUT TO:

40   INT. HEROT - MEAD HALL - NIGHT   40

THE THANES SING all the verses together now...picking up
the tempo...POUNDING their fists and cups on the table in
rhythm.

                          THANES
              The fattest of the Virgins,
              I knew her for a whore!
              I gave her all my codpiece,
              And still she wanted more!

BEOWULF, naked and laying on the floor, is
asleep...anyway, his eyes are shut.

THE THANES SING FASTER...

40   CONTINUED: 40

>   THANES (CONT'D)
>   Her sister was from Norway,
>   She cost me twenty groats!
>   She showed me there was more ways,
>   Than one to sow my oats!

AND FASTER...

BEOWULF opens his eyes...something is coming.

>   THANES (O.S.) (CONT'D)
>   (singing in verse)
>   Their mother was from Iceland,
>   And she was mighty hot!
>   She'd need a whole damn iceberg,
>   To cool her burning tw--

TWAAACKKK!!!

The SINGING abruptly STOPS. All eyes turn toward the great door.

TWACK! TWACK! TWACK...three very LOUD KNOCKS on the door.

No one in the room moves, then...

>   OLAF
>   G...G...Grendel!
>   He n...n...knocks.

The Thanes LAUGH raucously at Olaf's witticism.

Hondshew jumps from the table and backs toward the door...

>   HONDSHEW
>   That must be my sweet plum, Yrsa! She's
>   ready for me to taste her juicy fruit!

The Thanes LAUGH LOUDLY. Hondshew, drunk as a skunk, stumbles up to the double doors.

>   HONDSHEW (CONT'D)
>   Patience, my lovely! Give a thane a
>   chance to open...

>   WIGLAF
>   HONDSHEW! NO!!

But it's too late...

BLAAAMMM!!!!

The great timber bar EXPLODES into matchsticks.
Instantly, the two massive doors violently fly open on
their hinges...sending Hondshew sailing across the room.
The chain that held the timber bar dangles uselessly from
the pully.

GRENDEL leaps into the room...snarling and drooling.

Its SNARL is a horrific gaping grin of yellow canines.
Its sick skin glistens a wet, greenish gold. Its talons,
hard as marble. Simply put, Grendel is one scary
motherficker.

                    FREAKED-OUT THANE
          SWIFF ME! It's the frican' monster!!!

THE FREAKED-OUT THANE draws his sword, but Grendel is on
him...It STOMPS on the thane, instantly crushing him.

BEOWULF climbs up on a table and walks across the table
tops toward Grendel, very slowly and deliberately. He has
an easy smile on his face, like a man walking to a party.

GRENDEL LAUGHS as he picks up a thane with both hands and
punts him across the room...into the fire-pit. The fire
begins to rise and spit, taking its violent, WHITE
PHOSPHOROUS FORM.

ANOTHER THANE charges, but Grendel simply punches him,
sending him crashing into the mead vat and spilling it
into the fire-pit...a huge plume of STEAM AND SMOKE RISES
from the pit.

HONDSHEW, cut and bloody, and SCREAMING like a madman,
runs across the room toward Grendel...

                    HONDSHEW
          Aaaaarrrrrhhhhhhheeeeee!!!!!!!...

With his gigantic broadsword raised high above his head,
Hondshew leaps from a table, dives toward Grendel, and
with a LOUD CRACK, cleaves the sword blade into the
demon's skull!! But, of coarse, nothing happens...

GRENDEL grins at Hondshew. Who dangles helplessly from
the sword hilt. And before he can react...

GRENDEL grabs the thane with one claw, and with its
other, SNAPS the broadsword in two...leaving a chunk of
the blade still imbedded in its skull.

Then, in one swift motion, Grendel opens his rotting
jaws, sticks Hondshew's head in its mouth...and CRUNCH!!

(Mercifully, the billowing smoke from the fire-pit
obscures our vision.)

THE SURVIVING THANES GASP in horror.

GRENDEL CHOMPS and GNAWS...then, as THE SMOKE CLEARS, the
demon stops in mid-chew. Its eyes narrow at what it
sees...

BEOWULF, naked as the day he was born, standing on a
table. His hands on his hips in the classic Superman
pose. He smiles at the creature.

GRENDEL charges, raising its fist to crush Beowulf. But
Beowulf is too fast...he leaps to the other side of the
table as Grendel's fist SLAMS down on the planks, causing
the table to seesaw...sending Beowulf flying into the
rafters...then, from behind Grendel...

                    WIGLAF
          Die Demon!

WIGLAF slides under Grendel and strikes at its groin with
his sword, breaking the blade on the creature's tough
skin.

                    WIGLAF (CONT'D)
                  (flabbergasted)
          The swifan bastard has no pintel!!!

Indeed, Grendel has been neutered long ago. The gelded
GRENDEL spins and strikes at Wiglaf, who manages to hold
up his small shield just before the massive arm swats him
aside like a defenseless kitten.

Wiglaf slides backwards across the floor stopping inches
from the piss-pit

BEOWULF swings from an iron chandelier like a trapeze
artist, does a aerial somersault, and lands on Grendel's
back. He locks his arm around Grendel's neck in a fierce
chokehold.

GRENDEL SNARLS and jerks forward, causing Beowulf to
topple over Grendel's head and into its claw.

Grendel lifts Beowulf by the torso, about to bite his
head off, but in a maneuver made famous by Scottish
soccer hooligans, but originally invented by Swedish
heroes, Beowulf HEADBUTTS Grendel!

GRENDEL is slightly dazed. Seeing Beowulf has the
advantage, the surviving thanes stand down. This is
Beowulf's fight.

Beowulf leaps on Grendel's back. His hands around
Grendel's neck, squeezing: it's as if he's trying to
choke a tree...Straining, pulling himself up near
Grendel's ear, Beowulf groans out loud...

                    BEOWULF
               (groans)
          Yyyoouu fffilty ffu...

GRENDEL SCREAMS!!

BEOWULF is startled, but then quickly realizes Grendel's
weak spot. He pulls himself close to Grendel's deformed
ear...and YELLS right into it!

                    BEOWULF (CONT'D)
          YYyyaaaaaaaaahhh!!!!!

                    GRENDEL
               (screaming in pain)
          EEEEEEEEEEeeeeeeeeeeeiiiiiiiii!!!!

With one arm still around Grendel's neck, Beowulf uses
his free hand to box Grendel's ear...punching and
pounding it mercilessly!! Almost imperceptibly, Grendel
begins to SHRINK.

GRENDEL HOWLS in pain. It convulses and shakes,
desperately trying to dislodge Beowulf...smashing its
body into the timber columns.

BEOWULF holds on, continuing to pummel the creature.

GRENDEL, desperate, hurls backwards...into the fire-pit!

BEOWULF sees it coming, and springs up onto the rafters!

GRENDEL SHRIEKS as it lands on the hot embers...putrid
green and yellow smoke pours off its seared flesh.

Now contracted down to a mere 8 feet, Grendel leaps out
of the fire-pit and runs toward the door.

In another magnificent aerial move...

BEOWULF dives for the chain that lifts the door bar.(The
chain still holds a large chunk of timber). He swings on
the chain...flying right at Grendel's head!!!

GRENDEL lifts his claw to block the blow...SHATTERING the
timber into splinters. However, that caused Grendel's
wrist to slip through the loop in the chain!

BEOWULF dives for the other end of the chain, then swoops
down, cinching the chain tightly around Grendel's wrist.

CONTINUED: (5)

GRENDEL lets out a HORRIFIC SHRIEK and lashes the chain like a whip, RIPPING the pulley out of the ceiling.

Having had enough, it runs for the door, dragging the
chain behind...

BEOWULF, fearing that Grendel might escape, dives for the
chain and grabs it, he's dragged along the stone floor
like he was bare-foot water-skiing...

GRENDEL is at the great doors...

BEOWULF manages to hook the chain onto a large nail-
spike...

GRENDEL jolts to a stop just in the threshold of the
door...

BEOWULF pulls the chain with all his strength...

POP!! GRENDEL's shoulder is violently dislocated...

BEOWULF quickly lashes the chain around a support beam...

GRENDEL ROARS in agony. It tugs so savagely at the chain,
it jars the beam loose, causing stones, planks, and mud-
fill to shower down from the ceiling.

BEOWULF slides like he was coming in to home plate and
kicks the door closed with his foot, SLAMMING the heavy
wooden portal onto Grendel's arm...

GRENDEL lets out the SCREAM OF A CAGED HOWLER MONKEY!!

                    BEOWULF
              (holding the door shut on the
               flailing arm)
          Your days of blood-letting are finished,
          demon!

                    GRENDEL
          Let...Grendel...free!

Beowulf is shocked!!!

                    BEOWULF
          It speaks!!

                    GRENDEL
          I...not...monster here! Kill
          Grendel...man can't! What...thing are
          you!?

Beowulf presses the door against Grendel's arm and leans
in close to its mangled ear...

                       BEOWULF
                (almost whispering)
I am ripper and tearer and slasher and
gouger. I am the teeth in the darkness
and the talons in the night. I am all
the things you believed yourself to be.
                (louder)
Mine is strength and lust and POWER!
                (now yelling)
I AM BEOWULF!!

GRENDEL'S eyes become racked with fear.

BEOWULF SMASHES the door with great fury...the iron door
frame cutting Grendel's arm like a knife-edge...

GRENDEL SHRIEKS!! Its sinewy tendons to begin to
SNAP...its bones CRACK!!!

                    BEOWULF (CONT'D)
Think you now of the Thanes whose lives
you've stolen!

For emphases, Beowulf SLAMS the door against Grendel's
arm!! Grendel SCREAMS!!!

                    BEOWULF (CONT'D)
Think of them...
                (SLAM!)
as you die...
                (SLAM!!)
your demon's...
                (SLAM!! SLAM!!!)
death!!!

And with one powerful lunge...

BEOWULF SLAMS the door shut!! GRENDEL'S ARM lands on the
floor with a satisfying MEATY THUD.

BEOWULF stands there, staring at the arm for a
moment...when suddenly it grabs his foot. He kicks
wildly at it, finally shaking it loose.

THE ARM FLOPS around on the stone floor for a few moments
like a beached fish and then suddenly seizes into a
contorted position of agony.

BEOWULF stands against the door, breathing heavily. For
the first time, he seems freaked.

SEVERAL THANES, swords drawn, cautiously approach the
arm.

40   CONTINUED: (8)   40

WIGLAF pushes himself to the front...

                    WIGLAF
          Grendel's arm! You've done it!
              (turning to the other men)
          He's done it! He's torn the limbs from
          the beast! BEOWULF HAS KILLED HIM!!!

They all begin CHEERING.

Beowulf wipes the demon's green-black blood from his
face.

                                              CUT TO:

41   INT. HEROT - HROTHGAR'S QUARTERS - NIGHT   41

Hrothgar is in his bed, wide awake. Wealthow stands by
the window anxiously clutching a scarf.

WE HEAR the CHEER coming from the mead hall.

Hrothgar sits up...

                    HROTHGAR
          Is that a cheer? Could that be a cry of
          victory?

The door suddenly BURSTS open and Wulfgar runs in, eyes
glowing with delight...

                    WULFGAR
          My lord! Beowulf has killed the demon!

                    HROTHGAR
          Praise Odin!!

Small tears of joy form in Wealthow's eyes.

                    HROTHGAR (CONT'D)
          Call the scops. Spread the word! Tomorrow
          will be a glorious day of rejoicing!

Wulfgar quickly leaves.

Hrothgar walks up behind Wealthow. He puts his hand on
her shoulder -- almost a paternal gesture.

41   CONTINUED: 41

                         HROTHGAR (CONT'D)
               Our nightmare is over.
                    (he slides his hand toward
                     her breast)
               Come to bed, my sweet.

Wealthow whacks his hand away.

                         WEALTHOW
               Do not touch me.

                         HROTHGAR
               My kingdom needs an heir. I need a son.
               It's time you do your duty.

                         WEALTHOW
               How can I ever lay with you...knowing you
               laid with <u>her</u>.

Hrothgar looks very uncomfortable.

                         HROTHGAR
               I should never have told you.

We hear HAMMER BLOWS, rhythmic as sex.

                                                    CUT TO:

42   INT. HEROT - MEAD HALL - NIGHT   42

CLOSE ON: Grendel's arm is being NAILED into a massive
wooden beam in the mead hall.

BEOWULF wields the massive blacksmith's hammer. Beowulf
laughs, strangely, almost maniacal.

WIGLAF turns to look at the four dead thanes...laid-out
on their shields, covered with their capes. He looks back
at Beowulf hammering and cackling. He looks
concerned...who is the monster?

                                                    CUT TO:

43   INT. THE GREAT CAVE - NIGHT   43

Grendel comes stumbling into the safety of the cave,
making a DREADFUL, SOBBING SOUND.

Grendel falls into the pool, black blood from his missing
arm, pumps into the water, until everything is
black...then...

>   GRENDEL'S MOTHER (O.C.)
>   Oh Grendel, my son. My poor son.

GRENDEL'S MOTHER'S P.O.V.

THE CAMERA comes up from the pool, skimming the surface
of the water, gliding toward Grendel.

>   GRENDEL
>   Mama...mama...he hurt me...mama..

 Grendel is dying -- nearly dead.

>   GRENDEL'S MOTHER (O.C.)
>   I warned you. You must not go to them...

>   GRENDEL
>   He killed me, mother.

>   GRENDEL'S MOTHER (O.C.)
>   Who killed you, Grendel my son?

>   GRENDEL
>   He tore my arm away...it hurts
>   so...Grendel hurts so bad...

GRENDEL'S MOTHER'S GOLDEN HAND enters frame and strokes
its forehead. It's a beautiful hand, with webbed fingers
and golden scales, and long golden fingernails.

>   GRENDEL'S MOTHER (O.C.)
>   I know. Sleep now, my sweet son. Sleep
>   forever. Mother is here.

WE SEE GRENDEL'S MOTHER'S GOLDEN REFLECTION...rippling in
the water. Is she humanoid? Reptilian? It's hard to tell.

>   GRENDEL
>   Mama? He was so strong...so strong. He
>   hurt me.

>   GRENDEL'S MOTHER (O.C.)
>   He shall pay, my darling. Who was this
>   man?

>   GRENDEL
>   He was...so
>   strong...so...strong...he...his
>   name...Beowulf--

Her hand suddenly stops stroking Grendel's head.

43   CONTINUED: (2)   43

The life has gone from Grendel's eyes. They have misted
over, like the dead eyes of a rotten fish.

EXTREME CLOSE ON: Grendel's mother's lips.

                    GRENDEL'S MOTHER
                 (with vengeance)
          Beowulf.

                                                    CUT TO:

44   EXT. HEROT - STOCKADE RAIN DAY   44

CLOSE ON BEOWULF

He stands in the pouring rain with Wiglaf, watching a
burning funeral pyre. On the pyre are the four bodies of
Beowulf's thanes. The CRACKLING FIRE gets LOUDER as the
flames consume the dead.

Beowulf's 10 surviving thanes are present, along with a
few of Hrothgar's subjects.

                    BEOWULF
          They were great warriors.

Wiglaf's eyes begin to tear.

                    WIGLAF
          They died a most foul death.

                    BEOWULF
          They were murdered by a foul
          creature...from the depths of hell.

Wiglaf takes four daggers out from under his cape...

                    WIGLAF
          I've got their knives. We'll take them
          home...for their widows.

                    BEOWULF
          They will not be forgotten. The bards
          will sing of their glory forever.
                 (Beowulf takes Wiglaf by the
                  shoulder)
          Come. Let's drink to their memory. I want
          you to raise the first cup.

44   CONTINUED: 44

                    WIGLAF
     Nay, I'm not in the mood for merrymaking.
     I'll ride down to the mooring, to prepare
     the boat.

Wiglaf gives Beowulf a look...

                WIGLAF (CONT'D)
     We still leave tomorrow, on the tide? Do
     we not?

                    BEOWULF
        (nods)
     Aye.

                                CUT TO:

45   INT. MEAD HALL DAY   45

HROTHGAR is standing on his portable throne, positioned
under GRENDEL'S ARM. He's making a speech to BEOWULF.

BEOWULF'S THANES, WEALTHOW, UNFERTH AND THE ENTIRE COURT
are assembled. The great doors are open, and outside, the
rain is POURING down in sheets

                 HROTHGAR
     This hall has been a place of sadness and
     misery and blood. But today the monster's
     reign has ended. And we owe thanks to
     one man and one man alone: Beowulf. Come
     here, lad.

He puts his arm around Beowulf's shoulders. Beowulf
grins out at the crowd. It's hard to believe that this
grinning, friendly guy is the same naked lunatic who
ripped Grendel's arm off the night before.

                HROTHGAR (CONT'D)
     Beowulf, I love you like a son. With
     Grendel dead, you _are_ a son to me. And a
     son deserves his reward.
        (to thanes)
     Come on -- bring it out!

A couple of thanes haul a closed chest though the crowd.

YRSA, GITTE and Wealthow, off to one side, stare up at
Grendel's arm.

> YRSA
> (whispers to Gitte)
> They say Beowulf ripped it off with his
> bare hands.

> GITTE
> Mm. I wonder if his strength is only in
> his arms, or in his legs as well...all
> three of them.

Yrsa and Gitte GIGGLE like schoolgirls.

> WEALTHOW
> Well, after the feast tonight, I'm sure
> you can find out, Gitte.

> GITTE
> Me? It's not me he wants my queen.

Wealthow looks from one to the other. Yrsa agrees with
her eyes. Wealthow says nothing.

HROTHGAR

Opens the wood chest. Then, with a dramatic flourish,
lifts the Royal dragon Horn -- the one we saw at the
beginning, and hands it to Wealthow.

> HROTHGAR
> (with a touch of sarcasm)
> Why don't you do the honors, my queen?

Wealthow reluctantly takes the horn and presents it to
Beowulf.

> WEALTHOW
> For you...my lord.

The royal dragon horn is very beautiful. It glints and
glitters. For a moment, Beowulf is awed: He raises the
Horn on high, and the crowd goes wild.

Then, suddenly serious, Beowulf raises his hand, and like
a politician or a statesman...

> BEOWULF
> I find it hard to find in my heart the
> words I should say to thank you, great
> king. And all of you, I wish you could
> have been there last night, when I killed
> the monster. I was asleep when he
> arrived...

45   CONTINUED: (2)   45

As Beowulf tells them the story of his genius and ability
we TRACK BACKWARDS out into the POURING RAIN...and
find...

46   EXT. HEROT - STOCKADE RAIN DAY   46

WIGLAF OUTSIDE IN THE STOCKADE

He sits on his horse...watching his friends' bodies burn
in the CRACKLING PYRE.

Then Wiglaf kicks his horse, and gallops off, toward the
bridge.

                                                  CUT TO:

47   INT. HEROT - LONG HALL - NIGHT   47

Beowulf, the gold chain around his neck and the golden
horn on his belt, sits on the dais, watching his
SURVIVING TEN THANES with pride as they drink and wench
and celebrate their acquisition of dark age bling-bling.

Yrsa and Olaf stumble into frame, drunkenly groping each
other. Apparently, now that Hondshew is dead, Yrsa has
shifted her attentions to a very happy Olaf. He proudly
announces to Beowulf...

                    OLAF
          Yr...Yr...Yras here, p...promised to give
          my helm a wa...wa...waxin'

                    BEOWULF
          Good for you, Olaf.

                    OLAF
          Y..y..you know. This whole Death or
          Glory thing. The glory part is
          buh...buh...better.

Beowulf smiles and nods in agreement...ain't that the
truth.

                    YRSA
          Olaf! Come on!

Yrsa takes Olaf by the hand and walks him into the
shadows, where they kiss. Beowulf gets up and walks over
to the kings anteroom.

48   INT. ANTEROOM SAME   48

Beowulf steps out onto the balcony. In the moonlight, he
looks at the Royal Dragon Horn, stroking its surface,
tracing the dragon with his fingertip.

                    WEALTHOW (O.S.)
          You are not celebrating?

Beowulf turns to find Queen Wealthow standing in the open
doorway. He raises the horn to her.

                    BEOWULF
          I'll never let it go. I'll die with this
          cup of yours at my side.

                    WEALTHOW
          Nothing that is gold ever stays long. Is
          that all you wanted?

Beowulf looks at her with the eyes of a man who is sure
that he can have whatever he wants in the world.

                    BEOWULF
          Steal away from your husband in the
          night. Come to me.

                    WEALTHOW
          First driven by greed...now by lust. You
          may be beautiful, Lord Beowulf, but I
          fear you've the heart of a monster.

Beowulf is taken aback by her statement. She smiles
politely and gives the stunned Beowulf a kiss on the
cheek. Then, after a seductive glance she turns and
leaves Beowulf standing there alone.

                                              CUT TO:

49   INT. THE GREAT CAVE NIGHT   49

CLOSE On Grendel's very dead body, floating on the black
water of the cave.

Grendel's Mother's claw-like arms glide the corpse in the
pool, her reptilian form reflecting in the water.

She SINGS WORDLESSLY, a song of mourning, a WOEFUL DIRGE.

The once mightly Grendel, now nothing but a small and
withered carcass, is laid out on an ancient stone slab.
The slab is adorned with pieces of gold treasure and
human bones.

49   CONTINUED: 49

Grendel's Mother breaks off her song...

                    GRENDEL'S MOTHER (O.S.)
          He will come to me. I will see to it my
          son. He will come and I will turn his own
          strength against him. He will pay...

She begins SOBBING, then WAILING!!

Now THE CAMERA (Grendel's Mother's POV) begins to RISE
hurdling up to the cave ceiling. Her golden tail/talon
whipping and slashing as she ascends!!

He WAILING becomes a terrifying SCREECHING!! Like a
banshee!!!

                                                   CUT TO:

50   EXT. SEA SHORE   NIGHT   50

THE MOURNFUL BAYING from Grendel's Mother mixes with the
HOWL of the wind and the ROAR of the sea.

Wiglaf sits at the boat mooring next to a small campfire.
He HEARS the WAILING. He shudders.

51   EXT./INT. HEROT - MEAD HALL - DEEP NIGHT   51

Black night, spangled with countless stars.

MOVING P.O.V...We (THE CAMERA) descend to the mead hall
roof, as if flapping on huge wings.

We glide down the chimney of Herot, past the embers of
the fire, and into the main room...

The lamps are out. Beowulf's men, SNORING in the
background...

A WOMAN SIGHS...and THE CAMERA finds Yrsa and Olaf,
asleep, cuddling together under a fur blanket...THE
CAMERA PANS the room and finds BEOWULF, sleeping in the
dim firelight...WE PUSH IN VERY CLOSE...

A FEMALE FINGER enters frame and gently strokes his
cheek...Beowulf opens his eyes to find...

WEALTHOW standing over him, her perfect form silhouetted
through her sheer night dress...

                    BEOWULF
          My Que...

                    WEALTHOW
          Shhhhhh...

51   CONTINUED: 51

She presses her finger against Beowulf's lips. When she
speaks her VOICE has a DREAMY SOUND, with Old English
ECHOING in the background.

                    WEALTHOW (CONT'D)
                  (dream voice)
          I love you, I want you, only you, my
          king, my hero, my love...

Wealthow embraces him...kisses his cheek.

                    BEOWULF
          I don't understand...where is your
          husband?

                    WEALTHOW
          Dead.

                    BEOWULF
          Dead?! This is a dream. It's not
          happening. You're just a dream.

She pulls his tunic off....feeling his body.

                    WEALTHOW
          Me, darling? A dream?

She is on him...straddling him...lustfully and urgently
kissing him.

                    WEALTHOW (CONT'D)
          Give me a child. Enter me and give me a
          son.

She smiles a smile that SUDDENLY MORPHS INTO A HIDEOUS
SEA DEMON!!!!

                                        HARD CUT TO:

52   INT. MEAD HALL - MORNING   52

BEOWULF JOLTS AWAKE...sucking in air as if he'd been
underwater. Panicked, he looks around.

He's safe. It's early morning. But there's a LOUD BUZZING
SOUND. The DEEP BUZZING of flies. And a slow DRIP. DRIP.
DRIP.

Then, a PIERCING SCREAM!!! It's YRSA. She lifts her
trembling hand and points to the ceiling...

Beowulf looks up and GASPS!!!

CONTINUED:

All of Beowulf's men are HANGING FROM THE RAFTERS...DEAD!
Their bodies, limp and ragged, are dark silhouettes. The
DRIP noise is their black blood. A feast for the flies,
their BUZZ adds a horrific edge to the already surreal
scene of slaughter.

Beowulf jumps to his feet and draws his sword. He steps
slowly through the hall assessing the dead. Not a single
man is living. He alone was spared.

                    WIGLAF (O.S.)
          IN THE NAME OF ODIN!!!

Beowulf swings around to see...

WIGLAF, standing in the doorway, his sword
drawn...looking at the horrible butchery.

                    WIGLAF (CONT'D)
          Is Grendel not dead? Has he grown his
          arm anew?!!?

Beowulf looks at him, trembling, afraid to answer.

                                                   CUT TO:

INT. HEROT - HROTHGAR'S QUARTERS - DAY

CLOSE ON: HROTHGAR.

                    HROTHGAR
          It's not Grendel.

He's sitting on his bed, a deer skin wrapped around his
shoulders, his sword in his hand.

A contingent of guards stand inside the door. Wealthow is
at the window. Below, the bodies of Beowulf's thanes are
being carried out of the mead hall.

                    WIGLAF
          Not Grendel? Then who?

                    HROTHGAR
          Grendel's mother. It was the son you
          killed...I had hoped that she had left
          the land long ago.

Beowulf isn't happy about this.

                         BEOWULF
          How many monsters am I to slay?
          Grendel's mother? Father? Grendel's
          uncle? Will I have to hack down an entire
          family tree of these demons?

                         HROTHGAR
          She is the last. With her gone demonkind
          will slip into legend.

                         WIGLAF
                 (with disgust)
          Where they belong.

                         BEOWULF
          And what of her mate? Where is Grendel's
          father?

Wealthow looks at Hrothgar with an expression that says
"yes, Hrothgar, where is Grendel's father?"

                         HROTHGAR
          Gone. Grendel's father can do no harm to
          man.

Beowulf nods, suspicious.

                         UNFERTH
            Beowulf.

Unferth steps out of the shadows...

                         UNFERTH (CONT'D)
          ...I was wrong to doubt you before. And I
          shall not again. Yours is the blood of
          courage. I beg your forgiveness.

                         BEOWULF
                 (uncomfortable with Unferth's
                  sudden humility)
          Uh...Granted.

He turns to leave, but is stopped by Unferth's shout.

                         UNFERTH
                 (shouting)
          Cain! CAIN!!

Little Cain comes running in. Dragging the sword, he
trips and drops the it. Unferth cuffs him, and takes the
Sword.

CONTINUED: (2)

> UNFERTH (CONT'D)
> Take my sword. It's called "Hrunting".
> It belonged to my father's father.

> BEOWULF
> A sword like this will be no match for
> demon magic.

Unferth looks sadly at his father's sword. He begins
sheathing it.

> BEOWULF (CONT'D)
> Even so --

Unferth stops short of sliding his sword into its casing.

> BEOWULF (CONT'D)
> Something given with a good heart...that
> has its own magic.

Unferth smiles and holds the sword out for Beowulf.
Beowulf takes it and feels its weight.

> UNFERTH
> I'm sorry I ever doubted you.

> BEOWULF
> And I'm sorry I mentioned that you
> murdered your brothers...they were hasty
> words.

Beowulf pauses and regards the sword.

> BEOWULF (CONT'D)
> You know, Unferth...I may not return.
> Your ancestral sword might be lost with
> me.

> UNFERTH
> As long as it is with you, it will never
> be lost.

Beowulf turns to Wiglaf...

> BEOWULF
> And you, mighty Wiglaf. Are you still
> with me?

> WIGLAF
> To the end.

                                        CUT TO:

54   EXT. THE GREAT CAVE - DUSK   54

          A cave mouth, into which a river runs.

          It is a bizarre space, the last birds of twilight soaring
          about like fish in the sky. Their SCREECHES echo in
          spirals upward like whale song.

          Beowulf and Wiglaf, both holding flaming torches, pick
          their way across the rocks...

                              WIGLAF
                    Look.

          We follow his glance: at the entrance to the cave,
          abandoned and forgotten in the rocks, is a dried CORPSE.
          FROZEN BLOOD, blackens the snow. The corpse was abandoned
          by Grendel or its mother.

                              BEOWULF
                    This must be the place.

          Beowulf draws Unferth's sword, "Hrunting".

                              WIGLAF
                    She's probably a water demon. You don't
                    want to meet her in her element.

                              BEOWULF
                    I know.

                              WIGLAF
                    Do you want me to go in with you?

                              BEOWULF
                    No.

                              WIGLAF
                    Good. I'll wait up there.

          Wiglaf nods and heads back up the hill.

          Beowulf turns and walks into the cave, the torch blazing
          in his hand. The royal goblet hangs at his side.

55   INT. THE GREAT CAVE   55

          The inside of the cave is like some great cathedral of
          gray slate, stalagmites, and stalactites. Pools of
          minerals, millions of years in silent creation, become
          dazzling color shows in the light of Beowulf's torch.

55   CONTINUED: 55

He slowly enters into the great chamber that contains an
underground lake. Its waters are dark and placid.

Beowulf takes a step into the cave. His torch FLICKERS
OUT as if blown by an unseen, unfelt breath. He looks at
the golden horn on his belt -- it faintly glows. Beowulf
begins to disrobe...

TIME CUT:

56   INT. THE GREAT CAVE - POOL   56

Beowulf wades in the water carrying only Hrunting and the
glowing, golden horn. Moving closer and closer to the
narrowing end of the chamber. The water gets deeper, and
gets closer to the cave ceiling.

Soon Beowulf is chin deep in the reservoir and the cave
ceiling is no more than a foot from the surface of the
water.

He breathes in, submerges...

57   INT. THE GREAT CAVE - UNDERWATER   57

It is dark and blue. Beowulf begins to swim down the
channel of stone, using the glow of the horn as a torch
to guide his way.

Through the murky water Beowulf sees the bones of many a
Thane dragged into this liquid crypt and left to be
picked by the eels living here.

His breastplate has become an encumbrance in the tight
crawl-space. Beowulf claws at the straps, it falls
behind him as he advances.

His lungs are bursting now, his heart POUNDING in his
ears...He squeezes his way through. Birthing through
stone...and then, comes out in...

58   INT. THE GREAT CAVE - GRENDEL'S MOTHER'S LAIR   58

The lair of the mother seems to be within the belly of a
colossal prehistoric creature. Its calcium covered ribs
have long since become part of the stone. An ancient
treasure, much of it encrusted into the walls of this
cavern, glows with an unearthly phosphorescence.

From the shadows something that might be a giant gold
lizard slips up one of the walls of the ruin.

Beowulf steps up from the water. He pulls his sword.

The BODIES OF DEAD THANES are scattered in one corner,
their armor ripped open like sardine cans.   On the
ancient slab, in a place of honour, lies GRENDEL'S BODY,
one arm missing...quite dead.

Beowulf HEARS SCRATCHING on the heavy stone walls. He
spins to face the sounds, holding Hrunting before him.
Using the glowing horn as a torch.

A VOICE from above him says...

                    GRENDEL'S MOTHER (O.S.)
          I see you brought me treasure.

Beowulf looks up: there's nothing there but a golden
statue of a reptilian creature, inlaid with lapis lazuli
and woven golden thread.

Beowulf turns back to the other wonders of the cave when
he again hears a SCURRYING SOUND behind him.

He quickly turns -- the statue of the reptile seems to be
in a different position...but he can't be sure. Is it
just a trick of the light?

Then, ECHOING from the opposite side of the cave...

                    GRENDEL'S MOTHER (O.S.)
                    (CONT'D)
          What a beautiful golden horn. It glows
          so...delightfully.

                    BEOWULF
          Show yourself! What are you?

Crack!! Beowulf turns to see a FLASH of golden light
sever Grendel's huge head from its body...

As Grendel's head rolls to a stop, behind Beowulf,
something gold drops from the ceiling and SPLASHES into
the water.

Beowulf whips around and extends his sword toward the
pool...waiting. The water shimmers with a phosphorescent
glow. Then...

GRENDEL'S MOTHER rises from the pool. But she's no
monster, more like an ethereal Venus with glittering skin
and an aura of golden light. She's beautiful...a goddess.

                    GRENDEL'S MOTHER
          Are you the one they call Beowulf? The
          Bee-Wolf. The bear. Such a strong man
          you are. With the strength of a king.
          The king you will one day become.

                    BEOWULF
          What do you know of me, demon?

She moves toward Beowulf...walking on the surface of the
water...the long braid of her golden hair snakes
undulates like, well...a tail.

                    GRENDEL'S MOTHER
          I know that underneath your glamour
          you're as much a monster as my son
          Grendel. Perhaps more.

                    BEOWULF
          My glamour?

He strikes at her with his sword -- and in a blink of an
eye, she's GONE. Grendel's mother moves as fast as
thought...

                    GRENDEL'S MOTHER
          One needs glamour to become a king...

Now she's standing on the ruined stairs, and again,
walking towards him, and she keeps talking without
missing a beat...

                    GRENDEL'S MOTHER
          And I know...a man like you could own the
          greatest tale ever sung. Your story
          would live on when everything now alive
          is dust.

Beowulf is intrigued. And -- she's gone. Now she's just
behind him, whispering into his ear, like
Mephistopheles...

                    GRENDEL'S MOTHER
          Beowulf. It has been a long time since a
          man has come to visit me.

She approaches Beowulf like a cat descending on its prey.
Her long fingers caress the sides of Beowulf's face as
she did when he was sleeping.

Beowulf's eyes dilate. She has hold of his mind.

> BEOWULF
> I don't need...a sword...to kill you...

> GRENDEL'S MOTHER
> Of course you don't, my love.

She suggestively runs her fingertip along the edge of the
blade...

> GRENDEL'S MOTHER
> You took a son from me. Give me a son,
> brave thane. Stay with me. Love me.

This sends a shudder of horror into Beowulf's heart.
Beowulf shakes his head as if to clear it. But she's
whispering in his ear once again, whispering her
temptations:

> GRENDEL'S MOTHER
> Love me...and I shall weave you riches
> beyond imagination. I shall make you the
> greatest king that ever lived.

> BEOWULF
> (whispers)
> You lie.

She brushes the golden drinking horn with her hand,
slowly, suggestively. She circles Beowulf, her fingers
kissing his skin.

> GRENDEL'S MOTHER
> To you I swear: As long as this golden
> horn remains in my keeping, you will
> forever be king.

She reaches down, like a woman touching a man, and runs
her finger tips lightly along the sword's hilt...then
places its tip between the swell of her breasts.

> GRENDEL'S MOTHER (CONT'D)
> Forever strong, mighty...and all
> powerful. This I promise.

Instantly, the blade melts and drips like an eruption of
mercury, over her hand and onto the ground, where it
pools and puddles into reflections...

She moves in close, closer...

                    GRENDEL'S MOTHER (CONT'D)
          ...This I swear.

Each reflection shows Beowulf and the "GOLDEN
WOMAN"...LOCKED IN A PASSIONATE KISS!!

                                        SMASH CUT TO:

59   INT. MEAD HALL -- DAY   59

CLOSE ON: GRENDEL'S HUGE HEAD

As it tumbles out of the sack and onto the floor...a
woman SCREAMS.

Everyone is assembled in the mead hall of Herot. Beowulf
is at the front of the hall, with Wiglaf behind him.

                    BEOWULF
               (calming the lady)
          It's dead, my lady. It will harm you no
          more. After I finished off Grendel's
          monstrous mother, I cut off the brute's
          head.

HROTHGAR is staring at the head, a mixture of excitement
and disgust -- the head stares back at the room with
dead, milky eyes. And then joy.

                    HROTHGAR
          Our curse has been lifted...?

Everyone CHEERS. Hrothgar looks the happiest we have seen
him since Grendel's first attack, but his eyes are oddly
crazed.

                    HROTHGAR (CONT'D)
          Take this head from my sight -- nail it
          to the, no...

Hrothgar looks into the eyes of Grendel. In death it
bears an uncanny resemblance to him.

                    HROTHGAR (CONT'D)
               (shuddering with fear)
          ...into the sea!

Two Danish Thanes spike the head and carry it to the
balcony. As they toss it over the railing...a CHEER RISES
then...

SEGUES to the SOUNDS OF CELEBRATION...

60   INT. MEAD HALL -- LATER   60

A huge roasted pig is dropped onto a table. Mead flows.

We are in the final FESTIVITIES at the mead hall and it
has the atmosphere of a real party. Beowulf, Wiglaf and
the king's court are seated on the dais, at the table of
honor. Unferth leans over to Beowulf...

                    UNFERTH
          Beowulf, mighty monster-killer. There is
          something I must ask. Hrunting, my
          father's sword, did it help you destroy
          the hag?

                    BEOWULF
          It...it did. The demon would not be dead
          without it. I plunged Hrunting into the
          chest of Grendel's Mother. When I pulled
          it free from her corpse, the creature
          sprang back to life...so I plunged it
          back into the hag's chest and there it
          will stay, till Ragnarok.

Unferth nods, it is a noble enough image for him to relay
to his children's children. He takes Beowulf's hand and
kisses it.

                    UNFERTH
          Our people shall be grateful until the
          end of time.

Beowulf downs some mead...strangely guilty.

PULL BACK TO REVEAL Wealthow seated beside him. She
holds a jug of mead.

                    WEALTHOW
          I thought you might need some more to
          drink.

                    BEOWULF
          Aye.

                    WEALTHOW
          And the drinking horn. Do you have it?

                    BEOWULF
          No...I knew the greedy witch desired it
          so I threw the horn into the swamp, and
          she followed it. And that's where I
          struck.
                         (MORE)

                        BEOWULF (CONT'D)
                     (nods to Unferth)
              ...with the mighty sword Hrunting.
                     (he inhales)
              Once she was dead, I looked for it, but
              it was gone forever.

She looks at him, unsure. Hrothgar suddenly comes up from
behind him and takes him by the arm.

                        HROTHGAR
              Then find our hero another cup, my love.
              The hero and I must talk. And see to it
              that the mead keeps flowing.

Hrothgar, already drunk and gulping down mead, guides
Beowulf into the...

61   INT. ANTEROOM   BEHIND THE THRONE DAIS CONTINUOUS   61

                        HROTHGAR
              Tell me...You brought back the head of
              Grendel. But what about the head of the
              mother?

                        BEOWULF
              With her dead and cold, in the bog. Is it
              not enough to return with one monster's
              head?

                        HROTHGAR
              Did you kill her?

                        BEOWULF
              Would you like to hear the story of my
              struggle with that monstrous hag...

                        HROTHGAR
              She is no hag, Beowulf. We both know
              that. Answer me, damn you: did you kill
              her?

Beowulf looks Hrothgar dead in the eye. There is a long
moment between them.

                        BEOWULF
              Would I have been allowed to escape her
              had I not?

Hrothgar knows the answer, and it chills him to the bone.
He begins to step away.

61   CONTINUED: 61

                        HROTHGAR
                (trying to convince himself)
            Grendel is dead. That's all that matters
            to me. Grendel will bother me no more.
            The hag is <u>not</u> my curse. Not any more.

Beowulf looks at Hrothgar for a long, knowing moment.
Then, Hrothgar removes the golden circlet from his head.
He looks down at it.

                        HROTHGAR (CONT'D)
            They think this band of gold is all there
            is to being king. They think because I
            wear this, I'm wiser than them. Braver.
            Better.

He puts it back on his head. Then he walks back to the
mead hall, his eyes more crazed then ever.

61A   INT. MEAD HALL   61A

He bellows out:

                        HROTHGAR
                (at the top of voice)
            Listen! Listen to me! Because my lord
            Beowulf is a mighty hero. Because he
            killed the demon Grendel, and laid its
            mother in her grave. Because he lifted
            the curse from this land. And because I
            have no heir...

He looks over to Wealthow, who looks slightly scared.

                        HROTHGAR (CONT'D)
            ...I declare that on my death I leave all
            that I possess -- my kingdom, my
            hall...and even my queen. It all goes to
            this... hero.

                        UNFERTH
            But -- my lord --

                        HROTHGAR
            I HAVE SPOKEN! When I am gone. Beowulf,
            son of Edgethow, SHALL BE KING!!

A moment of shock. Then, CHEERS.

Wealthow gives Hrothgar the most bewildered look -- he
winks.

Everyone surrounds the stunned Beowulf, paying tribute
and congratulating him.

61A   CONTINUED: 61A

Wealthow, baffled at this turn of events, looks to
Unferth who is gritting his teeth. She then looks into
the king's anteroom, beyond which is the balcony.

WEALTHOW'S P.O.V.

Hrothgar is standing at the open ledge balcony. He has
his back to his entire country, facing the ocean. He
takes off his circlet, places it on the stone
balustrade...AND JUMPS!!!

Wealthow SCREAMS.

                    WEALTHOW
                  (shrill)
          HROTHGAR! Hrothgar--!

Her eyes go wide and she runs to the...

62   EXT. ANTEROOM BALCONY -- NIGHT   62

She looks over the edge. On the rocks below, is
Hrothgar's body. Dead. Deep beneath the sea WE SEE
something golden slithering, like a huge eel, or the form
of a woman...

Beowulf, Unferth, and the others run to her side. They
look over the edge with wide, horrified eyes.

Hrothgar's body is seen briefly in the crashing waves --
and then he's gone, lost to the sea, swept out in a
powerful surge.

There is a moment of STUNNED SILENCE on the ledge. The
only SOUND is the CRASH OF WAVES on the rocks below.

                    WEALTHOW
              (weeping, full of denial)
          He. He must have fallen.

Unferth, who is beyond understanding, holds her back from
the ledge. Then, he picks up Hrothgar's circlet and turns
to the Thanes behind him -- all silent and wide-eyed,
Wiglaf at the front of the crowd. Unferth can barely
choke the words out:

                    UNFERTH
          All hail -- *King Beowulf.*

He places the golden circlet on Beowulf's head. There's
a long, long pause, and then -- CHEERS!

62   CONTINUED: 62

EXTREME CLOSE ON: Beowulf as he stands and looks at his
subjects. He is the king. And then...

                                          MATCH CUT TO:

MANY YEARS AFTER

63   EXT. DANISH COASTLINE - BLUFF - DAY   63

EXTREME CLOSE ON: KING BEOWULF, the golden circlet on
his head.

Now decades older. He is in very good shape for his age.
His hair is streaked with grey and white, his skin is
liver-spotted, and marked with old scars, long healed.
He is still tall and proud as the young man he was thrity
years before. His pepper-and-salt beard is tightly
trimmed.

PULL BACK TO REVEAL that Beowulf and OLD WIGLAF are atop
their horses on a small bluff that overlooks the
shoreline.

AN ARCHER sitting on horseback, behind Beowulf, charges
his bow. Then, on Wiglaf's COMMAND...RELEASES HIS
ARROW...

THE CAMERA FLIES WITH THE ARROW...soaring backwards away
from the clifftops revealing MORE ARCHERS and the KING'S
COMMAND...

WE CONTINUE WITH THE ARROW, PULLING BACK over the sand
until suddenly...WE LAND in the middle of a FEROCIOUS
BATTLE.

BEOWULF'S THANES are in the process of annihilating A
BAND OF FRISIAN INVADERS...using swords, hammers, axes
and horses...

KING BEOWULF

watching it all from the line of the moor, shudders and
closes his eyes in disgust.

                    KING BEOWULF
            This isn't battle, Wiglaf. It's
            slaughter.

                    OLD WIGLAF
            The Frisians want to make themselves
            heroes, your majesty.
                    (MORE)

63   CONTINUED: 63

                         OLD WIGLAF (CONT'D)
               They want the bards to sing of their
               deeds.

                         KING BEOWULF
               It's going to be a short song.

                         OLD WIGLAF
               Can you blame them? Your legend is known
               from the high seas and the snow barriers
               to the great island kingdom. You are the
               "monster slayer".

                         KING BEOWULF
                    (with longing disdain)
               We men are the monsters now.

Beowulf shakes his head...sad.

                         KING BEOWULF (CONT'D)
               The time of heroes is dead, Wiglaf. The
               Christ God has killed it...leaving
               humankind nothing but weeping martyrs and
               fear...and shame.

At that moment, down on the beach, a VOICE erupts from
the LINGERING BATTLE...

                         FRISIAN LEADER(O.S.)
               Show me to King Beowulf! I would die by
               his sword and his alone...show me to
               Beowulf!!

Beowulf spurs his horse, and shouts...

                         KING BEOWULF (CONT'D)
               Leave him!

64   EXT. DANISH COASTLINE - ON THE BEACH   64

THE FRIESIAN LEADER is still alive. The rest of the
Friesians are dead, or dying. The Frisian leader is
kicked in the head by a laughing mob of thanes who have
him surrounded and are humiliating him by not killing
him. They all LAUGH with every WHACK.

Beowulf arrives, scowling...

                         KING BEOWULF
               What is this? You think it sport to mock
               your opponent in this fashion? Let him
               die quickly...with some honor left
               intact.

He turns, disgusted, and begins to ride away...just as
Wiglaf has caught up.

> FRISIAN LEADER
> Kill me yourself, if you would have me
> killed...coward!

Beowulf stops his horse, but remains with his back to his
thanes and the Frisian leader. He just sits there,
holding the reigns to his horse...we can't see his face.

Wiglaf interjects.

> OLD WIGLAF
> Balls! The king can never engage in
> direct battle.
>   (ordering to his thanes)
> Kill the invader now. Do it quick and
> put his head on a spear.

Beowulf's men, feeling a little less boisterous, raise
their weapons to comply.

> KING BEOWULF
> Stop!

Beowulf turns his horse around.

> KING BEOWULF (CONT'D)
> You think me a coward?

> FRISIAN LEADER
> I think you've forgotten how to wield an
> axe in battle. I think you're an old
> man.

Beowulf dismounts his horse, never taking his eyes off of
the Frisian leader.

> OLD WIGLAF
> My lord, the king can never engage in
> direct battle!

> KING BEOWULF
> Silence!
>   (he turns to the Frisian
>   leader)
> So you want your name in the song of
> Beowulf? You think that it should end
> with me killed by a Frisian raider with
> no name?

> FRISIAN LEADER
> I am Finn, of Frisia, and my name shall
> be remembered forever.

> KING BEOWULF
> (matter of fact)
> Only if you kill me. Otherwise you're
> nothing.

Beowulf draws his sword and plants it in the sand, point
down. He walks toward the Frisian.

> OLD WIGLAF
> Give the king a weapon!

> THANE IN THE CROWD
> Take mine!

> ANOTHER THANE
> No mine!

> YET ANOTHER THANE
> Kill him with my sword!

A number of swords are held out, but Beowulf turns down
them all. As he approaches he keeps his eyes focused on
the Frisian, who has an axe in his hands and a growing
smile on his face.

Then, Beowulf does the most unexpected thing...he begins
to strip himself of his armor, letting it drop to the
sand as he approaches. His torso is horribly scarred and
hacked, as if he's taken a thousand sword cuts in his
time on this earth, and all of them have healed.

The Frisian's smile turns into an expression of
confusion.

> KING BEOWULF
> You think you're the first to try to kill
> me? Or the hundredth? Let me tell you
> something, Frisian, the gods won't allow
> me death by your feeble blade. The gods
> won't let me die by a sword...or be taken
> by the sea. The gods won't allow me to
> pass in my sleep...ripe with age.

Beowulf has removed all of his armor, revealing his white
tunic underneath. He rips it open, exposing his chest.

                         KING BEOWULF (CONT'D)
                            (cont'd)
               Plant your axe here, Finn, of Frisia.
               Take my life.

          Beowulf holds open the fabric as he approaches him. The
          Frisian, holding the axe up, begins to step backwards.

                         FRISIAN LEADER
               Take a sword and fight me like a man.

                         KING BEOWULF
               I don't need a sword. I don't need an
               axe. I need no weapon.

                         FRISIAN LEADER
                            (starting to really get
                             intimidated and nervous)
               Someone give him a sword...or I'll...
               I'll--

                         KING BEOWULF
               You'll what?! Kill me?
                            (suddenly Beowulf SCREAMS
                             with rage)
               Kill me! Kill me! Do it! Kill me!

          Beowulf has pushed the Frisian back to the waterline.
          The man is standing ankle deep in the ocean.

          The Frisian is holding the axe above his shoulders,
          shaking nervously. He tries to raise it further to
          strike the death blow...but fear holds him back. He
          drops it into the sand and then falls to his knees,
          defeated.

                         KING BEOWULF (CONT'D)
               You know why you can't kill me, friend?
               Because I died years ago...when I was a
               young man.

          Beowulf closes his tunic and looks at the man, piteously.

                         KING BEOWULF (CONT'D)
                            (to his war captain)
               Give him a piece of gold and send him
               home...he has a story to tell.

                                                       CUT TO:

65   EXT. CASTLE ARCH-BRIDGE DAY   65

Beowulf stands on top of a massive stone arch-bridge,
rising 100 feet above Castle Herot, it spans two turrets,
the large one is Beowulf's quarters.

He leans over the stone wall, looking out at the grey
winter sea. Flakes of snow are dizzying down.

URSULA, King Beowulf's young mistress, comes up behind
him. He does not register her presence.

                    URSULA
          Your majesty? Are you hurt?

                    KING BEOWULF
          Not a scratch.
                    (he kisses her)
          You know, Ursula. When I was young, I
          thought being King would be about
          battling every morning, counting the
          golden loot in the afternoon, and swiving
          beautiful women every night. And
          now...nothing's as good as it should have
          been.

                    URSULA
          Not even the "swiving a beautiful woman
          every night" part, your majesty?

                    KING BEOWULF
                    (laughs)
          Well, some nights, Ursula. Some nights.

                    URSULA
          Perhaps tonight?

                    KING BEOWULF
          No...
                    (a rueful laugh)
          Tonight I feel my age upon me.
          Tomorrow. After the Celebration. We can't
          forget what tomorrow is? Can we now?

                    URSULA
                    (seriously)
          Your Day. When the Saga of Beowulf is
          told...of how you lifted the darkness
          from the land.
          And the day after, we celebrate the birth
          of Christ Jesus.

65   CONTINUED: 65

He smiles, and tenderly strokes her face.

                    WEALTHOW (O.S.)
                (icily)
          I see you've survived.

Beowulf turns to find...

Queen Wealthow and a PRIEST (in long cardinal robes and a
large gold cross) coming across the bridge...

                    KING BEOWULF
          Alas, my queen. The Frisian invaders have
          been pushed into the sea. And you are not
          a widow...yet.

She smiles sweetly and says...

                    QUEEN WEALTHOW
          How comforting, my husband.

WE HEAR A HORN BLOW...

                                              CUT TO:

66   INT. HEROT VILLAGE -- MORNING   66

In the frosty cold, breath steaming, Old Wiglaf stands on
a stone plinth calling out an announcement:

                    OLD WIGLAF
          On this day...in honour of our glorious
          King...let us tell the saga of King
          Beowulf. How our fearless lord slew the
          demon Grendel, and the demon's hag
          mother...

THE CAMERA PULLS BACK, GLIDING HIGH ABOVE Castle Herot,
it is Herot of Beowulf's era...larger, more fortified,
impressive with it's two stone turrets.

In the distance King Beowulf stands alone on the arch-
bridge.

WIGLAF'S VOICE ECHOES beyond the castle keep...

                    OLD WIGLAF (CONT'D)
          Let his deeds of valor inspire us. On
          this day, let fires be lit and sagas
          told...

66   CONTINUED: 66

About a half-mile from Herot...THE CAMERA FINDS the tall
steeple of...

67   EXT. UNFERTH HALL -- SAME   67

Unferth hall is an impressive manor built of stone and
timber. Its newest addition is the huge cross which
adorns the steeple. THE CAMERA BOOMS down to find...

OLD UNFERTH hobbling out to his court yard.

                    OLD WIGLAF (O.S.)
          I declare this day...BEOWULF'S DAY!

CLOSE ON OLD UNFERTH

                    OLD UNFERTH
          Where the hell is that fool with the
          horses? Cain? Hurry it up!

Unferth's son, GUTHRIC(35) and LADY GUTHRIC, AND THEIR
SIX CHILDREN are climbing into a primitive sled, waiting
for their horses. It begins to snow.

Guthric bears the same cantankerous attitude as his
father. He also wears a large cross.

                    GUTHRIC
          Beowulf's Day. Bloody, stupid, old fools
          day more like. He's as senile as father.

                    LADY GUTHRIC
          He is the king.

                    GUTHRIC
          Do you know how bloody sick I am of
          hearing about bloody Grendel and bloody
          Grendel's bloody mother?
          What the hell was Grendel anyway? Some
          kind of giant dog, or something? And
          what was Grendel's mother? She doesn't
          even have a name!

                    LADY GUTHRIC
               (wearily)
          Can we just go.

                    OLD UNFERTH
               (approaches the sled,
                yelling)
          Cain! CAIN!!

                        GUTHRIC
                  (taking up the cry)
         CAIN! WHERE THE BLOODY CHRIST ARE Y...

WHACK! Unferth hits Guthric with his walking stick.

                      OLD UNFERTH
                (now yelling at Guthric)
         Don't you blaspheme in my presence!!

At that moment two of UNFERTH'S HOUSE GUARDS appear,
dragging OLD CAIN through the snow.

                         GUARD
         He ran off again, my lord.

OLD CAIN, ragged, shivering, wearing a tattered blanket
to keep out the cold. He's dragged before old Unferth.

                      GUARD (CONT'D)
         ...we found him on the edge of the moors.

The two guards push Cain to the ground. As he falls, his
blanket flips open...something golden GLINTS.

                      OLD UNFERTH
         What have you got there?

Cain curls to try and hide his treasure, but it's too
late.

                    OLD UNFERTH (CONT'D)
                 (raising his walking-stick,
                  to strike)
         Show me, damn you...

Cain holds up...the GOLDEN DRAGON HORN.

Old Unferth's eyes open wide as saucers...

CLOSE ON THE HORN. It glints and glitters in the light.
And then the ENTIRE IMAGE surrounding the horn FADES TO
BLACK...LEAVING ONLY THE HORN ON SCREEN...

WE HEAR Wealthow's voice, ghostlike, ECHOING in the
darkness...

                   QUEEN WEALTHOW (O.C.)
                  (ethereal)
         So it's come back to you, Beowulf...

Now the SURROUNDING IMAGE FADES IN...

67   CONTINUED: (2)   67

And we find...QUEEN WEALTHOW HOLDING THE GOLDEN HORN.

68   INT. ANTEROOM   NIGHT   68

Wealthow stands at the foot of the stairs in the king's
anteroom, along with King Beowulf, Wiglaf and Old
Unferth.

This is where the first scene from the movie left off.

                    QUEEN WEALTHOW
               ...After all these years.

Wealthow hands the horn to Beowulf. He takes hold of the
horn very gingerly, as if it where somehow tainted...

                    KING BEOWULF
               Where is this slave who found it?

OLD CAIN is roughly thrown to the floor by Unferth's
guards.

                    OLD CAIN
                    (trembling)
               Please...please don't kill me?

                    KING BEOWULF
                    (shows Cain the horn)
               Where did you find this treasure?

                    CAIN
               I...I'm sorry I runned away, master.
               Please don't hurt me no more.

Old Unferth viciously kicks Cain...

                    OLD UNFERTH
                    (yells)
               ANSWER YOUR KING!!!

                    KING BEOWULF
               STOP!!!

Beowulf bends down and holds the golden horn before the
terrified slave...

                    OLD CAIN
               I...I didn't steal it...I swear.

                    KING BEOWULF
                    (quietly)
               Where?

68   CONTINUED: 68

                            OLD CAIN
                   U...up...on the moors...

69   EXT. THE MOORS - FLASHBACK NIGHT   69

            Cain is running like hell across the moors. The SOUNDS OF
            A SEARCH PARTY are HEARD in the distance.

                            GUARD (O.C.)
                   Cain! Cain! Can you hear me! You don't
                   want to stay out on the moors! There are
                   things out here that'll eat your heart
                   for breakfast!

            Cain passes the rock shaped like a reptile skull, near
            Grendel's cave, when suddenly, the ground gives way
            beneath him and he is seemingly swallowed into the Earth.

70   INT. THE BARROW - NIGHT   70

            Cain is under the ground. It's dark...but Cain realizes
            that we are somewhere that glimmers....that glimmers...

            GOLD!

            It's a treasure horde: rings and bracelets, necklaces
            torques and plates, coins and statues and goblets, piled
            all around. Helmets and mail-shirts, swords, daggers and
            spears, shields and harps, statues of hawks and
            horses...the world glows in gold.

            Cain moves through the gold like a dark shadow....

                            CAIN
                   Such riches...

            Then he sees something so wonderful that it takes his
            breath away...

            CAIN reaches out, tentatively, for THE GOLDEN HORN.

            END FLASHBACK...

71   INT. ANTEROOM - NIGHT   71

                            OLD CAIN
                   ...but I was going to bring it back...I
                   swear.

KING BEOWULF
That's all? No demon? No witch?

Cain shakes his head.

KING BEOWULF (CONT'D)
...no woman?

Wealthow's eyes flash in Beowulf's direction.

Again, Cain shakes his head.

Beowulf stands...and walks away.

CUT TO:

72   INT. HEROT - BEOWULF'S CHAMBERS - NIGHT   72

CLOSE ON: King Beowulf, he stirs in his troubled sleep.
He's tangled in his sheets, and in his hand he clutches
the dragon horn.

Ursula is beside him, watching him toss and turn. Then
she pulls on a robe of fur, and walks out onto...

72A   EXT. THE ARCH-BRIDGE - NIGHT   72A

She steps out into the moonlight, but stops short...

Wealthow is standing in the middle of the bridge. She
also wears a heavy fur cape.

QUEEN WEALTHOW
(looking at the stars)
Another restless night?

Ursula nods, terrified. Wealthow turns to her.

QUEEN WEALTHOW (CONT'D)
It's all right, girl. I'm not going to
eat you.

URSULA
He has bad dreams...they've been coming
more often.

WEALTHOW
He's a king. Kings have a lot on their
conscience.

There's an awkward pause in the conversion. Ursula is
frightened to actually look at the queen.

CONTINUED:

                              URSULA
                    He calls your name in his sleep.

                              WEALTHOW
                         (unimpressed)
                    Does he?

                              URSULA
                    I believe he still holds you in his
                    heart.

                              WEALTHOW
                         (condescending)
                    Do you?

Another long pause...

                              URSULA
                    I often wonder. What happened...

                              WEALTHOW
                         (finishes Ursula's question)
                    ...to us?

Ursula barely nods, suddenly dreading the answer.

                              WEALTHOW (CONT'D)
                         (turns back to the stars)
                    Too many secrets.

Then, as if on que, we hear a LOUD RUMBLE...and...

FIRE LIGHTS UP THE NIGHT SKY!!!

Ursula and Wealthow look to see...A STREAM OF FLAME!

In the distance, A GUSH OF FIRE...RAINING FROM THE SKY!!!
The flames hit the ground, and a village BURSTS INTO
FLAMES.

                              WEALTHOW (CONT'D)
                    God helps us.

                                                      CUT TO:

73   EXT. KING BEOWULF'S CASTLE - BAILEY - DAWN   73

KING BEOWULF, staring in horror...

                              KING BEOWULF
                    What. Tell me. What did this?

A flood of REFUGEES pours into the castle-keep. They are
MEN, WOMEN and CHILDREN, all in bad shape...burnt or
scorched.

A WOMAN WITH A BABY runs into frame. She has wide,
terrified eyes.

                    WOMAN WITH BABY
          It came from the sky in the night, my
          lord! It burnt our houses and farms!!!

                    MAN #1
          I saw our whole village burn!! Children
          screaming as they died!!

                    MAN #2
          I saw it, your majesty, vomiting fire and
          smoke!!!

                    KING BEOWULF
          Damn you all. What was it!

                    OLD UNFERTH (O.S.)
          The dragon.

OLD WIGLAF grabs Beowulf by the shoulder and points to...

OLD UNFERTH, burnt and smoldering, being carried though
the castle gate by one of his guards. Unferth's charred
hand clutching his cross. Almost mad, his eyes are locked
on Beowulf...

                    OLD UNFERTH (CONT'D)
          My son. His wife. My grandchildren. All
          dead. Burned in the night. But not me.
          Not me.

                    KING BEOWULF
          You say a dragon did this?

                    OLD UNFERTH
          You had an agreement...and nothing would
          harm you. But now you have the golden
          horn...and the agreement is now
          ended...and my son is dead.

                    KING BEOWULF
          Who said THIS?!!?

CONTINUED: (2)

                          OLD UNFERTH
                Sins of the fathers. That's the last
                thing I heard...the last thing, before my
                family was burned alive...the sins of the
                <u>fathers</u>.

Beowulf grabs Unferth and shakes him...

                          KING BEOWULF
                Who!! WHO SAID THIS!!!

Unferth gives him a long crazed look, then says...

                          OLD UNFERTH
                <u>He</u> did.

King Beowulf and Old Wiglaf lock eyes. Beowulf's face
fills with dread...

                                              CUT TO:

74   INT. KING BEOWULF'S QUARTERS - KING'S ARMORY - DAY   74

King Beowulf is standing in front of his wall of weapons:
His great bow, shield, sword and wolf/bear skin cape.

As he straps on his adorned breast-plate, he gives orders
to Old Wiglaf and his THANE OFFICERS...

                          BEOWULF
                Take up positions along the northern edge
                of the great gorge. That's our only
                hope...if I fail.

Wiglaf nods. He and his men leave.

Beowulf pulls his sword and shield down from the wall,
along with a huge bearded ax, a long leather strap is
wrapped around the handle.

Beowulf is suiting up...becoming a warrior again.

The door flies open and Ursula rushes in, tears streaming
down her cheeks.

                          URSULA
                        (sobbing)
                Don't go! I beg you!

Beowulf turns to her and gently holds her face.

                    BEOWULF
        You are free to go. I release you. Find a
        good man and bear him children...bear him
        a son.

                    URSULA
        I don't want anyone else. I want you.

                    BEOWULF
        I'm not the man you think me to be.

                    URSULA
        You're a great man, and a hero. This I
        know to be true.

                    KING BEOWULF
        Then you're as much of a fool as the rest
        of them.

Ursula bursts into tears and runs from the chamber.

Beowulf turns to see his reflection in a polished sheild.
He looks deep into his own tortured eyes. In a half-
hearted, pathetic gesture, he lifts his sword and
slashes at the air.

An ironic CLAPPING ECHOES in the chamber. It's Queen
Wealthow, standing in the open doorway.

                    QUEEN WEALTHOW
        Very impressive, dear. But the armor
        looked better on you when you were
        younger.

                    KING BEOWULF
        I'm sure it did.

Wealthow approaches the king...

                    QUEEN WEALTHOW
        Why don't you take that poor girl and
        live out your remaining years in
        peace...Let some young hero save us.

                    KING BEOWULF
        And start the whole nightmare all over
        again?
                (he shakes his head)
        No, I visited this horror upon my
        kingdom...I must be the one to finish
        her.

74   CONTINUED: (2)   74

                              QUEEN WEALTHOW
                   Her...? Was she so beautiful, Beowulf? A
                   beauty so costly?

He looks sadly into Wealthow's eyes...

Beowulf nods, then...

                              KING BEOWULF
                   Beautiful, and full of fine promises. I
                   was weak. I am sorry...so sorry.

He looks sadly into Wealthow's eyes...

                              BEOWULF
                   I have always loved you, my Queen.

                              QUEEN WEALTHOW
                   And I you.

They smile warmly at each other, then...

                              BEOWULF
                   Keep a memory of me, not as a king and
                   hero, but as a man...fallible and flawed.

King Beowulf pulls his cape on with a confident flourish.

75   EXT. THE GREAT CAVE - DAY   75

Just as it was thrity years ago. King Beowulf and Old
Wiglaf, alone, ride up on horses. The horses shy, sensing
something. They won't step a foot closer to the mouth of
the cave.

                              BEOWULF
                   This is the place.

                              OLD WIGLAF
                   This is where we came when you killed
                   Grendel's mother...

                              BEOWULF
                   You know my Wiglaf, I have no heir. If
                   I'm killed by this demon...you shall be
                   king. I have arranged it with the
                   Heralds...they have my authorization.

                              WIGLAF
                   Don't speak of such things, my lord.

Beowulf sighs, a sadness comes over him.

                              BEOWULF
                   Wiglaf, there is something you must
                   know...

75   CONTINUED: 75

Suddenly, with a fury we have never seen, Wiglaf cuts
off Beowulf in mid-sentence...

                    OLD WIGLAF
                  (shouting)
          NAY!!! THERE IS NOTHING I MUST KNOW!! You
          are BEOWULF! Beowulf the mighty! The
          hero! The slayer and destroyer of
          demons!!!!
          Now let's kill this flying devil where it
          sleeps, and get on with our bloody
          lives!!

Wiglaf takes a breath and collects himself. Beowulf
stares in stunned silence.

                    OLD WIGLAF (CONT'D)
          Now, do you want me to go in with you?

Beowulf, who is speechless, shakes his head.

                    OLD WIGLAF (CONT'D)
          Good. I'll wait there.

76   INT. THE GREAT CAVE - GRENDEL'S MOTHER'S LAIR   76

King Beowulf emerges from the water, as he did when he
was young. It seems bigger and emptier than before.
Everything seems further away. We can hear WATER DRIPPING
SLOWLY. He looks to the golden horn he's holding in his
hand.

He SHOUTS something, mouths "Come forth. Show yourself!"
But NO SOUND COMES OUT. Then, delayed we hear...

                    KING BEOWULF
                  (echoing)
          Come forth. Show yourself!

Suddenly, he's walking in EXTREME SLOW-MOTION: His feet
hit the water and throw up showers of slow droplets...

He looks down. The reflection in the water is that of
Young Beowulf. He drops a rock into the water: It
ECHOES and BOOMS. When the ripples have stopped, it's
his old face staring up at him from the water.

Now behind him stand a number of DEAD THANES...men we saw
killed earlier. They stand there, pale and bloody
corpses, some of them missing limbs. They speak in a
ghostly SLOW-MOTION...

                    HONDSHEW
          Hail Beowulf, who killed the monster
          Grendel.

                    THANE #2
          Hail Beowulf, who slew Grendel's mother.

                    THANE #3
          Hail mighty Beowulf, the wisest king, and
          the mightiest.

                    THANE #4
          Hail Beowulf, who left us for dead.

                    OLAF
          Hail the Great King Beowulf, liar and m-m-
          monster, lecher and f...f...fool.

                    THE THANES TOGETHER
          Hail! Hail! Hail! Hail!

King Beowulf stares at them, speechless, as they tell him
the things he would rather not think.

He turns to shout at them, but they've vanished.

Now, from above, there's a LOUD FLAPPING SOUND...an
enormous GUST OF WIND hits Beowulf, almost knocking him
down. Then, from inside a dark tunnel...A SOFT MALE VOICE
ECHOES...

                    VOICE (O.S.)
          How strange. When I listened at windows
          and from rooftops to the talk of the
          mighty King Beowulf, all the talk was of
          a hero, valiant and wise, courageous and
          noble. But...you're nothing...an empty
          nothing.

                    KING BEOWULF
          I am Beowulf.

A TORCH FLAMES in the tunnel, showing us...a thin,
beautiful, GOLDEN YOUNG MAN. Average in size, not at all
physically imposing, with curled leather and gold straps
all over his naked skin. He looks very much like Young
Beowulf.

Beowulf recognizes the likeness...and shudders, he knows
whose son this is.

                    GOLDEN MAN
          You are shit.

                    KING BEOWULF
          What are you?

                    GOLDEN MAN
          I'm something you left behind...Father!

King Beowulf reacts to this.

                    KING BEOWULF
          Here. Take your damned horn back. Leave
          my land in peace.

Beowulf throws the horn into the tunnel. It lands at the
Golden Man's feet. The Golden Man shakes his head.

                    GOLDEN MAN
          It's too late for that.

The Golden Man slowly presses his naked foot on top of
the horn...instantly, the horn begins to melt, forming a
pool of golden liquid on the stone floor...then, the
molten gold MELDS INTO THE GOLDEN-MAN'S FOOT like
mercury.

                    GOLDEN MAN (CONT'D)
          How will you hurt _me_ father? With your
          fingers, your teeth...your bare hands?

                    KING BEOWULF
          Where's your mother. Where is she? Show
          yourself, bitch!

                    GOLDEN MAN
          Nobody sees my mother unless she
          wishes...not even me.

                    KING BEOWULF
          This is madness.

                    GOLDEN MAN
          You have a wonderful land, my father. A
          beautiful home. And women. When I
          listened at windows, they spoke of your
          women. Your wise queen. Your pretty
          bedwarmer. I wonder -- which one do you
          think I should kill first?

                    KING BEOWULF
          Why? Why are you doing this?

                    GOLDEN MAN
          Because...I hate you, father.

CONTINUED: (3)

As the Golden Man walks toward Beowulf...he begins to
GROW LARGER, just like Grendel...

                    GOLDEN MAN (CONT'D)
          You have your kingdom and your
          treasure...your glory and your women. But
          where was I in your grand plan?

Before Beowulf opens his mouth to answer...

                    GOLDEN MAN (CONT'D)
          If you engraved my hate on every star in
          the sky, on every grain of sand on every
          beach from now until the end of time, you
          would still not have the smallest inkling
          just how much I HATE YOU!

The Golden Man starts to TRANSFORM...MORPH INTO A GOLDEN
DRAGON!!! As his mouth becomes more reptile-like, his/its
lips no longer move...this last sentence BELCHES from its
throat...

                    DRAGON-MAN
          WATCH AS I BURN YOUR WORLD!!!

HOT, ORANGE FIRE SPEWS FROM ITS MOUTH...but...

KING BEOWULF dives into the pool, as flames roil the
water...

                                              CUT TO:

76 EXT. THE GREAT CAVE ENTRANCE   DAY   77

King Beowulf dives out of the cave! A ball of fire
singeing his ass!

EVERYTHING RUMBLES, like an earthquake, and then...

THE DRAGON ERUPTS out of the earth, scattering rocks.

Now we see THE DRAGON. The knotwork that covered the man
becomes the scale-patterns of the creature. It's the size
of a whale. With huge, golden scales and teeth the size
of a man's forearm. Utterly beautiful, utterly
terrifying...

Wiglaf's jaw drops as he reins his frightened horse...

                    OLD WIGLAF
          Odin's swifan balls !!!!

CONTINUED:

Beowulf leaps on his horse...

                         KING BEOWULF
                    It's headed for Herot!!!

THE DRAGON, SCREECHING AND GROWLING, beats its wings with
tremendous force...AND BEGINS FLYING...toward a clearing,
slowly rising above the treetops...

EXT. FORREST

BEOWULF rides right beneath the dragon's talon. Ducking
and bobbing to avoid getting hit by the its barbed tail,
he reaches for the dragon's claw...

THE DRAGON climbs above a growth of tall trees...

BEOWULF stands on his horse...pulls the bearded ax from
his belt and hooks the dragon's talon with its spiked
blade. Beowulf quickly unravels the leather strapping and
holds it with all his strength as...

THE DRAGON rises...lifting Beowulf off his horse...the
dragon's razor sharp tail gaffs Beowulf's horse in the
belly and sends it tumbling into Wiglaf's horse...Wiglaf
goes down...

BEOWULF dangles just below the treetops...swinging and
flailing from side to side to avoid hitting the trees. He
pulls his sword with his free hand and uses it like a
machete to hack away the tree limbs...

OLD WIGLAF jumps back on his horse and gallops toward the
castle...

EXT. ABOVE FORREST

THE DRAGON ROARS and BELCHES fire as it flies along,
incinerating the trees...

BEOWULF looks up and sees the "soft spot" in the dragon's
neck...every time the dragon breaths fire, this area of
thin membrane GLOWS...

EXT. ABOVE CLEARING

THE DRAGON reaches a clearing and Beowulf can see the
gorge in the distance, and the great wood bridge spanning
it. The dragon SWOOPS DOWN toward the gorge. Beowulf
HEARS a commander SHOUT...

80   CONTINUED: 80

                              COMMANDER (O.C.)
                    Archer's ready!!!!

BEOWULF'S army of ARCHERS rise-up from the tall
grass...their bows charged...aimed at the dragon!!!

                              COMMANDER (O.C.) (CONT'D)
                    ...NOW!!!!!

THE ARCHERS release a volley of arrows...

THE DRAGON SCREAMS, then SPITS a line of fire into the
arrows...incinerating most of them...

THE ARCHERS let-go with another hail...but this time...

THE DRAGON climbs...just above the arc of the WHIZZING
arrows...lifting the suspended Beowulf directly into the
line of fire...

81   EXT. GORGE - GREAT WOOD BRIDGE   81

Having no choice, Beowulf lets go and drops into the
gorge, right inside its ledge...he miraculously grabs
hold of a protruding root...breaking his fall. His sword
CLATTERS onto the rocks below...

HUGE CROSS-BOWS, mounted on wagons, are rolled out from
behind hay-stacks...they unleash their giant spears...

THE DRAGON ROARS an angry bellow as it dives into the
gorge...right over Beowulf, almost slicing him with it's
tail...

82   EXT. OLD KING'S ROAD   82

OLD WIGLAF gallops full out, down the king's road...

83   EXT. GORGE - GREAT WOOD BRIDGE   83

BEOWULF claws himself out of the gorge and runs toward
the massive wooden bridge...

GIANT CATAPULTS are triggered, throwing huge nets over
the gorge in an attempt to ensnare the dragon...the huge
net lands on top of Beowulf, knocking him to the
ground...he curses.

CONTINUED:

THE DRAGON, really pissed now, lets out a tremendous
BELLOW, as it flames the hemp netting...however, the
burning nets continue to force the dragon down into the
gorge...

BEOWULF makes it to the bridge and runs to the center of
the span...he sees...

THE DRAGON barrels down the gorge, toward the
bridge...spitting fire at the attacking warriors, raking
the troops and setting them ablaze...

BEOWULF pulls his dagger and leaps up on the bridge
railing...

THE DRAGON swoops beneath the bridge...headed for the
sea...

84   EXT. ABOVE GORGE - GREAT WOOD BRIDGE   84

BEOWULF JUMPS and lands on the dragon's back, stabbing
his dagger into it for traction.

THE DRAGON growls and looks back with its golden eyes at
the man on its back -- BEOWULF.

                    BEOWULF
               (screams maniacally)
          ARE YOU READY TO DIE?! YOU FILTHY PIECE
          OF...

THE DRAGON SCREECHES A HELLISH WAIL as it swoops down in
a great arc...picking up speed...breathing a heavy plume
of burning hydrogen, the dragon sprays the timber bridge
with liquid fire, igniting it like it was made of
matchsticks.

MEN ARE ON FIRE and running...some drop and flop around
in the snow...some die where they stand...

A RETREATING SQUAD OF THANES running along the cliff
ledge, suddenly find themselves in the path of the
Dragon's shadow...

THE DRAGON dives down and drops on top of RUNNING THANES,
CRUSHING some with its belly, IMPALING others in its
talons, and RAMMING the rest off the cliffs like rag
dolls...knocking them into the sea and rocks below.

THE DRAGON turns back to Beowulf, giving him a "howd'ya
like them apples" smile...

84   CONTINUED: 84

                          BEOWULF (CONT'D)
              Damn you!! I'll have your lizard head on
              a spike!!!

THE DRAGON pitches and rolls...then it flies inverted,
attempting to knock Beowulf off its back...

But Beowulf still holds.

85   EXT. KING'S ROAD   85

OLD WIGLAF, on his horse, THUNDERS for the burning
bridge...

86   EXT. ABOVE KING BEOWULF'S CASTLE   86

BEOWULF AND THE DRAGON soar up alongside Castel Herot...

URSULA runs out onto the arch-bridge...she gasps in
horror at the sight of the monstrous dragon...

BEOWULF is now climbing behind the dragon's head. It
twists madly trying to spit fire at him, but Beowulf is
just out of reach...

THE DRAGON arches around and plummets down...down toward
the sea...It tucks its wings and hits the water...

87   EXT. UNDER THE SEA   87

BEOWULF is dragged deep into the dark water...his face
twisted into a grimace, he holds on to the Dragon's
braided scales by sheer strength of will...the force of
the rushing water tears off his armor and his tunic,
leaving him wearing only his chain-mail.

THE DRAGON dives deeper and deeper, all the way down to
the sea-floor...the dragon continues to SPIT FIRE
underwater, causing large plumes of noxious gas and steam
to lash Beowulf's face...suddenly, the dragon's fire-
breath LIGHTS-UP...

88   EXT. UNDER THE SEA - A SHIP WRECK   88

A Viking vessel manned by skeletons. One side of it is a
mass of broken and sharpened SPARS....the Dragon twists
in the water and heads right for it...

88   CONTINUED: 88

BEOWULF is about to slam into the Spars!! Holding his
breath with full cheeks, Beowulf pulls his dagger out of
the dragon's back and PUSHES OFF...

THE DRAGON smashes into the ship wreck, destroying
it...sending debris and flotsam swirling...

BEOWULF, now in his element, clamps his dagger between
his teeth and dives into the roiling wreckage and comes
up with an IRON CHAIN, twenty feet long with a primitive
ANCHOR-HOOK on one end...

THE DRAGON thrashes around in the wreckage...

89   EXT. UNDER THE SEA   89

BEOWULF swims for the surface...

THE DRAGON spots Beowulf, then with a mighty thrust of
its wings, rockets toward him...

BEOWULF PUMPS and strokes like the hero that he is, but
the dragon is closing in...

THE DRAGON bullets through the water...hatred glowing in
its eyes...

BEOWULF nears the surface, swimming with all he's got...

THE DRAGON opens its massive jaws..fire and bubbles of
heated hydrogen streaming from the corners of its
mouth...now, right on Beowulf's heels, THE DRAGON chomps-
down...but BEOWULF lunges to the side and swings the
anchor into the demon's mouth...hooking the anchor in its
jaw!!!

SEAWATER EXPLODES as the Dragon breaks the surface and
rises...

INTO THE AIR ABOVE THE SEA

90   EXT. ABOVE SEA   90

BEOWULF, dangling from the chain attached to the anchor,
sucks in oxygen.

THE DRAGON keeps climbing...BEOWULF wraps the bottom
length of chain around his lower left arm...

THE DRAGON sees Ursula on the castle bridge-way...its
eyes narrow.

91   EXT. GREAT WOOD BRIDGE   91

    WIGLAF gallops up to the burning bridge...just as its
    chard timbers give way...and an entire side of the bridge
    collapses into the gorge...

92   EXT. ABOVE KING BEOWULF'S CASTLE   92

    BEOWULF, the chain wrapped around his left wrist,
    clambers along the Dragon's spine...like a dark-age's
    wing-walker...

    THE DRAGON AND BEOWULF soar high above the Castle
    Herot...

    URSULA stands in the center of the bridge, stunned by the
    scene of carnage below.

    THE DRAGON reaches the apex of its climb, for what seems
    like an eternal second, then dives toward Ursula!!!

    BEOWULF holds on to the chain with all his strength, his
    cheeks and beard blown back by the wind...

    Below us, Castle Herot...growing fast as we drop toward
    it at astonishing speed!! THE WIND SCREAMING through the
    dragon's wings...

    URSULA is still on the bridge, paralyzed with fear,
    helplessly watching the dragon dive toward her...

    THE DRAGON dives at Ursula...its mouth opens wide...deep
    in its throat the dragon's igniters (formed from precious
    metal) start sparking, and...

    THE DRAGON VOMITS AN ENORMOUS FIRE-BALL AS IT ROARS
    toward Ursula...

    BEOWULF, barely holding on, ripped by the wind, watches
    helplessly...

                         BEOWULF
                       (screams)
                  Noooooo!!!!!

    THE DRAGON reacts: Is that son-of-a-bitch still on my
    back?

    Just as the wall of flame is about to hit Ursula...she's
    knocked down, out of harms way...BY QUEEN WEALTHOW!!!!

92   CONTINUED: 92

The fire splatters across the stone bridge like
Napalm...Wealthow quickly helps Ursula up...they run
toward the opposite side of the bridge.

93   EXT. GREAT WOOD BRIDGE   93

WIGLAF

Reacts to the fire in the distance...and as the dragon
swoops around to take another shot at the women, he sees
BEOWULF, HEROICALLY RIDING THE DRAGON'S BACK!!!

Wiglaf looks at the remains of the burning bridge...a
section of path, maybe three feet wide, and a railing are
still standing...but on fire!!

Wiglaf spurs his horse and gallops across the burning
ledge, as timbers and planks fall away behind him!

Then, suddenly, with only a few yards to go, the section
in front of him collapses!! leaving a gaping hole!!!
Wiglaf drives his heels into the horse...his mighty steed
jumps for the far edge of the gorge...but isn't going to
make it...

So, Wiglaf leaps from the stirrups, flips over the
horse's head...and lands on the cliff ledge...the horse
bellies into the ledge, kicking and flailing...

Using all his strength, Wiglaf pulls the horse by the
reins, up over the ledge to safety. He leaps into the
saddle and speeds away...

94   EXT. KING BEOWULF'S CASTLE ARCH-BRIDGE   94

WEALTHOW runs with URSULA toward the opposite tower...

THE DRAGON snarls, barring its teeth...setting its wings
to slow...it draws a bead on the two women...

BEOWULF cinches the chain around his wrist, pushes off,
and jumps onto the dragon's wing...he draws his dagger
and stabs the creature's webbed wing...suddenly he's
sliding down the wing, like Captain Blood cutting the
sail of the ship.

The tear in its wing causes the Dragon to spiral out of
control...looping Beowulf (and the chain) around its
neck...creating a choke-chain LEASH!!

94   CONTINUED: 94

THE DRAGON recovers from the spin, lurching Beowulf to an
abrupt stop...inches above the pointed tip of a castle
flag standard.

The creature seems to LAUGH, now climbing straight
up...to the bridge...and the two fleeing women.

WEALTHOW sees the Dragon taking aim...she and Ursula
cling to each other...both terrified!!

THE DRAGON rears back to spit...

BEOWULF swings on the chain as his body slaps against the
dragon's scaly breast-bone...

THE DRAGON SPEWS its deadly fire. The flame ROARS through
its gullet causes the thin skin at the center of its neck
to GLOW!!!

BEOWULF sees this...THE SOFT SPOT! Under the dragon's
neck!! Beowulf draws his dagger...

THE DEMON'S FIRE-BALL surges toward the bridge...

WEALTHOW AND URSULA dive out of the way, in the opposite
direction...THE FIRE-BALL HITS THE BRIDGE...missing the
women, but cutting off their escape...the flame singeing
their gowns.

At that moment...

BEOWULF SLICES OPEN THE DRAGON'S THROAT...right at the
SOFT SPOT! He looks inside the wound...just beyond the
trachea, behind a transparent membrane...sits THE
DRAGON'S BLACK HEART...it's the exact same shape and size
as a human heart, pumping the demon's black blood!!!

BEOWULF thrusts his dagger at the heart...but the dragon
vomits another stream of fire...

                    BEOWULF
               (screams in pain)
            AAAaahhh!!!!!

THE FIRE SEARS BEOWULF'S HAND and the dagger is belched
out with the fire...

THE FIRE-BALL SPLATTERS in front of the fleeing women...

WEALTHOW AND URSULA ARE TRAPPED between two pillars of
fire...there's no way to escape!!

94   CONTINUED: (2)   94

THE DRAGON narrows its eyes, its mouth forming a
malevolent smirk...moving in for the kill...

BEOWULF dangles helplessly from the chain...

THE TWO WOMEN hold each other tightly...

THE DRAGON cocks its head to spit, but...

COUGHS AND CHOKES...AND SPITTLES OUT a weak, limp
flame...the bulk of demon's hydrogen gas blowing though
the wound in its neck.

THE DRAGON SCREAMS IN RAGE and STRIKES AT THE WOMEN...its
jaws wide open, bearing its fangs...

THE WOMEN dive to the ground and squeeze against the
inside wall...

THE DRAGON SNAPS...missing them...but taking a hug bite
out of the stone railing behind them...

BEOWULF thrusts his charred hand into the dragon's wound
in a desperate attempt to grab the creatures heart...but
it's more than a foot out of reach...the chain wrapped
around his wrist like a hand-cuff...he can't reach any
further.

THE WOMEN tuck against the wall...

THE DRAGON snaps at them again...

BEOWULF CRIES OUT in frustration.

                    BEOWULF (CONT'D)
          NOOOOooo!!!!!

But then...

                    OLD WIGLAF (O.S.)
          MY LORD!!!

BEOWULF sees...

95   EXT. KING BEOWULF'S CASTLE   95

OLD WIGLAF...riding up under the dragon, holding a
charged bow, with a long dagger lashed to its arrow.

WIGLAF lets the arrow fly...a perfect shot, straight at
the dragon's wound...but...

96   EXT. KING BEOWULF'S CASTLE ARCH-BRIDGE   96

THE DRAGON lurches violently toward the women...and THE
ARROW is going to miss its mark. It arcs
downward...falling short, but at the last second...

BEOWULF swings out his leg...allowing THE ARROW to plunge
into his calf muscle...

BEOWULF SCREAMS from the pain, but quickly retracts his
leg and retrieves the dagger...

Beowulf thrusts the dagger through the dragon's wound!
Slashing open the membrane, he STABS THE DAGGER AT THE
DRAGON'S HEART!! But...

Unbelievably, BEOWULF'S REACH IS STILL SHORT...four
inches short. He tugs desperately at the chain,
stretching his arm and wrist to gain more length, but to
no avail...

In a mad rage, THE DRAGON CHOMPS and bites at the stone
wall...sending chunks of rock and stone flying...

WEALTHOW AND URSULA, terrified, cover their heads...one
or two more dragon bites, and the wall will be
gone...when suddenly...

A strange calm comes over Beowulf...he knows what he must
do...he reaches the dagger under his chain-mail at his
shoulder...and BEGINS CUTTING HIS ARM!!

The pain is excruciating, as Beowulf slices and hacks at
his underarm...his blood seeping through the chain mesh.

OLD WIGLAF watches from below, unable to believe what
he's witnessing...

THE DRAGON CACKLES with glee...it rips another huge chunk
of stone out of the wall...

WITH A FINAL CUT of the dagger...BEOWULF SEVERS HIS OWN
ARM!! He drops **a good five inches**, his arm and torso held
together by the chain-mail.

KING BEOWULF, now with an expression of serenity on his
face like we have never seen, swings on his severed arm
and thrusts the dagger into the dragon's throat!!! But...

At that moment, a torrent of rocks and stone tumble down
the dragons gullet...KNOCKING THE DAGGER OUT OF BEOWULF'S
HAND!!!!!

96   CONTINUED: 96

EVERYTHING SHIFTS INTO SLOW MOTION:

Beowulf screams in anguish...

                    BEOWULF
          NNNNAAAAYYYYY!!!!!

THE DRAGON'S FANGS SNAP an inch above Wealthow's
head...the two women, now totally exposed...

THE DRAGON'S SHADOW looms over them...moving in for the
kill!!

WEALTHOW AND URSULA look up in horror as the dragon's
mouth slowly descends...

OLD WIGLAF, aghast, looks away...

The air, or perhaps Beowulf's head, is filled with the
GOLDEN MAN'S LAUGHTER...something he said in the cave...

                    DRAGON (V.O.)
               (echoing, ghostlike)
          How will you hurt me, my father? Your
          fingers? Your teeth? YOUR BARE HANDS?

BEOWULF, in a super human, heroic effort...plunges is arm
into the dragon's wound...

THE DRAGON lets out A BELLOW OF PAIN AND FEAR...its
yellow eye's roll back in its head...as...

KING BEOWULF RIPS OUT THE DRAGON'S HEART...WITH HIS BARE
HAND!!!

The dragon's chin slams down on the remnants of the
bridge, inches from the trembling women...it begins
tumbling, wildly, out of control, down and down and
down...the rocks and the sea fly up at us, in one long,
nightmarish hurtle. Then, with a CRASH...

Beowulf and the Dragon SMASH into the rocks at the edge
of the sea.

97   EXT. THE ROCKS   97

WAVES crash over them both, and when the waves retreat
the Dragon has become the Golden Man once more. There's
an open wound extending from his neck down to his chest.

                    DRAGON-MAN
          Father?

Beowulf throws his good arm around his dead son's head, cradling it.

> KING BEOWULF
> I'm sorry...

And another wave CRASHES over them. When it recedes, Beowulf is alone, mortally wounded, on the rocks. The Golden Man is gone...having been taken by the waves.

King Beowulf's grey hair and face and beard are soaked by the waves, so it's hard to tell if he's crying or not. But he is.

We hear the CRUNCH of boots on pebbles, and Old Wiglaf comes into view...

> OLD WIGLAF
> I told you we were too old to be heroes.
> Let's get you to a healer.

He struggles over to Beowulf and tries to help him, but Beowulf resists.

> KING BEOWULF
> No. Not this time, old friend.

> OLD WIGLAF
> You're Beowulf. A little thing like this
> isn't going to finish you off.

> KING BEOWULF
> No. I'm done.
> (then, he seems to be
> hallucinating)
> Do you hear her?

Wiglaf may not hear it...but we do. It's a far off VOICE SINGING. A haunting song that seems to resonate throughout the land. The Siren Song.

> OLD WIGLAF
> I hear nothing...

> KING BEOWULF
> The song. It's Grendel's Mother -- my
> son's mother -- my...

He stops, distracted by pain, and whether he was going to say "lover" or "mother" or "nemesis" we will never know...

> OLD WIGLAF
> No, lord. Don't say such things. You
> killed Grendel's mother. When we were
> young. It's in the saga...

Beowulf cuts him off with a painful yell...

> KING BEOWULF
> A LIE!! You know it was...a lie.

Wiglaf reveals nothing. His face stoic, his eyes
enigmatic.

> KING BEOWULF (CONT'D)
> Too late for lies, Wiglaf. Too late--

And Beowulf is dead.

DISSOLVE TO:

98   EXT. SEA SIDE -- FUNERAL BOAT -- SUNSET   98

Beowulf's body, looking like an old hero in his fur cape,
rests on a pile of golden treasure...on a Viking
ship...in full sail.

A scop, the young boy from the first scene, his voice a
perfect treble, begins to sing...

> BOY
> (sings)
> Across the whale road he came
> And made our land his hearth and home...

Four thanes dressed in their finest armor, cast the boat
out to the icy sea.

Old Wiglaf stands on a rock out-crop. THE GOLD CROWN of
Herot upon his head. Beowulf's crown, and Hrothgar's
before him.

Wealthow and Ursula hold hands tightly, united by their
grief.

Old Unferth, a broken man, stands holding on to Old
Cain's shoulder.

> BOY (CONT'D)
> (sings)
> With glory and for good he died
> Protecting us from evil's might
> And so his saga will be told
> Until the sun goes dark and cold...

CONTINUED:

Beowulf's funeral ship drifts toward a rocky outcrop,
forming a natural arch. A cedar bonfire is burning on
top.

As the boat passes under the arch, the embers are pushed
over the side, creating a heart-stoppingly beautiful...

WATERFALL OF GLOWING EMBERS

...A beat, and the ship erupts in flame.

The setting sun, like a huge crimson eye on the horizon,
frames the burning boat into a silhouette.

The boy's song ends. And into the silence, Wiglaf speaks.

                    OLD WIGLAF
          He...he was the bravest of us. The
          prince of all warriors. His name will
          live forever. He--

Wiglaf breaks down.

                    WEALTHOW
          His song...shall be sung forever....As
          long as the Earth endures, his tales
          shall be told.

And the mourners turn back, heading towards the castle.

Beowulf's ship is now out into the open sea, burning.

Wiglaf pauses. He seems to hear something, a distant
KEENING...he looks out to sea.

The wordless keening becomes the SIREN SONG...of
GRENDEL'S MOTHER!

She's sitting on the prow of the burning boat. Beautiful,
naked and perfect. In the flames...Grendel's beautiful
mother...untouched by time...kisses her lover goodbye.

The boat lists and begins to sink. And just before it
goes down, she stands on the rising bow, and executes a
perfect arching dive. And as the Age of Heroes comes to
its end...the siren vanishes beneath the waves.

Wiglaf looks down...waves lap at his feet...when
suddenly, The Golden Drinking Horn appears...washed up by
the waves.

Wiglaf's eyes widen as he cautiously lifts the horn out
of the sand, then looks back out to the sea...

And rising out of the water is Grendel's Mother, golden
and beautiful...with her long, exquisite finger, she
beckons Wiglaf...

A strange look flickers across the old warrior's eyes...a
look we haven't seen before...

And Wiglaf steps into the water...walking toward her...

Just as the last of the setting sun, for a moment, burns
green as any emerald, and the darkness falls we...

                                        FADE OUT:

 Afterword

BY NEIL GAIMAN

I know that there is a relationship between a script and a film, but I also know that it's not always the relationship that the viewing public imagines. It's not the relationship between a play performed and a script, or even of a house and an architect's plan. If anything it's the relationship between a battle plan and a battle.

There are those who believe that the art form of Hollywood is movies. I believe this—except on my cynical days, when I believe that the art form of Hollywood is contracts, and that occasionally movies get made as an unavoidable part of the contract-making process.

When I was a young man I went out to Hollywood with a book, convinced that I was smarter and better and wiser than any other young man who had gone out to Hollywood and fallen afoul of the system, and I watched as my weeks turned into a rough assemblage of every Hollywood cliché you've ever heard of. "You'd have to be mad to want to do this," I thought, and I went away again.

In his introduction to these scripts, Roger Avary is much too honest about the process of getting this script made. This is because Roger is a Holy Madman. When he dies, no matter what amazing things he does between now and then, they will mention in the obituaries that he concluded his short Oscar acceptance speech by saying, "I'm gonna go now 'cause I really got to take a pee." And he did. He says it was because he really had to take a pee.

If you read these two scripts, and bits, and Roger's introductions, you will learn an awful lot about the filmmaking process. You'll read two different battle plans for two different battles.

In 1997 we sat down in Mexico (mosquitoes in clouds, and they would make it through the netting in the night and be flying around lazily, blood-gorged, in the morning) to write a low-budget, live-action film, to be shot on location somewhere cold. It would have been rough and ready and cheap: Gilliam's *Jabberwocky* and *Monty Python and the Holy Grail* were our touchstones when we talked. Roger would have directed it. He grew a beard in order to look like a Viking when he directed, and to appear in crowd shots. He looks like a Viking when he has a beard, after all.

And then, eight years later, we found ourselves making a film in a soundstage and inside computers, with a huge budget, a dream cast, and a director in Bob Zemeckis who is so far from mad, so amiable and willing to collaborate, that it's frankly suspicious.

If I tag along with Roger (who is a Holy Madman. Did I mention that already? They walk through battles unscathed. Roger would not go to Florida because of the giant methane bubble beneath the gulf of Mexico, and when I made him go to Florida with me he kept one eye out for tidal waves the entire time, which made Florida so much more interesting for me than it has ever been, before or since) we have adventures, and things become a lot more interesting. So I tag along with Roger. You would too.

Also, I get to write rude songs, although only part of one of them made it into the finished film. But you get two of them here. Which is reason enough for you to read this book, even if you aren't interested in how films are made.

Appendix

---

SONGS

WE ARE BEOWULF'S ARMY

(to be sung like a rough and ready rugby song)

There were a dozen virgins,
All Friesians and Franks!
We took 'em for a boat-ride,
and all we got were wanks!

OOohh,
We are Beowulf's army,
we are mighty thanes,
we'll steal your cattle,
and take your girls,
then we'll do it all over again!

The prettiest of the virgins,
she was the fairest Swede!
I told her I'd an urgin',
for where to spend my seed!

<u>*Singing*</u> *we are Beowulf's army,*
we are mighty thanes,
we'll steal your cattle,
and take your girls,
then we'll do it all over again!

The oldest of the virgins,
she was a Vandal lass!
I showed my mighty weapon,
and she showed me her ass!

<u>*Singing*</u> *we are Beowulf's army,*
we are mighty thanes,
we'll steal your cattle,
and take your girls,
then we'll do it all over again . . .

The fattest of the Virgins,
I knew her for a whore!
I gave her all my codpiece,
And still she wanted more!

<u>*Singing*</u> *we are Beowulf's army,*
we are mighty thanes,
we'll steal your cattle,
and take your girls,
then we'll do it all over again . . .

A virgin was from Norway,
She cost me twenty groats!
She showed me there was more ways,
Than one to sow my oats!

<u>*Singing*</u> *we are Beowulf's army,*
we are mighty thanes,
we'll steal your cattle,
and take your girls,
then we'll do it all over again . . .

There was a girl from Iceland,
And she was mighty hot!
She'd take a whole damn iceberg,
To cool her burning twat!

<u>*Singing*</u> *we are Beowulf's army,*
we are mighty thanes,
we'll steal your cattle,
and take your girls,
then we'll do it all over again..

NAIL 'EM TO THE WALL

(from a lost draft)

Hrothgar is a hero
Hrothgar is a king
He's not afraid of dragons
Or any other thing
When giants came to Hrothgar
So big and strong and tall
He'd cut their bloody bollocks off
And nail them to the wall.

Oooooh
Nail 'em to the wall,
Nail 'em to the wall,
He'd cut their bloody bollocks off and nail them
   to the wall.

Hrothgar was a young man
Hrothgar went to fight
He killed a dozen monsters
In one tremendous night
When dragons came at Hrothgar
He'd battle, bust and brawl
then he'd rip their scaly tails off
And nail them to the wall . . .

Ooohhh . . .
Nail it to the wall,
Nail it to the wall,
He ripped its evil head right off and nailed it to
   the wall . . .